21
IMMORTALS

21 IMMORTALS

INSPECTOR MISLAN
AND THE YEE SANG MURDERS

ROZLAN MOHD NOOR

ARCADE
CrimeWise

An Arcade CrimeWise Book

First North American Edition

This is a work of fiction. Names, places, characters, and incidents are either the products of the author's imagination or are used fictitiously.

Originally published in Malaysia by Silverfish Books

Arcade Publishing books may be purchased in bulk at special discounts for sales promotion, corporate gifts, fund-raising, or educational purposes. Special editions can also be created to specifications. For details, contact the Special Sales Department, Arcade Publishing, 307 West 36th Street, 11th Floor, New York, NY 10018 or arcade@skyhorsepublishing.com.

Visit our website at www.arcadepub.com.

10 9 8 7 6 5 4 3 2 1

Library of Congress Cataloging-in-Publication Data

Names: Rozlan Mohd. Noor, author.
Title: 21 immortals: Inspector Mislan and the yee sang murders / Rozlan Mohd Noor.
Other titles: Twenty-one immortals
Description: First North American edition. | New York, NY: Arcade CrimeWise, [2020]
Identifiers: LCCN 2020009736 | ISBN 9781950691401 (hardcover) | ISBN 9781950691654 (ebook)
Subjects: LCSH: Police—Malaysia—Kuala Lumpur—Fiction. | Murder—Investigation—Malaysia—Kuala Lumpur—Fiction. | Kuala Lumpur (Malaysia)—Fiction.
Classification: LCC PR9530.9.R69 A613 2020 | DDC 899/.28—dc23
LC record available at https://lccn.loc.gov/2020009736

Cover design by Erin Seaward-Hiatt
Cover photograph: © Gionnixxx/Getty Images

Printed in the United States of America

21
IMMORTALS

1

IT IS EARLY SUNDAY morning, and Inspector Mislan Latif, an investigator with Major Crimes, had just completed a twenty-four-hour shift, during which he handled two homicides and one armed robbery. He ambles along the empty corridor to his office from the restroom after freshening up and taking a leak.

It was a relatively quiet Saturday shift, with only three crimes reported, unusual for a weekend night in Kuala Lumpur. He is not complaining, though. It is one of the many lessons he has learned working on the city's Major Crimes desk: "Never complain about a no-case shift." No sooner does he think that than the phone rings. He looks around; the incoming shift is late. "A month's salary says they're in the canteen or at some roadside stall enjoying a long Sunday breakfast, or even still in bed sleeping off a late Saturday night," he grumbles. He picks up the receiver and answers, "Mislan."

It is the front desk. "Good morning, sir, we have just received a 302."

It's a murder report. "Look, my shift is over. See if you can find the incoming team in the canteen."

"Sorry, sir, the murder took place during your shift. The report was made at 0712, but the station only called it in now. Your assistant, Sergeant Johan, is already at the scene."

"What's the address?" he asks impatiently, annoyed at the delay in receiving the information. He is so looking forward to a well-earned relaxing Sunday after a long shift. He has promised his son, Daniel, a lunch outing and a movie; now he's not sure if he can keep it. It's going to be another bean in his "jar of broken promises."

"One-oh-four-A, Ampang Hilir," the front desk officer replies, taking no offense at Mislan's disapproving tone.

"That's near where I live. Listen, if anything else comes up, please track down today's shift and give it to them," he says, replacing the receiver a little harder than he intends. He grabs the backpack that he carries for a briefcase and catches the elevator to the ground floor. He looks for the standby police car but doesn't see one. He assumes it has, probably, been driven out by the incoming shift, or the driver, for breakfast. The police car is assigned to the investigating officer on duty, and because his shift is technically over, the car and driver are now at the disposal of the next team. Investigators and their assistants frequently use personal vehicles to conduct investigations after shift hours, at their own expense, whereas the brass are driven in police cars at taxpayers' cost twenty-four hours a day, seven days a week. He walks around to the back of the building to his car in irritation, gets in, and turns the ignition key.

He takes Jalan Hang Tuah to Jalan Imbi, passing Berjaya Times Square on his right to drive via the new Kampung Pandan street. As he approaches the traffic lights at the T-junction to Ampang Hilir, he slows, unsure if he should go left or right. The light turns green, and he decides to turn right. He drives slowly, looking for the presence of police. Then, a thought occurs to him: Ampang Hilir is one of the several residential areas in the city preferred by expatriates.

"Damn it. Is the victim a white guy?" he says aloud to himself.

Traffic is light, as city denizens are still sleeping off their Saturday-night hangovers, ecstasies, fantasies, and exhaustions. It takes him twenty minutes to reach his destination, a drive that usually takes twice as long, or more, on weekdays. Mislan sees a large crowd in front of the address—large by Sunday-morning standards, anyway. The size of the crowd, and the presence of several television network vehicles, tells him this is no ordinary murder. He fears that the victim is indeed an expatriate, with all the associated hassle of Foreign Ministry involvement. However, he doesn't recall the desk officer telling him there was anything peculiar about the case. He makes a mental note, one he knows he will never follow up on, to have a word with the supervising officer on the quality of reporting by desk officers. Driving slowly past the address he observes two Mobile Patrol Vehicles parked in an inverted V in front of the gate, acting as a barricade, with two uniformed officers standing guard. He looks for a place to park, and gets one about a hundred yards away. He swears at the inconvenience of it; if he were in a police car, he would be able to drive right up to the door. He kills the engine, picks up his backpack, and, as he steps out of the car, he speed-dials his assistant on his cell phone.

Sergeant Johan answers at the first ring. "Sir?"

"Jo, what's going on? Why the big media crowd?"

"It's better for you to see it, sir. I don't know how to describe it. I have never seen anything like this before."

"Is the victim a Caucasian?"

"No, they are Chinese. Why?"

"Nothing; just give me two minutes," he says, relieved. The Mobile Patrol Vehicles officers at the gate give him away when they salute and he acknowledges. The media "news vultures" instantly come alive and swamp him. Cameras, video flashlights, and questions assault him.

"Are you the investigating officer for this case?"

"Can you tell us what has happened?"

"Is anyone dead?"

He pushes his way through the crowd, saying, "No comment," repeatedly. The MPV officers step aside, and he walks between them, squeezing past the vehicles without looking back. He never did like the media; always sensationalizing everything. He has had his share of butt-chewing because of them. To him, they have only one objective: increased circulation. That is what mattered, not the sensitivity of the case, not whether they were complicating or obstructing investigations, or influencing trial proceedings, or destroying the reputations of victims and those related, despite whatever they claim.

At the front door, he is introduced to the MPV officer who had responded to the distress call. He recognizes Lance Corporal Jaafar Abdul from a previous encounter.

His assistant investigating officer, Sergeant Johan Kamaruddin, is at the entrance to the dining room speaking on his cell phone. When their eyes meet, his assistant beckons to him with his eyes. He notices another MPV officer standing next to his assistant, partly hidden by a wall. The officer snaps to attention and gives him a smart salute, stepping forward. With eyes glued to the dining table, Mislan acknowledges the salute with a wave. As his brain digests what he sees, he feels a strange morbid fascination that makes the hair on the back of his neck bristle. Ironically, something inside him also finds the scene amusing, and he nearly chuckles. What lies before him is not the usual rancid, messy, gruesome, bloody crime scene, but a creepy silent-death play that is macabre yet poetic. Eerie yet, in some twisted way, humorous. However, closer examination of the victims' faces makes his amusement disappear. A chill runs down his spine, and he shivers. All the victims seem to have a Mona Lisa smile: knowing, secretive, blissful, and oblivious to the excitement about them. The inspector feels as if he is at Madame Tussauds. Only, these are real people, very dead. He hears someone speaking to him. It is Johan. "Seen anything like this before, sir?"

He shakes his head slowly. "They're all dead?" He has seen his share of bodies, but this case is something else. He cannot get a grip on it.

"I'm afraid so."

"Any live vics?"

"Nope."

"Have you done the prelim?"

"Yes, briefly." He flips open his notepad. "No sign of break-in. No alarm, no CCTV installed. Looks like nothing valuable was taken; the vics all wear expensive watches and jewelry."

"Why are the paramedics here?" He points at a man wearing a jacket. "Hey, you," he calls. "Yes, you. Can you and your team leave? There's no one alive there."

After the jacket-man and his partner leave, he instructs the MPV officer not to allow anyone in without his approval. The officer, obviously captivated by the scene, moves reluctantly to the doorway, but cannot resist looking back at the dining table occasionally.

Going into the dining hall for a closer look, he nods at Chew, the Forensic Department supervisor. "What do we have here?"

"I just got here. I'm as clueless as you are."

"Have you gone through their personals?"

"Yup, everything's here, nothing missing."

"You got the phone?"

"Phone, wallet. I've bagged them all. Why?"

"The phone; can I have it, just the father's? Dusted it yet?"

"Nope, thought I'd do it at the lab." He calls out to one of his technicians responsible for cataloguing and bagging evidence and tells him to get the phone dusted and signed off to the inspector.

"Is that *yee sang*?" He points to the food on the table.

"Yup, expensive *yee sang* with extra fresh salmon."

"Chew, isn't *yee sang* eaten only during Chinese New Year?"

"Traditionally, but I suppose there's nothing wrong with eating it anytime you want. In my family, we don't."

"Isn't it food for prosperity?"

"Prosperity, longevity, and many other good things, depending on what you believe or wish for. I don't know, I'm not into it."

"What do you mean, you're not into it? It's a Chinese thing, isn't it?"

"It's tradition, not religion. We're not much into tradition in my family."

"Don't you make *yee sang* at home?"

"Nope. We eat it at a restaurant, or buy takeout. I don't know if you can buy any at this time of the year. Maybe a restaurant will make it for you if you placed a special order."

"Found any wrapping for the *yee sang*?"

Chew asks his team if they had done the kitchen. One of the technicians replies that he didn't find anything. Garbage bags were empty, as if they had just been changed.

"Maybe they're telling us something," he says, making a note. "Are you calling the coroner?"

"I think not, but if you want me to, I will."

"How long will it be before you can give me something?"

"Don't think I can give you anything soon, not until we get back to the lab and do some testing. All I can say is that this house is not the primary scene, and the people who did this are serious sickos."

"Cause of death?"

"No visible injury or bleeding, so my best guess now is 'no idea,'" Chew replies, tittering. "I think it's poison, but we'll know only after the coroner gets the bodies on his table. Can you step over here for a moment? Come smell the body," he says, gesturing to the victim he is examining.

"You're kidding, right?"

"No, go ahead. Take a whiff," he insists.

He takes a quick sniff, then looks at the Forensics supervisor, baffled. "What?"

"Nice, eh?" he says, moving to the next victim, sniffing.

"You're sick, Chew," he says. "For heaven's sake, they're dead. You should start spending more time with the living."

"They smell nice, don't they? Someone has taken a lot of trouble to do this."

"*Mmm.* You might have something there. Finish here, and let us start doing some real police work." Mislan says with a laugh, making his way out to the living room.

"Check out all the perfumes, colognes, powders, and creams in their rooms. Bet you'll get the same scent," Chew calls after him.

In the living room he lights a cigarette, mindful of Johan's disapproving stare. It is against crime scene rules; precautions against contamination or introducing unrelated evidence.

"The maid called this in?"

"The neighbor at 106A, Mr. Mohamad Salim. Maria, the vic's maid, went to his house as he was about to leave for work and told him about it."

"Where are they now?"

"I told them to wait at 106A."

"Who's watching them?"

"No one. Don't worry, I've told them not to call or talk to anyone, especially the press," he says, sensing the lead investigator's concern.

"Has the boss been informed?"

"Not yet, leaving that to you as the lead."

"Let's wait a little longer until we have something to tell. Meanwhile, why don't you debrief the officers who initially responded to the call? Ask if they saw anything. I'll take the maid. Tell Chew to let us know when he's done."

A forensic technician hands him an evidence bag with the victim's phone. Signing for it, he asks if there were prints. The technician shakes his head, says it had been wiped clean. He figures the killer must have erased call logs and text messages as well. The killer was meticulous.

With one hand cupping the ashes and the other hiding a lighted cigarette in the cave of his palm—a trick he learned smoking in the school toilet—he walks to the front door. When they see him emerging from the house, the news vultures start hurling questions at him. The two officers guarding the gate have their hands full stopping them from pushing their way in. He takes several deep breaths, lets loose a few low curses, and braces himself before stepping onto the driveway. Once outside the gate, he pushes his way through the mass of bodies, hands with microphones and tape recorders, almost knocking a camera operator into the gutter. He notices the crowd has grown bigger, as the neighbors are out now. At the rate the crowd is growing, he thinks he will need to call his boss soon before she hears about it from other sources. He glances at his watch. It is four minutes to nine. He figures he is good for another half an hour.

Walking up the driveway of 106A, he calls out, "Assalamualaikum." *Peace be upon you.*

Several voices from inside the house answer, "Waalaikumsalam." *Peace be upon you, too.* The front door opens, and a well-dressed gentleman in his late forties emerges.

"Mr. Mohamad Salim? I'm Inspector Mislan from Major Crimes," he says, extending his hand. The man nods, shakes his hand, and invites him in. He removes his shoes, releasing a pungent odor from his overnight socks, before stepping into the house. He sees two women in the living room. He easily identifies Maria as the woman perched at the edge of a sofa.

Mohamad Salim introduces the woman sitting in the middle as

his wife. Mislan nods to her in acknowledgment. Telling his host of his wish to speak with Maria, he asks if there is anywhere he can do it in private. He is led to a small room near the kitchen that looks like a study. He thanks his host, and motions for Maria to follow him.

She sits on the worn-out single settee in the room with her head bowed, staring at the floor, her hands clasped tightly on her knees. He closes the door, swivels the leather chair, and drops heavily into it, facing her. The ancient leather chair creaks like an overused bed in a cheap brothel. The noise startles Maria, and he recognizes the expression: fear; one he has seen hundreds of times in the eyes of witnesses to shocking crimes. He knows she will be traumatized for a long time, if not for life.

"Maria, I'm Inspector Mislan. I need to ask you some questions. Are you up to it?"

She nods without raising her head.

He can see her knuckles turning white as her grip tightens. "Please relax. I only want to ask you a few questions, then I'll let you rest," he says as gently as he can. "What's your full name?" he asks, switching on the digital recorder he carries in his backpack.

"Malau Kayana. My Christian name is Maria."

"Filipino?"

"Yes."

"Where were you last night?"

"My friend's house. Saturday's my usual day off. I normally leave in the morning and come back in the evening. This week I asked ma'am if I can go off on Friday evening. Ma'am said okay, but I have to come back early Sunday morning because ma'am and family are going away."

"Why did you need to go off on Friday evening?"

"It was my best friend's birthday, and we were having a party at the Crossroads at the Concorde Hotel."

The mention of Crossroads stirs memories of his ex-wife; it used to be a place they hung out at, too. She loved the Filipino bands with their well-rehearsed routines and choreographed dances. It was a place where the old went to feel young, watch the young, and hoped to hook up with the young. It was also a popular hangout for Filipinas on weekends; a place for dancing, drinking, and chatting up white male tourists.

"I'll need your friend's name, address, and contact number. What was your employer's name?" he asks, bringing himself back to the interview.

"Mr. Tham," she replies, writing her friend's name, house address, and contact number on a notepad the inspector hands her.

"Do you know his full name?"

"I only call him Mr. Tham."

"Do you know where they were going?"

"I heard Master Lionel say Langkawi."

"It's okay, I'll find out later. What time did you get home?"

"About seven. I came through the kitchen. When I arrived, the lights were on, and I thought the family was already up, getting ready to leave for their vacation. I came in and was walking through the dining hall to my room when I saw them at the table. I said good morning, but no one answered. I thought, maybe Mr. Tham was angry with me for coming back late. I went closer to say sorry and saw they were having some New Year's food, not breakfast. That's when I knew something was wrong. I looked at their faces, and they looked like smiling ghosts, no one talking or moving. It was so scary. I ran out, and I came here for help because I didn't know what to do or who to call." Tears roll down her cheeks, though she tries to stop them with her palms.

"It's okay, you did right. Was there anyone in the house when you came home, apart from the family?"

"No. When the police came, they took me to the house. They checked the house, but there was no one. I'm sorry, I shouldn't have run out."

"If you had remained, you might not be here talking to me," he says, more to himself. "How long have you worked for the family?"

"Two years."

"Was that the entire family at the table?"

"Yes. Mr. Tham, ma'am, and little Master Lionel. He was ten." She starts sobbing openly, unable to hold back her emotions.

He waits for her sobbing to lessen before asking, "Where's your passport?"

"Here," she says, unzipping her handbag, handing it to him.

"I'll hang on to this for a while and return it once I've made copies.

That's all I need now. I'll send someone when I want you to come to the house and show me around," he says as he stands, returning the ancient chair to its original position.

Maria follows him out. He thanks the host and starts walking back to 104A. At the gate he stops, turns to Mohamad Salim, and asks, "Did you, by chance, see or hear anything last night?"

"No, I'm sorry," Mohamad Salim replies apologetically.

"How about your wife, your children, or your maid?"

"We have talked about it, but no one saw or heard anything. My children are not staying with us now. All studying abroad. Sorry."

"It's all right, I didn't think so. Anyway, please do not speak to anyone about this, just to be on the safe side. I might have to speak to you again. Not today, though."

"I understand."

He looks at his watch and thinks his boss would be up by now. He speed-dials her.

"Yes, Lan." He likes her addressing him by his shortened name.

"Morning, ma'am, hope I didn't wake you."

"Morning. No, you did not. What's up?"

"A multiple 302 at Ampang Hilir. Came in just as I was closing shop."

"Multiple! We've not had that for a while. What's it about? Drugs?"

"It's not the usual. It's difficult for me to explain over the phone. You have to see this."

"Just give me what you've got," Superintendent of Police Samsiah Hassan persists.

"D10 called in Forensics HQ and they're still working on it, so I have nothing much yet. The vics are a family of three: father, mother, and a son, aged ten. They are propped at the dining table, all dressed up for dinner. The father's name is Tham. As I said, I've not got much yet. The case was called in by the neighbor, one Mr. Mohamad Salim, when the victim's Filipina maid, Maria, went to their house for help after her find."

"Tham, Ampang Hilir! Could it be Robert Tham?"

"As I said, I've not got anything yet. One thing's sure; the news vultures are in full force. Who is Robert Tham?"

"The RT fashion line. You wouldn't know unless you've got teenage daughters. It's a trendy clothing line like MNG, Guess, and Zara," she says. "Make that a priority. Ask who the vics are and call me back. I'll be over in twenty-five," she tells him, hanging up before he can respond.

Mislan is sure it's going to be a long Sunday. He feels exhausted, hungry, and sorry for Daniel, who must be looking forward to a fun-filled day with his dad. The ringing of his cell phone jolts him. Pressing the answer button, he says, "Yes, Jo."

"Forensics is done with the vics; they're starting on the house now. Chew's saying it's going to be quick. Do you want me to hold them till you're here?"

"Let me speak to Chew."

"Hang on."

He hears Johan calling Chew. "Inspector Mislan wants a word."

A few second later, the Forensics supervisor answers.

"Chew, are you done?"

"Yup. Nothing much we can do here anymore, need to do most of our work back at the lab. Do you want to arrange for the vics to be moved to the morgue? I have to go now, got another scene to process. I'll leave two of my people here to help in the transfer and do the house. By the looks of it, I don't think we're going to find anything useful."

"Anything you want to tell me before you split?"

"Only that this house is not the primary crime scene. I've told you that already. Find me the primary scene, and we'll give you something."

"Time of death?"

"Considering the room and body temperatures, not more than seventy-two hours. It's unofficial. The coroner may be able to narrow it by checking the livor mortis or lividity and analyzing digestion."

"Chew, do me a favor. Can you put the burner on this? I'd like to have something for the brass before the media gets it. Let me know when you have anything, please."

"Sure."

Switching off the cell phone, he lights a cigarette and walks back to Mohamad Salim's house. As he approaches the driveway, the front door opens and the gentleman comes out.

"Yes, Inspector, back so soon?" he asks, baffled.

"Sorry, just needed to know a little about the victims. Was he Robert Tham?"

"Yes, Tham Cheng Loke, but I think he is better known as Robert Tham. You know the RT chain of stores? I thought you knew."

"Yes, I did, just wanted to confirm it," he lies, quickly covering his ignorance.

"Thanks, again." As he starts walking back to 104A, he calls his boss to tell her she is right, it is the Robert Tham. He suggests she might want to call the station and ask for additional uniformed personnel to help with crowd control.

2

THE CRIME SCENE IS one of those upmarket bungalows owned by the superrich. Luxury town houses and condominiums have sprouted everywhere along this stretch and the surrounding areas, turning it into a residential address beyond the reach of most Malaysians. Even the old disused mining pool at the end of the street, once a garbage dump, has been transformed into a landscaped park by City Hall. 104A is near the former landfill, facing a vacant lot. Protected on all sides by high brick walls, a solid gate, and dark-tinted windows, the house is obscured from prying eyes. Mislan recalls driving along this street when 104A was under construction not long ago, wondering who the owner was and how much one needed to earn to own a house like that. Certainly more than an inspector's salary, he remembers thinking. Strange that it took a tragedy like this to provide him with an answer to his question. He knows now who owned it.

The onrushing news vultures catch him off guard. On reflex, his shooting hand goes for his sidearm. Fortunately, he recovers quickly and manages to avoid a spot in the front pages of tomorrow's newspapers. "Inspector, can you tell us what has happened here?" someone shouts. Cameras click continuously. No doubt, they are feeling the heat from their editors for a story. "Inspector, are you anti-press?" He knows they are only trying to provoke him into saying something silly, but he is not biting, not today. He puts on his best phony smile and walks up to the two officers at the gate. They step aside for him but block the news vultures. He mumbles his thanks and moves on.

From the hall, he can hear Johan talking with the forensic technicians in the dining room as they pack their equipment. He slides into one of the soft comfortable divans in the living room, wondering how he should handle the investigation. The head of Major Crimes will be arriving any minute, and he has nothing to go on, nor has he any idea how to proceed.

"What the hell is this about?" he asks himself aloud, attracting the attention of the officer standing guard at the dining room. Mislan dismisses him with a wave, and the officer returns to whatever he is watching. He surveys the living room and is amazed at how large and spacious it is, with its split-level floor, high plaster ceiling, and large windows. The room has cream-colored leather divans, rococo coffee tables, ostentatious ornaments, concealed lighting, a large plasma-screen TV, granite flooring, and thick throw carpets. He estimates the living room alone must cost more than his three-bedroom apartment. He pulls out his pack of cigarettes but thinks better of it. Just as he puts it back into his pocket, he realizes from the shouts of the news vultures outside that the head of Major Crimes has arrived.

Dragging himself off the comfortable divan, he calls out to his assistant as he strides toward the front door.

"Morning, ma'am," he greets his boss.

"What is it you have that you cannot describe over the phone?" she asks, dispensing with formalities, more curious than annoyed.

"This way, ma'am." He leads her to the dining room. Johan and the guard stand at attention and salute her, which she acknowledges with a smile. She stops abruptly at the door as if restrained by an unseen arm and stares in disbelief and shock. She brings her hands to her mouth, and a muffled "Oh, my God" escapes through her fingers. Noticing people watching, she lowers her hands and repeats softly, "Oh, my God."

They stand at the entrance, staring at the dining table, silent. The victims are dressed in their Sunday best, the late Mr. Robert Tham in a dark-blue Italian suit, white Armani shirt, a matching Dunhill tie, and with a blue satin handkerchief in the breast pocket. The late Mrs. Tham wears a bloodred silk cheongsam with a gold border, a pink pearl necklace, earrings, and bracelets. Even her shoes match her dress. Little

Lionel is in beige Guess pants, white long-sleeved shirt, pink tie, and black shoes. They are all seated holding chopsticks as if enjoying a *yee sang* dinner. The table is set with the best china, crystal wineglasses, water goblets, and silver cutlery. An open bottle of Bin 79, white, sits in an ice bucket next to the table, with the glasses of the late Mr. and Mrs. Robert half filled. Lionel's glass has water. Closer inspection shows that the *yee sang* has strips of fresh salmon all tossed and mixed, ready to be eaten. Lionel even had pieces of *yee sang* in his mouth. What gets Mislan's attention are the eyes. They are glazed, staring at nothing; wide open but not seeing, like the eyes of dead fish on ice in supermarkets. He feels he wants to reach out and close them.

"That's Robert all right. I've seen his face in magazines," Superintendent Samsiah says. "Has the forensic investigation been done?"

"Almost. Chew's the supervisor, but he has gone to another scene. The technicians are helping with the transfer of the bodies to the coroner. Chew says he needs to run more tests before he'll give us anything. We haven't started doing the house yet."

"Is that *yee sang*?" she says to no one in particular.

"Yes."

"What's the story here? What's all this supposed to mean?"

"What? The *yee sang*, or the staging?"

"Both."

"I've asked the same question many times. At this point I'm drawing blanks."

"I thought *yee sang* is served only during Chinese New Year. It has to mean something."

"I thought so, too. Chew says it's tradition, not religion, and that it has something to do with prosperity, longevity, abundance, vigor, and many other such things."

"They're all dead, so what good will all those things be to them?"

"I don't know: maybe in their next lives. Anyway, we may know more after we've gone through the house, but I'm not betting on it."

"Why is that?"

"Chew says this house is not the primary scene, and I agree with him."

She nods. "Anything taken?"

"Doesn't look like it, but we've not done a thorough search yet. I'll need Maria, the vic's maid, to help me see if there is anything missing, or if there is a safe in the house."

"I'm going to let you do your work now. Let me know when you have something. I'll have to brief the OCCI." Superintendent Samsiah reports to the officer in charge of criminal investigations.

"How about the media?" he asks, jerking his thumb toward the front of the house. "They're getting impatient. They'll want something to feed their printing machines soon."

"Feed them nothing until the OCCI has been briefed. It'll be his call."

"I'll arrange for the vics to be transferred under concealment then."

"How are you planning to do that?" she asks, amused.

"I'll get a Black Maria to confuse them. That should work."

"Good. Just clear things up, ASAP." Before leaving, she takes another look at the table and shakes her head in disbelief.

Mislan calls the district police station to ask for a Black Maria. Cadavers usually rode only in the back of a Land Rover. The corporal tells him that a Black Maria will not be available on Sunday unless pre-arranged, and that he needs to get clearance and will revert. As Mislan waits for the reply, he tells his assistant and the forensic technicians to prepare the victims for transfer. He briefs them on his plan to use a Black Maria to confuse the news vultures, and to avoid visuals of body bags in tonight's news. Corporal Shuib Ahmad from the station calls to tell him that his Black Maria request has been approved and asks for the address. He tells Corporal Shuib to instruct the driver to back up to the front door on arrival. He walks up to Johan and discusses his plans. He wants the victims sent to HUKM, the Universiti Kebangsaan Hospital, instead of the General Hospital, as they usually did. He calls the HUKM mortuary asking for the forensic pathologist on duty. After he's made to wait for thirty seconds, a woman's voice answers, "Dr. Safia speaking." He is in luck; he and Dr. Nursafia Roslan are close, both officially and, of late, socially. After his wife left about a year ago, they had been out for drinks and dinners several times. He liked her company, and she his, but it had not moved beyond that.

"Morning, Doctor, Inspector Mislan from Major Crimes here."

"Hey, why so formal? What's up, Lan?"

"I've got a bite-me case this morning. Need to send it to your place instead of the GH to avoid the press. You running a full house?"

"I've got two routines waiting. How sensitive is it?"

"Robert Tham. Heard of him?"

"*The* Robert Tham?" she quips. She sounds excited.

"Fie, don't get too excited, and be sure to be seated when they arrive. Don't want you falling and getting hurt."

"They?"

"Three: father, mother, and son. Long story. You have to see them yourself."

"You're kidding, right?"

When he does not reply, she says, "Lan, now you're freaking me out!"

He laughs. It feels good to laugh after the last few hours.

"When are they getting here?"

"Within the hour. Fie, can you alert security? I don't want the press getting shots of them. By the way, I'm sending them in a Black Maria. Security would direct them to the emergency entrance, like they are detainees. Can you speak to security to direct them to your place once they get there?"

"Why the secrecy?" She is bursting with curiosity.

"For one, it's the Robert Tham. Second, it's the entire family. Third, is the condition in which they were discovered. Tell you what, if you don't have anything on tonight, how about dinner? We can talk more."

"I should finish here by six. Why don't you pick me up at 7:30?"

"Sure. Fie, sorry to put them on your table."

"Don't be. Thanks for roping me in. See you tonight."

"All right, then. See you."

At the mention of dinner, his stomach starts rumbling. He has not eaten anything yet. Maybe he should get Maria to fix him something after the victims are shipped out.

When the Black Maria arrives, Johan and the forensic technicians are ready. The driver backs the vehicle up close to the front entrance to create a tunnel, blocking the view of the news vultures. The victims, all zipped up in body bags and ready, are quickly carried in. "Jo, can you ride with the vics? Make sure the media get no shots for the papers. Dr. Safia is expecting them."

His assistant gives him the thumb-ups and climbs into the back of the Black Maria with the body bags.

"Call me when they're safely inside," he shouts as the vehicle slowly moves out.

He watches some news vehicles tailing the Black Maria and a few others making a dash in another direction, probably rushing off to the GH to await its arrival, to plant themselves at strategic locations or bribe their way in. A few will linger and risk losing a story at the hospital in the hope of a bigger one here. Mislan waits until the vehicle is out of sight before instructing one of the officers to bring the maid from 106A. He releases one of the MPV officers from crowd-control duties and wonders what happened to the reinforcement he asked for earlier. Maybe the station is shorthanded today. Whatever the reason, it isn't important now. Mislan peeks outside and is relieved at the sight of the dispersing crowd. He walks to the front gate, lights a cigarette, and watches Maria being escorted over, with three news vultures following. Maria walks with her head bowed, using her handbag to shield her face from the cameras.

As they reach him, he asks Maria if she has the remote control for the gate. She nods, pulls out one attached to a keychain with several other keys. He presses the red button to shut the gate, and the remaining desperately optimistic news vultures slowly go away.

With Maria's help, Mislan and the forensic technicians walk through the house. They start with the master bedroom, where he sees a king-sized bed, slippers by the bedside, an LCD television, a minibar, walk-in wardrobes complete with shoe racks, and a bathroom with a large Jacuzzi and towels on the rack. Clothes in the wardrobe are neatly hung or kept folded in drawers. The jewelry box, perfume bottles, cosmetics, and hairbrushes are neatly laid out, exactly where they're supposed to be. The lights and air-conditioners are turned off, and only the curtains don't seem right. They are drawn. He thinks it must have been an oversight by the killers. They must have left the scene before day-break, so they hadn't found it necessary to let the light in.

The technicians dust the room for prints and swab for blood in the bathrooms, coming up empty. They take samples of perfumes and cosmetics for analysis and to match traces taken from the victims. Lionel's room and the two guest rooms are moderately, but tastefully, furnished. Everything is orderly, neat, and undisturbed, like the master bedroom.

Maria says that nothing is missing, as far as she can tell. No sign of break-in, struggle, or of intruders having been in the house. Maria doesn't know if there is a wall safe, so they look behind all the picture frames, bookshelves, and anywhere they feel one could be hidden. Satisfied that there isn't one and that he was going to get nothing else from the scene, Mislan tells Maria to inform him if she is going to stay elsewhere, asks her for her contact number, thanks her, and leaves.

3

IT IS 3:30 IN the afternoon when he finally comes home to Daniel's scornful greeting; deservedly so, he thinks. Hugging Daniel, he asks, "Have you eaten, kiddo?"

Daniel nods. "Where have you been, Daddy?"

"Daddy had a case to attend to. What did you eat?"

"Maggi," his son says, his voice muffled.

"Intant noodles?!" he retorts, shaking his head. "How many times has Daddy told you not to eat too much Maggi? It's not good for you."

"It's my first this week."

"Yeah, right. You had it two nights ago. Daddy saw you. Daddy is going to call Mummy and tell her, then she will scold you. You want that?"

"No, Daddy, no," Daniel pleads. "I didn't ask for it. It was Sis," he says, shifting the blame to the maid.

"Don't blame Sister," Mislan admonishes him, and goes to his bedroom.

"Daddy, are we going out?" Daniel asks, following him. Before he can reply, Mislan's cell phone rings. He looks at the screen, and signals for Daniel to be quiet with a finger to his lips.

"Ma'am?"

"Tune in to five-o-one, Astro Awani."

"Give me a sec," he says, hastens to his bedroom, and hunts for the remote. He finds it between the cushion and the backrest of his wing chair. A woman newscaster standing in front of the victim's house is reporting on Robert Tham, a successful businessman with several companies under his wing. The RT clothing line is the company's main business, with retail outlets in all the larger shopping malls nationwide. After she finishes, the anchor returns with other local news.

"You there, Lan?" It is his boss again.

"Yes, but I missed the first part, though. Did they say anything about the case?"

"A bungled break-in that turned bloody. According to them, it is not confirmed, but members of the family are feared dead. I'm expecting the OCCI to call any minute. Do you have any updates for him?"

"Nothing much more than I had this morning: no sign of forced entry or a break-in, no struggle, and nothing noticeable was taken. You can rule out a burglary or robbery. The house was not fitted with an alarm or a CCTV. They moved in only six months ago. Forensics doesn't think the fingerprints they have lifted will be of any significance. They say the house is not the primary scene, and have found nothing of importance. I have sent the vics to HUKM instead of the GH to avoid the media. Besides, they do have better facilities. Dr. Safia is the forensic pathologist in charge. I've asked her to put some gas on it, and not to say anything to the press."

"Anything else?"

"I'll be talking to Dr. Safia later, to see if she can give me something. Chew says the earliest he will have anything is Tuesday."

"All right, get some rest. Call me if Dr. Safia tells you anything that I can pass on to the OCCI," she says, with a soft sigh.

"Will do."

Then the phone goes dead. He drops his backpack on the floor, ejects the clip from his sidearm, checks the chamber to make sure it is empty, and puts everything inside his bedside drawer.

"Who was that?"

"It was Daddy's boss, you busybody."

"Now can I watch my channel?"

"Yes. Daddy is going to take a shower now. We can go out in a little while, okay?" he says, feeling tired and guilty.

"Can we go bowling, please, with a cherry on top?" This is Daniel's favorite plea of late, a line he has learned from television.

"It will be crowded, kiddo. We won't get a lane."

"Please, Daddy, please, with a cherry on top," he pleads, hands clasped prayer-like, smiling his cutest.

"We'll see." That satisfies his son.

It was on an ordinary Friday in June last year that his wife left them. She went to work in the morning, called up in the afternoon to say she was at a friend's birthday party, then came home on Sunday to collect her clothes. He had not seen it coming, even in his dreams. He tried to discuss it, reason with her, and even pleaded for her to reconsider. He told her Daniel was too young and needed his mother, but she had decided. She said she had given it much thought, and that she needed to find herself. It all happened quickly. The next thing he knew, they were divorced, and reality kicked in.

Daniel was five and a half and could not understand why his mother didn't come home as she used to. Mislan, too, was at a loss. After his mother left, Daniel slept with him when he was home. He drove his son to school whenever he could. He played kiddy softball and kiddy rugby and wrestled with him in bed. The last time they played on the bed, Daniel pinned his father down for a superfast count of three.

Before Daniel was born, he and his ex-wife, Lynn, decided they would speak only English to Daniel, to make it his first language. So Daniel doesn't speak much Malay at home except with the Indonesian maid.

It was a decision he and his ex-wife had made for Daniel's future. They had decided that their son would learn enough Malay in school, as that was the medium of instruction. They wanted their son to be modern and liberal, and not to grow up a narrow-minded bigot. If "Mummy" and "Daddy" were part of the deal, so be it. Besides, English is the global language, and its mastery is essential for Daniel to compete and seize opportunities that come his way.

The politics of language always tire Mislan. He blames politicians for creating the mess. Even in the police force, his coworkers who cannot speak English are sidelined, even if they are good at everything else. Overseas postings and career advancements are difficult for those who don't speak the language. Yet, it is not their fault. Mislan had worked hard to teach himself English by attending night classes. So, he and his ex-wife had been determined to give Daniel the gift of a language they had been denied. Daniel wouldn't be less Malay even if English was his first language, they'd decided.

Coming out from the shower, Mislan is greeted by the ringing of his phone and Daniel's disquieting stares. It's Johan. Everything is under control at HUKM, but the reporters are still around, looking for a story. He tells his assistant to ask Dr. Safia to bag everything she finds on the victims and pass them on to Chew before knocking off for the day. Turning to Daniel, he says, "It's Daddy's friend," before being asked. "So what's the plan for today?"

"Can we watch *Transformers*?"

"Don't think we can, kiddo. Daddy has to meet a friend later."

"Can I come?"

"It's work, kiddo. I'm going to be late. You'll get restless and keep asking me, 'Can we go home, can we go home?'" he says, mimicking him playfully.

"Dad-dy!"

"So what do you want to do?"

"Watch *Transformers*."

"Told you, I have to work, kiddo."

"DVD!"

"Oh, okay. Thought you meant the movie. Here, or in your room?" Daniel points to the TV. "Go get the DVD," he says, relieved at not having to go out.

He loads the DVD in the player, and they lie in bed, Daniel's head on his chest as they watch cars, trucks, planes, and all sort of vehicles and appliances transform into robots, act like humans, and speak English. Ten minutes into the movie, Mislan dozes off.

He wakes up at 5:30, to see the DVD player turned off. Daniel is gone. He notices that the maid's house keys are missing from the holder next to the front door and realizes she has taken his son down to the pool. Feeling guilty for dozing off, he changes into his beach shorts and goes down to the pool to join Daniel.

4

DUE TO A CHANGE in plans, their venue is shifted to Coffee Bean at Ampang Point, and Dr. Safia will go there by herself. He is the first to arrive. He gets himself a double cappuccino and sits in the smoking area facing the street. Five minutes later, he sees Dr. Safia drive by slowly, looking for a place to park. Then he sees her walking toward him, talking on the phone. Dr. Safia is a woman of medium height, slim, with light-brown skin, shoulder-length hair, and pleasant soft features. For a person who works daily with stiffs, she smiles plenty. He remembers that her hair used to be wavy with a streak of brown, but now it is straight and black. He feels he should say something complimentary about her hair and score some points. She stops at the entrance, acknowledges him with a smile, and keeps talking on the phone. She seems agitated, speaking in a low harsh tone with animated hand movements.

She then turns off the phone, throws it into her handbag, which, he thinks, is large enough to fit a fourteen-pound bowling ball. Perhaps it is in fashion: large handbags.

She smiles and says, "Hi, been waiting long? Sorry."

"Not really. Can I get you something?" He smiles back.

"It's all right, I'll get mine." She gropes again inside her handbag, finds her wallet, drops the bag on the chair next to him and says, "Watch it for me, please." Then she adds, "You want anything else?"

"No, thanks. I'm fine." He watches her as she heads to the counter and gets in line. She looks good, even from the back; firm butt, straight back, and he wonders if she has anyone special in her life at the moment.

She comes back with an iced mocha latte and an order plate. "I've not had dinner," she says, sliding into her seat. In the process, her knee brushes against his thigh, giving him a rush in his groin. He looks at her face but sees nothing to indicate it was intentional. He cautions himself against over-reading signals. She leans over and pulls out a pack of cigarettes from the handbag and puts it on the table.

"Busy day?"

"Something came up at the last minute. Some rescheduling. Had your dinner?"

"Late lunch. Who was that on the phone?" he asks nonchalantly.

"A friend," she answers in a matter-of-fact way, hinting she has no desire to talk about it.

"Angry boyfriend?" he says, pushing it.

Sucking at the straw of her iced mocha latte, she gives him an it's-none-of-your-business look. He knows not to push it and that it's time to change the subject. Just then a waiter comes with a plate of salad, which he puts in front of her before taking the order plate away.

He waits until she has taken a few bites before asking, "You want to go first?"

"Why don't you speak while I eat?"

He tells her about the crime scene, the *yee sang* dinner, and the little else he knows. He finishes his story before she has gone through half her Caesar salad. She puts down her fork, sucks again on her straw, and, with her brown eyes fixed on him, says, "Spooky."

He nods. "Yah."

"Are you holding back on me?" Dr. Safia teases him.

"As I said, I've got nothing. Forensics can only tell me something on Tuesday. That's if they can get anything worth telling. I'm lost. No fucking idea where to start. Sorry about my language."

"No shit. Sorry. Heard you have a powerful mojo. What's it telling you?" she says, smiling. The way she said it makes him smile and relax a little.

"My mojo? Where did you hear that?"

"You're not the only police officer I know." She says it in a come-on-be-jealous tone. "I've been out with one or two of them. Your name came up in one of the conversations."

"If they're saying bad things about me, they are all lies. The good parts are all true," he says, laughing.

Dr. Safia puts down her cutlery and pulls out a cigarette. He takes the cigarette from her hand, lights it, and hands it back to her.

"So what have you got for me?"

Blowing out smoke, she says, "First things first: I've done what you ordered. Bagged everything loose on the bodies and given it to Sergeant Johan. I've sent the stomach contents for analysis. The results should come in tomorrow morning. That'll give me a better time of death. For now, I'll put it between forty-eight and seventy-two hours."

"Thanks."

"Don't thank me until I give you the diamonds," she says. "Chew's guess is right, cause of death was poisoning. I didn't find needle marks on the bodies, so it was not by injection. No sign of trauma around the mouth, so we can rule out forced consumption. The color of the blood, whatever little I managed to extract, was consistent with poisoning. By the way, blood has been drained from all the bodies and replaced with embalming fluid." His eyebrows arch, and she knows he is impressed. "I managed to get sufficient blood from their hearts. That has been sent to Toxicology along with samples of hair and liver tissues. We should identify the poison soon. My guess is that it was ingested through inhalation."

"What do you mean inhalation?"

"Breathing. Gassed."

"You mean like a gas chamber?"

"I don't know if it was a chamber, but they were gassed," Dr. Safia replies with narrowing eyes.

"How?"

"That's your area, now," she says, dragging on her cigarette slowly.

"About this embalming, doesn't one require a funeral parlor, or something, to do it?"

"Legally, yes, but we're not talking about something legal here, are we?"

"No, we're not," Mislan admits. "If not at a funeral parlor, where?"

"I don't know. It's my first case, too."

"The embalming fluid . . . can you buy it anywhere, I mean retail?"

"I think not, but if you know your chemistry, you could probably make it. It's nothing special. You can probably find cocktail mixes on the net."

"Is there any way to identify where it comes from? I mean, signature mixes or chemical compositions that'll point you to a particular funeral parlor or mortician?"

"I'm not sure. I can check it for you if you want."

"That'll be good."

"What do you think?" She is excited that she's contributing to the case.

"It's a long shot, but if we can narrow down the embalming fluid, that'll give us somewhere to start. How soon can you get me the information?"

"It's too late for me to call anyone now. I'll do it tomorrow morning and tell you. You think that's the diamond?"

"It could be, Fie. Either way, you've done well," he says, lighting another cigarette for her. This time, he lights one for himself, "Got anything more?"

"A lady shouldn't have to carry so many diamonds on her. You know that." He senses a come-on.

"Nice hair. It suits you," he says, cashing in, changing the subject. It catches her off guard and makes her blush. She smiles and savors the compliment. Their conversation then drifts to hobbies, movies, and songs. Personal questions are avoided, though. Time flies. It's been a while since he's been out with a woman or, for that matter, with anyone. The few occasions he did go out with Dr. Safia were more work-related pit-stops for a meal or a drink. After his wife left, he buried himself in the job and devoted whatever little time he had remaining to Daniel.

He is having such a wonderful time; he hates to leave, but he knows he will have to soon, so he can file his twenty-four-hour report on time.

5

He pulls into the Kuala Lumpur Police Contingent Headquarters in Jalan Hang Tuah at 10:45 p.m. and parks his car close to the lobby. It is Sunday night, and the parking lot is empty but for a few vehicles belonging to the investigating team on shift and the skeleton staff on duty. On normal working days, he would be fortunate to even find a spot within the compound. Acknowledging the greetings of the guard, he takes the elevator to his office on the seventh floor to find the front desk officer not at his post but sitting with the shift investigator, having a leisurely chat.

Like all investigators in Major Crimes, Mislan does not have a private office. He shares a desk, telephone, and computer with his assistant in the open office space. The brass say that the "open" system cultivates team building, "sharing is caring" and all that shit. Perhaps, that is the reason for the brass not working as a team, he sneers, with their private offices, computers, and direct phone lines—no sharing, no caring.

"Working late?" quips Chief Inspector Krishnan, tapping his watch.

"Just need to file my twenty-four-hour report, then I'm out of here."

"The Yee Sang Murders?"

"It's got a name?"

"Have you not watched the news? The cute newslady called it that. She said something about a robbery while they were having *yee sang* for dinner and that the entire family got whacked. What's the story?"

"Don't know yet, too early to tell. Did you, by any chance, catch the newslady's name?"

"Nope, too busy looking at her cleavage to notice her name. Catch it at midnight. I'm sure they'll air it again, she's too cute not to," Krishnan says.

"All right, thanks." He turns on the computer, lights a cigarette, and waits for the system to boot up. The old desktop computer hums and whines like a wounded animal before coming to life. He logs in with his username and password, clicks open the twenty-four-hour report template, and starts filling it in. The twenty-four-hour report is a summary of cases to be forwarded to the Control Centre, which then compiles them and distributes the information to relevant officers and divisions for information or action. Cases of public interest and national security are sent to certain individuals and the Malaysia Control Centre.

Completing the questionnaires, he writes the Report Heading, a header with a two-line summary of the case. He classifies it as a 302 and hits the Enter key, sending the report digitally to preaddressed recipients. He signs out and turns off the computer. Before leaving, he stops by the front desk and pulls out the message box. He finds his stack and flips through them. Noting that all the messages are from television networks and the press, he drops them back into the box and leaves.

Once inside his car, he takes out the notepad and writes in it, Cause of death: poisoning by inhalation. Type of gas: unknown. Victims were embalmed, modus operandi unknown. Replacing the notepad in his backpack, he starts the car and heads home. He thinks of calling Dr. Safia when he stops at a traffic light. He wonders if they could continue from where they had left off. Then he banishes the thought. He tells himself he is expecting too much.

6

AS HE WALKS PAST his boss's office at 7:30 in the morning, he notices she is already at her desk going through the twenty-four-hour reports. She signals him to enter.

"Morning, ma'am," he greets her, standing at the doorway.

"Morning, come in and sit down," she says, pointing to chairs in front of her table. "You didn't call me last night, so I suppose you have nothing new?"

"Sorry, the meeting went a on little longer than I expected. I didn't want to bother you so late at night," he says lamely.

She raises her eyebrow, and gives him a knowing smile. "Bet it did. So how did it go?"

"Dr. Safia has uncovered two unusual facts about the murders. She is following up on them. I'll be discussing them with her today. Meanwhile, we'll be checking the backgrounds of the vics, especially Robert Tham, to see if we can develop a theory."

"And Dr. Safia's findings are?"

"She says all the vics were poisoned by inhalation, and that they were embalmed."

Mislan expects her to be surprised; instead, she merely leans back expressionless, silent.

Finally, she says, "I'm taking you out of roster for a week. That'll give you sufficient time to make some headway, or to solve this."

"Are you not going to ask me about the embalming?"

"Nope. I thought they looked a little fresh. It kept me awake all night. Embalming did occur to me. I've seen many dead people, you know," she says, reminding him she was a ground officer once. "I've also seen embalmed bodies. At funerals. Anyway, I knew you'd uncover the reason for their fresh look. That's going to mess up the time of death, though, the embalming."

"I don't know, will it? Guess Dr. Safia will handle that."

"All right, then."

"Thanks. Are you expecting closure on this?" he asks. He knows the consequences of failure. He also realizes the slack she is cutting him by taking him off the roster for a week. That decision is unlikely to be popular with the other investigators. With him off the roster, it will only increase their caseloads. Over the week, casual comments and friendly teasing could easily become ugly scorn, and, if he failed to get closure, it would worsen. "I appreciate the slack time, but don't you think it's better to wait until I have a solid lead at least?"

"How are we going to get a solid lead, if you are not out there looking?"

"You're the boss," he says, knowing she may have reasons he is not privileged to know.

"I'll announce it at morning prayer," she says, referring to their daily early morning meeting of officers, dismissing him. As he leaves, she says, "Heard your case has a name: the Yee Sang Murders. Nice."

"Yah, heard it, too," he says, shrugging without looking back, but he is sure she is smiling at him, teasing.

Sergeant Johan Ismail comes in with two packets of *nasi lemak* and puts one on his desk.

"What's this for?"

"For not making me work on Sunday night," Johan says mischievously.

Mislan picks up his packet of fragrant rice cooked in coconut milk and walks to the makeshift pantry, a tiny area next to the emergency exit with an old desk and several chairs pushed against the wall. He makes coffee for both of them, and sits for his *nasi lemak* breakfast.

"This tastes good. Where did you buy it?"

"From a stall near my house. What are we doing today?"

"I'd like you to start with a profile on the vics, the father first. Try D7." That was Vice, Gaming, and Secret Society. "After that, talk to Narcotics and Commercial Crimes. Let's shake the bushes and see what comes out. I'll see if Special Branch has anything on him."

"Do you have a theory? I mean, the killers did go to quite a lot of trouble."

"You're saying 'killers.' What makes you think there was more than one killer?" Mislan says, probing his assistant's reasoning.

"There has to be. It's not a one-person job. At least two people must have been involved."

"If it's 'they,' do you think there's a message? A warning? Are we to expect more vics?"

"Could be, but whoever the message is for might not get it, or might retaliate."

"Retaliate? You mean a war?" Mislan asks, raising his brows.

"May come to that."

"What about the motive? A business deal gone bad?"

"Possible, or it could be over a drug deal, gambling, vice, anything."

"How so?"

Before Johan can answer, Mislan hears his name being called. Chief Inspector Krishnan points to the meeting room, indicating that morning prayer is about to begin. He folds his *nasi lemak* wrapper and puts it aside. He tells Johan he will clean up later.

Morning prayer kicks off at 8:30, starting with the latest twenty-four-hour reports of serious crimes. The meeting is usually short, allowing investigators to attend court proceedings and other matters. This morning, he expects to be the star attraction, and it bothers him that he has nothing of substance to mention. Chief Inspector Krishnan starts the meeting with his briefing. It is quickly dispensed with, and all heads turn to Mislan. It is his turn. Awkward silence follows as they wait for him to start. When nothing happens, like spectators at a tennis match, all heads turn to the head of Major Crimes, as if it is her turn to serve. She laughs heartily, breaking the silence, surprising them.

"Thank you for the moment of silence. I'm sure the late Mr. Robert

Tham and family would have appreciated that. Mislan, do you want to update us on the Yee Sang Murders?" All heads turn toward him in unison.

Just as he is about to start speaking, the door swings open, and the Officer in Charge of Criminal Investigation, Senior Assistant Commissioner Burhanuddin Sidek, barges in unannounced. Chairs are hastily pushed back as investigators, caught unawares, jump to attention. Only Superintendent Samsiah is not surprised. She stands calmly, greets him, and offers him her chair, creating a domino effect, with the investigator at the far end left standing. The standing investigator then scurries out to find a chair for himself, not wishing to miss the excitement of the morning. Mislan figures the heat must have been turned up a few degrees for the high priest of crime to come prowling in the villages for sacrificial goats.

"Inspector Mislan, are you the lead in this case?" the OCCI inquires pompously, being the first to sit.

He nods.

"Have you seen the papers today?" he asks sarcastically.

"No, sir. I haven't had the opportunity."

The OCCI looks at Superintendent Samsiah, who just nods.

"Well, there is a picture of the scene, with an inset of a photograph of the victim, with the headline, *RT Owner Murdered*." The OCCI pauses as if expecting applause, but when none comes, he continues. "The way I read it, the press is leaning toward the triads. I'm getting calls from some concerned public figures fearing the worst: repercussions, retaliations, more killings, even a gang war." He pauses. "Where are we on this?" he asks, turning dramatically toward the head of Major Crimes.

Unperturbed by the OCCI's melodrama, she says calmly, "We were about to hear the update." Without waiting for a response from the OCCI, she says, "Mislan, why don't you update us?"

All eyes are now on him. Clearing his throat of imaginary blockages, he begins, "The vics are Tham Cheng Loke, also known to the public as Robert Tham, and—"

"Let's skip the bio. I've read the twenty-four-hour report," the OCCI snaps impatiently. "Tell us what you've got, and what is 'vics'?"

"He means 'victims,'" Superintendent Samsiah explains, to the amusement of the other investigators.

Mislan is tempted to ask "Have you really read the twenty-four-hour report?" but does not, and only glares at SAC Burhanuddin. In the few seconds of silent staring that follow, he swears he can hear the investigators breathing and Chief Inspector Krishnan's stomach growling. Even cell phones seem to know not to ring. A tapping sound draws his attention to Superintendent Samsiah, who gives him one of her let-it-slide stares.

Yielding, Mislan continues, "We have nothing much to go on, now. The pathologist is making some inquiries on the embalming methods. I'm expecting some answers soon, by Tuesday at the earliest. The Forensic Department cannot give us anything yet. Meanwhile, my assistant is doing a background on the vics, to see if we can discover a motive."

"Who's the pathologist?"

"Dr. Nursafia Roslan from HUKM."

"Have you spoken to the chief pathologist?"

"No, I don't see the necessity. I've worked with Dr. Nursafia on several cases before this. She knows her stuff. She is putting this on the front burner, and samples have been sent to the toxicologist for analysis."

"What are the leads?"

"They're 'findings,' not leads yet. I prefer not to make it public now. If you wish, I can brief you on a need-to-know basis." He looks at his boss.

She agrees, and he hears low murmurings of disappointment from the other investigators. With that, the morning prayer ends. As the investigators file out, he whispers to one of them to get Johan to come in.

As the last investigator leaves, the OCCI says, "You're going to lose many friends."

Mislan ignores the remark, knowing his fellow investigators would act the same way to protect their cases from being leaked to the press or elsewhere. To him, SAC Burhanuddin Sidek is just another ass-kissing-pencil-pusher who is full of it and a publicity junkie who has decorated his office walls with framed newspaper clippings of himself. His office has been nicknamed the "ego chamber" by those who have visited it. He was one of several hundred senior police officers who were reassigned when the Police Field Force, a paramilitary outfit during the "Emergency" period, was downsized. Many went into management, General Duties, or Traffic, but, by the intervention of mysterious hands, SAC Burhanuddin became the city's crime-fighting supremo with no crime-fighting experience, except from watching television. His appointment caught many veteran crime fighters by surprise. Many put in transfer requests, and many retired. It was rumored that his wife was well-connected.

Mislan hears a soft knock on the door. Sergeant Johan enters and stands at attention. Superintendent Samsiah acknowledges his salute and points to a chair. Then, looking at Mislan, she says, "Shall we?"

Speaking to SAC Burhanuddin, he introduces his assistant investigating officer, explaining the need to invite Johan. He pauses for SAC Burhanuddin's response, not expecting any, then he continues, "Dr. Safia's professional opinion is death by poisoning. Chew, the Forensic supervisor, has the same opinion. As there was no sign of force, no needle mark on the bodies, or bruising at the mouths, Dr. Safia suspects the poison was administered by inhalation. They were gassed."

"What do you mean, she suspects? Doesn't she know?"

"That's her professional opinion. She has sent samples of tissues, blood, and nostril hair to toxicology and expects something by today. In investigation methodology, until the results are back from the lab, it remains an opinion," he says, watching the OCCI looking on, clueless. From the corner of his eyes, he sees Superintendent Samsiah hiding a smile with her hand. He continues, "Dr. Safia says the vics were embalmed."

"What does that mean?"

"The victims' blood had been removed and replaced with embalming fluid. It's what morticians do in funeral parlors."

The OCCI nods with disinterest.

"Raw materials for embalming are readily available. She's trying to determine whether the fluid used on the vics carries a signature."

"Does she know the embalming process?"

"She's doesn't. She's looking for someone who might. Meanwhile, we're building a profile on Robert Tham. We're reaching out to D7, Narcotics, and the Special Branch for a theory."

"How far back do we need to go?" It's Superintendent Samsiah.

"As far back as we can."

"Do you need me to talk to them?" she offers.

"We're good for the moment. I'll take you up on your offer if we're stonewalled."

"Is that all?" the OCCI interjects. "You expect me to go to the press with that?" He turns to Superintendent Samsiah. "I can't go to the press with that! What about suspects?"

"Suspects! We don't even have a motive," he says, not hiding his annoyance.

The OCCI looks at Superintendent Samsiah and says, "Are you not putting someone with more experience on this?"

"Mislan remains the lead. I'll supervise," she answers, calmly. "I've pulled him off the roster to focus on this case and—"

"Are you not going to reconsider your decision?" the OCCI cuts her off.

Her face hardens. She shakes her head.

"I think you're making a mistake. It's your career on the line," the OCCI says, making a clear threat. He pushes himself up with his hands on the meeting table, indicating that the meeting is over.

They remain seated until he leaves.

"Thanks, ma'am, but he's right. I'll understand if you want to give this to someone else."

"Just do your job. Let me worry about my career," she says curtly, and leaves.

7

RT FASHION HOUSE IN Bukit Bintang occupies an old colonial bungalow that has been remodeled into commercial property. Mislan parks in a "visitors" spot and stands by his open car door for several minutes, admiring the luxury vehicles in the lot.

He then picks up his backpack, closes the car door, and walks to the front door. He notes that it is monitored by a closed-circuit camera. A key-access pad with an intercom by its side has a sticker that says "Please Press for Assistance." Standing by the door, he examines the two sides of the bungalow. A camera mounted at each end is aimed at the parking lot and the gate, probably to capture images of vehicles entering and leaving the compound. He sees no guardhouse and no security guard on duty either. He wonders who monitors the cameras and how long the recordings are stored before being overwritten.

A woman's voice coming through the intercom startles him: "Can I help you?"

"I'm Inspector Mislan. I'm here to see the person in charge," he speaks into the intercom.

"Do you have an appointment?"

"No," he replies, holding up his authority card to the camera. He hears the whirring of hydraulics as the camera zooms in for a close-up of the card. A few seconds pass before he hears a clicking sound and the same voice invites him in.

The living room, waiting room, lobby, or whatever it is termed in a bungalow that is now an office, is dimly lit. It looks like a comfortable living room but is decorated with the professional flair of an office. The furniture and fixtures look as if they have been designed by the same person who did the victim's house: soft leather sofas and glass-topped coffee tables with stainless-steel legs, all expensive. Display cases, with RT's latest award-winning designs, line one wall. Posters in large frames line another. The door clicks as it locks itself behind him, and the same voice asks him to register. Seeing no reception counter, he turns toward the voice to see a Plexiglas window built into the wall with a silhouette behind it. Pressing his authority card against the Plexiglas, he says, "Can I speak to the person in charge?"

The silhouette does not answer; instead, it pushes a register book and a pen through an opening below the Plexiglas. He writes his name, contact number, and designation and leaves the column for the person he wants to meet blank. He pushes the register book back, and the silhouette says, "Please have a seat, I'll inform Miss Irene." He hears the word *Miss* and feels offended, convinced that a wet-behind-the-ears clerk is being sent to talk to him. Corporate people only meet the brass. Inspectors, to them, are too far down the ladder. Walking back to the sofa, he sees a hospitality counter with several jars of cookies and a range of hot and cold drinks. He wants some coffee but is afraid he might not be able to work the strange-looking contraptions. He is dying for a smoke and looks for an ashtray. He doesn't find any. He asks the silhouette if smoking is permitted. The answer is: "No."

He hears a click and turns around to locate the source. He sees a tiny green blinking light on the wall as a door opens and a smartly dressed middle-aged woman enters.

"Inspector Mislan, I'm Irene Rijanti," she says, extending her hand.

He shakes her long soft hand, saying, "Thank you for seeing me. Do you have somewhere we can talk in private?" She is not what he expects.

"Yes, we can use my office," she says, turning back to where she came from, and punches some numbers on a camouflaged keypad. He hears another click, and the door she came through reopens. She leads him to another area that looks more like the living room of a movie celebrity than an office. She walks with an air of confidence and the elegance of a woman who has been on a thousand catwalks. The flirtatious sway of her rear, the bouncing of her long curly hair, and the lingering scent of her perfume tease, taunt, and intoxicate. Irene Rijanti looks like one of those women who age but never grow old, never become outdated or irrelevant.

When his cell phone rings, Irene turns and looks at him without breaking her stride, and asks if he needs to answer the call before coming in. He nods, and takes a few steps back. Through the corner of his eyes, he sees Irene stop at the secretary's desk, lean close, and say something to her, looking in his direction a few times.

"Yes, Jo."

"I think we've got something good from D7. The vic was SS. I'm going to D7 to get copies of the file."

"Good." So Mr. Robert Tham was a member of a secret society. "How about reports from the others?"

"Nothing yet. I'll drop by their offices after D7. Maybe they need some persuasion."

"Good, you do that. Tell me if they're not handing it out."

He walks into Irene's office, notices the empty secretary's chair, and pokes his head through her door. She invites him in. Irene steps out from behind her boomerang-shaped glass table, sits in one of the soft leather singles, and beckons him to take the one next to hers. The missing secretary reappears with a mug of coffee and an ashtray. After depositing them on the coffee table in front of him, she leaves, closing the door.

"Thought you would like some coffee, and I heard you ask if you could smoke in the lobby," Irene says.

"Thank you, that is kind of you." He is impressed. They have, obviously, been watching and listening. He offers her a cigarette, lights hers, and gets one himself. He takes a long drag and reaches for his coffee.

"It's black. I take it that police officers drink only black coffee," Irene says with a chuckle. "Learned it from TV. Hope I'm right, but if you want cream or, perhaps, tea, my secretary can get it for you."

"No, coffee is good. I suppose you know why I'm here?" he starts, bring out his digital recorder. "Do you mind if I tape this interview? I'm getting too old to remember details."

Irene hesitates. "Interview? Sorry, I don't understand. I just got back from Hong Kong late last night. Business. I thought you are here about the donation Robert pledged."

"I'm so sorry, I thought you knew or were informed by your staff. Mr. Tham and his family are deceased. We found the bodies yesterday." He watches her face for signs but sees only genuine shock. Her jaw drops, and her eyes go watery. He gives her a moment before saying, "I need to ask you a few questions. Are you up to it?"

Irene nods awkwardly, takes an extra-long drag on the cigarette, squashes it in the ashtray, and asks, "What happened?"

"We're still working on it, trying to piece things together to get a clearer picture. The maid found them when she came back on Sunday morning. When was the last you saw Mr. Tham?"

"Thursday evening, before I left for Hong Kong. Our meeting finished late."

"Did he appear, or act, different?"

"No, he was his usual self. Last week was tiring, problems at our factory in Indonesia. Robert managed to resolve most of it. If anything, I would say, he was relaxed, talking about his coming family weekend getaway. He was looking forward to it."

"May I know what the problems in Indonesia were?"

"Equity. That is the biggest hassle in setting up business over there."

"Could that have led to Mr. Tham's death?"

She laughs. "No, Inspector. That'll not benefit them. Robert's death will be a loss to them financially."

"The vacation, did he mention where they were going?"

"I believe to Langkawi."

"Did he have a driver?"

"No, he drives himself. He says drivers are liabilities; they talk too much. You know what he means." Irene smiles, regaining her composure.

"Is there anything you can tell me about Mr. Tham? Anything that might help us in our investigations?"

"I don't know what to tell. I met Robert about nine years ago at a charity function. I was then a buyer for a foreign label. We started talking, Robert expressed interest in starting a line of his own, and I wanted out of my dead-end career. We clicked, and a year later RT was born. After that, RT started creating waves in the industry, and we now manufacture in Hong Kong, China, Thailand, and we are about to set up in Indonesia. We are well established in Southeast Asia, Australia, South America," she says with obvious pride.

"What about enemies? Did Mr. Tham have any?"

"I don't know. As in all businesses, competition is tough. The fashion industry is no different, possibly even worse. I am sure some are envious of our success, but I don't know whether they can be termed enemies."

"Did Mr. Tham have any other businesses?"

"Yes, but they were not linked to RT. That was one of my conditions for joining him, that his other businesses were his, and not linked to RT. Robert kept his promise; his other businesses were never run from here, and I have never been involved."

"What kind of businesses? Do you know?"

"I know he has a real-estate company, RT Realty. He started it to offset the sales commission of this bungalow, then continued it as a business. I have heard he is a partner in a used car business, but I don't know the details. He did mention something about venturing into entertainment. You know, karaoke lounges and pubs, but I don't know whether he did."

"Is there anyone I can talk to who knows more about his other businesses? Maybe his partners."

"I don't know. We never did talk about any of that, and he does not believe in having a secretary. Handles all his calls and business affairs himself."

"What about families?"

"I'm sorry, Inspector. I don't know. I remember hearing that he is an only child and that his parents are dead. Robert never spoke about them, and I was not introduced to anyone. Robert was private about his past, and that suited me fine. So I don't know anything about Robert's family. I have never been invited to his house, not even for Chinese New Year. It's strictly RT business between us."

"How about you?"

"What about me?"

"I mean, are you a partner, shareholder?"

Smiling, Irene says, "I'm a partner, a small partner. I own ten percent of the company. The rest is owned by Robert. What are you getting at? That I killed Robert to take over the company?"

He laughs. "Did you?"

"What do you think, Inspector?" Irene looks amused.

"At this point, I don't know what to think. So, without Mr. Tham, who holds ninety percent of the shares, who benefits?"

"I don't know. I know it's not me."

"How about the operations, signing checks and all?"

"It has always been me handling the operations; I suppose that will continue until someone comes and shows me that he, or she, owns the ninety percent."

"Are you married?"

Irene laughs out loud. "Is that for the investigation, or for your knowledge? I was, Inspector. Now you're going to ask me if I'm seeing someone, right."

"Nope, but since you have brought it up, are you?"

"I'm available. How's that?" she teases him.

"That's it for now. I won't take more of your time," Mislan says, trying to sound formal and failing. Handing her his call card, he says, "Please call me if you think of something." With that, he retrieves his recorder, slings on his backpack, and stands. Irene opens a gold card-holder and gives him her business card.

She then walks him to the lobby where they shake hands and he thanks her again. When the front door opens with a click, he stands in the doorway and asks her who owns all the vehicles. She points to a blue BMW Z4, saying it is hers, whereas the silver Porsche Cayenne and white Mercedes E240 Kompressor belonged to Robert Tham.

"Which car did he normally drive?"

"Both of them. He changed cars as he pleased. He said it was for safety reasons. That's odd."

"What?"

"The Cayenne. I thought Robert was going to use it on his vacation. Maybe he changed his mind. Typical of Robert, you can never be certain of what he'll do until he does it. Always changing his mind at the last minute."

8

As he waits for the air-conditioner to cool his car, Mislan speed-dials Sergeant Johan and instructs him to wait at the station guardhouse. When he takes out the digital recorder from his shirt pocket, he realizes it is still running. He switches it off and puts it in the backpack. He keys in another speed-dial number, this time for Dr. Safia, to ask if she is game for a quick lunch, to which she says, "Yes, a very quick lunch." He puts his car into gear and drives past the touristy Bintang Walk before taking a right toward Pudu. An immediate left into Jalan Galloway leads him to his headquarters in Jalan Hang Tuah. He sees Johan at the guardhouse and pulls over, signaling to him with two flashes of his headlights.

"Where are we headed?" Johan asks, climbing into the passenger's seat.

"HUKM. Have you got anything from D7?"

Johan unbuckles his clutch bag and extracts a few sheets. "Tham aka Robert Tham aka Lan-si (Arrogant) Tham was a member of the 21 Immortals. Recruited at seventeen, he was active in Chow Kit. He has been linked to several protection-money rackets, extortion, and assault cases, but was never charged. He became the lieutenant of the South Side in '82 when Four Finger Loo rose to the position of Tiger General. In '88 he was rumored to be the Tiger General in the north, that is, Perak and Penang. After the SS operation of '95, his file went inactive."

"What do you mean 'went inactive'?"

"It's not closed, just inactive. It was like D7 had no further interest in him."

"What do you make of it? You think he was recruited, or did he snitch and make a deal?"

"The D7 officer who made these copies is an old-timer. He asked me why I was interested. Told him it was routine, but you know how they like to talk. He said he remembered the big sweep. D7 bragged that they had a big fish at the time. Maybe it was him."

"You think the killing was payback by the 21?"

"Maybe. Secret societies are notorious for it. Many of those rounded up are now free. It's the only motive that makes any sense."

He nods. "Who was the case officer?"

"Inspector Song Chee Chin, now with the Petaling Jaya police."

"Is anyone handling it now?"

"Nope. It has been made inactive and archived."

"I knew Song when I was in the district. He was in charge of SS. We worked on the Jalan Campbell gang fights together. I'll call him, run your theory, and see what he thinks. Meanwhile, Jo, please check Maria's story. Get the help of a detective on standby," he says.

"How did it go at RT?" Johan asks.

"It went. They usually see nothing, hear nothing, and know nothing. I don't buy it, though. How could anyone work with someone for nine years and know nothing about him, his business, friends, or family?"

"What's there not to buy?" Johan says, amused. "I once lived with a girl for two years. I knew nothing about her until one day a man showed up with a four-year-old child claiming to be her husband and the boy, their son."

Bursting into laughter, Mislan says, "You're joking, right?"

"I'm not shitting you. It's the truth," Johan replies.

"Then, what happened?"

"I told the guy he had the wrong house. After they left, which took some convincing, I packed her things, carried them to her car, and told her never to come back."

"You're a class act, Jo. Did you ever see her again?"

"Nope. Guess she must have moved in with another ignorant bastard. A pity, though. She was good under the sheets," Johan says, shaking his head, laughing and swearing.

They are silent for the remainder of the journey. He is preoccupied with Johan's story: a file not closed but inactive, and the case officer transferred to Petaling Jaya. Maybe Johan is right; it is payback, but why the charade? What is the message?

Traffic is heavy, and it takes them more than forty minutes to make the journey of eleven kilometers. The Department of Forensic Pathology is next to the morgue, at the back of the hospital complex, with its entrance hidden from public view. He parks his car in the lot reserved for government vehicles. An ancient-looking, sleepy security guard seated at the entrance does not bother to approach them to verify their identity or credentials.

He calls Dr. Safia. "Hi, your office or the canteen?"

"Why don't you wait for me in the canteen? Give me ten. I have to shoot off this report."

"All right." He takes his backpack and gestures for Johan to follow him. They walk toward the main building past the physiotherapy center, take the elevator to G, and go to the canteen. The *nasi campur* line is long. It is lunchtime. He looks at Johan, and as if reading his mind, the sergeant nods and they head for the snacks and sandwiches counter where there are two large women queuing. He chooses some snacks and two packets of tuna sandwiches, pays for them, and tells Johan to get some drinks while he locates a table where they can have some privacy.

He finds one by the window. He realizes that it overlooks the morgue only after settling down. Smiling, he thinks of the irony: The hospital has it right, a canteen overlooking a morgue.

"What are you smiling at?" Johan says, as he puts down the drinks.

"Nothing."

Johan looks out of the window, curious. Just then Dr. Safia emerges from the building across. "She's a looker, eh," he remarks. "Word around the office is that you two are an item."

"Just friends," the inspector says curtly, killing further conversation on the subject.

Mislan sees Dr. Safia standing at the canteen's door, her eyes searching over the heads of the crowd. He waves to her and watches as she walks toward them, her unbuttoned bleached-white hospital gown floating by her side with each rhythmic sway of her body. Her movements are graceful, and her smile never leaves her face. She handles the dead daily, she always smiles. What makes her so? Why did she become a pathologist? Were they more than just friends?

"Thanks for your time," he says.

"No problem, I need the distraction. Sergeant Johan, how are you?" she extends her hand.

"Hi, Doc. I'm fine, thanks," Johan replies, standing instantly to shake her hand.

"We just got some snacks and sandwiches. You want something else?"

"Not to worry, these are fine."

"You okay with coffee?" Johan asks.

She nods.

He waits for her to sip her drink. "Anything new so far?"

"Just got the toxi report. It's confirmed. Cause of death: hydrogen cyanide poisoning through inhalation," she says unwrapping the tuna sandwich. Noticing he is about to ask her another question, she holds up the sandwich and says, "Hold on. For the deceased to have that level of hydrogen cyanide in their system, they must have been directly exposed to it in an enclosed area. Hydrogen cyanide, or HCN, as you know, is lethal, colorless and odorless. The deceased wouldn't have realized its presence. My guess is they were in an enclosed, airtight area when the gas was introduced. Now you may ask your questions."

"Are you saying it cannot be sprayed on them in an open environment?"

"I suppose if you hold down the victim, you can spray it directly into their faces. You'll have to wear breathing apparatus, or you'll suffer the same fate. HCN dilutes fast in the open, so the level of concentration may not be enough to kill them as quickly as you want to."

"Hmm. What about the embalming fluid?"

"I spoke to Professor David Teh from the University of Malaya, an expert. He's willing to look at the report and give us his opinion. I've faxed it to him. I'll call him later to see if he can tell us anything."

"Great, and you'll let me know soon after, right?"

"You'll be the first." Dr. Safia smiles.

"Back to the COD, let me get this right: you said the vics were poisoned with hydrogen cyanide. By inhalation, but it wasn't sprayed on them. You figure they were in a sort of airtight chamber? This case is going nowhere. I've got more questions than answers." He takes out his cigarette pack.

Johan points to the no smoking sign behind him, and shakes his head. He looks back, smiles, and returns the pack to his pocket.

"Like what?" Dr. Safia takes another bite of the sandwich.

"The killers must have built an airtight chamber with gas piping and all. You'll need special skills or knowledge for that, won't you?"

"I don't know. Maybe."

"Hydrogen cyanide, is that easily available?" the sergeant asks.

Turning to face Johan, Dr. Safia says, "Yes, it's in the seafood we eat, but at a safe level. It's also used in manufacturing paper. You could produce it in a lab, I suppose. Don't know about canning it under pressure for a gas chamber, though. That's something else for which you might need special equipment and expertise. During the Second World War, Nazis used it against the Jews; some reports say Saddam used it against his enemies. About the chamber, I think a walk-in freezer will serve the purpose; it is airtight and piped."

"Yes, let's consider that . . . I mean the freezer thing . . . there were no defensive wounds on the vics, right?" It is more a statement than a question. "You didn't find any signs of struggle, bruising, lacerations, or broken nails. If they were locked in a freezer, wouldn't they know something bad was happening? Wouldn't they have started banging, kicking, or pulling at the door after a while? That'll surely have left some bruise marks."

Dr. Safia nods. "Unless the gas was released as soon as they were locked in."

"Even then it'll take time to fill the chamber. I'm sure they would have started kicking and banging the door the moment they were thrown into the chamber. No, I can't buy that theory."

Johan nods his agreement. "How long does this HCN take to knock you out?"

"It's lethal, depending on the concentration level. It takes a few seconds to a minute for systemic chemical asphyxiation. It attacks organs that are most sensitive to low oxygen levels: the central nervous system, the cardiovascular system, and the pulmonary system."

"Wow, Doc. English please, I failed my science in school," Mislan says, laughing.

"The brain, heart, and lungs," she says, amused. "All you need is one breath, and that's it. It was a favorite with spies during World War II and the Cold War. Don't you watch spy movies? How, when they are captured, they pop cyanide pills into their mouths to avoid torture?"

The two policemen chuckle at the way she says it.

"Doc, if the vics were put in a chamber together, won't there be markings on their bodies from hugging one another tightly just before death?"

"I thought of that, too, but there were no marks on their bodies to indicate they did. Don't forget they were embalmed. That could be a reason for the marking not being visible."

"Really?"

"Yes, but we would still be able to detect markings if they were there."

"But you didn't."

"Nope."

"Could they have been gassed separately?"

"Possible," she agrees.

He shakes his head. "The killer would need three gas chambers, and with only one it would have taken too much time to finish the job. Impossible."

The others agree.

"Why not poison their food?" Johan asks.

"Unpredictable and unmanageable. Poison is good if there is only one vic. I don't think the killers wanted to take the risk of some people not eating or drinking the poison once they saw what was happening to others," Mislan replies shaking his head.

"Then why not just shoot or stab them; simple, no hassle, and sure?" Johan suggests.

"Too messy, room for mistakes, and leaves evidence. No, these killers were good. This crime was very well-planned; it was not an impulse kill-ing. It needed intelligence, preparation, and determination. A master-piece. Something special, but I just don't understand it," Mislan admits.

"You sound like you admire them. I have to go now; I'll leave it in the good hands of Inspector Sherlock and Watson to figure it out." Dr. Safia stands. "Got a group of young deputy public prosecutors coming to watch me do my magic. Hope there are some cute ones attending."

"I respect their means, not their end," he says, smiling. "Thanks, Fie. Please don't forget to call me when Professor Teh has something."

She gives him the thumbs up as she walks toward the door. Watching her, Johan comments, "Stunning, isn't she? Brains and beauty. What else could you ask for?"

When Mislan ignores him, Johan asks, "Now what?"

"Now, we go get some real food. I'm hungry."

9

ONE THE WAY BACK, Mislan takes a detour through Jalan Cheras and Kampung Pandan and drives to Seri Ratu, the famous Indonesian *nasi padang* restaurant. It was also one of his ex-wife's favorite eateries. It brings back memories of happier times with her. He thinks of her, the streets they traveled, the shops and restaurants they liked, the songs they sang, and the special times they shared. He still sees her, talks to her, smiles at her in his mind, in his memories, and is often swept away by grief and longing. It is a part of his life where time refuses to move on. How could he ever be resigned to never seeing her again?

"Something's wrong?"

He sees Johan looking at him.

"Just wondering if I left something in the car," he lies, quickly recovering.

They find a table, and two waiters immediately approach, each bearing a large tray, with several plates of food, which they place before them. When the waiters finish, more than twenty dishes are spread before them. Johan is astounded, "How are we going to eat all this?"

"You eat what you want, and the food not consumed will not be charged. Or, you could tell the waiter to remove dishes you don't want. That's how it's done in Indonesia."

With his anxiety put to rest, Johan starts eating, but Mislan has lost his appetite. He is troubled by Dr. Safia's report. Something about the method bothers him. He cannot put his finger on it, yet it nags him. It is probably the key to the case. Unless he pins it down, he is no nearer to solving the case than he was when he filed his twenty-four-hour report. He has no theory, no leads, and many unanswered questions. Maybe the OCCI is right after all. Maybe the case should have been given to someone with more experience. Maybe he should go talk to his boss and surrender.

"Are you all right?" Johan asks for the second time since they arrived.

"Yes. Why?"

"You're not eating. Something bothering you? It's Dr. Safia, isn't it?"

"It's not Dr. Safia, not what your dirty mind is thinking," he says, guessing where his assistant was leading the conversation. "It's what she said. Anyway, looking at all the food makes me full. You go ahead and stuff yourself."

Watching his assistant eat, his mind drifts again to his ex-wife. How she used to enjoy the food here, especially the grilled fish and prawns. She loved seafood. Although he is allergic to prawn, he never stopped her from ordering and enjoying them.

Johan's phone rings and he answers it with his mouth full. After several "hmms" and "okays," he explains that the call was from the standby detective. Maria's story checks out. "What's our next move?"

"I don't know. Just can't make sense of the case. I'm going back to the office, to go through what we have so far. Maybe there is something we have missed. I want you to run down the secret society lead. Track down Four Finger Loo and any other known members of 21. See if we can get some inside story on the vic. At this point, that's all we can do; dig deeper. I'll see if Inspector Song can point us in the right direction."

After Johan finishes his meal, Mislan signals for the bill. As he waits for it, he notices a woman in her early thirties staring at them. She looks familiar, but he can't place her. She's dressed casually in jeans and designer T-shirt, and, when their eyes meet, she smiles. She's probably Indonesian, he thinks, smiling at the way Johan is eating like a foreign tourist. Maybe it is his lucky day; a woman is hitting on him. Not having been with a woman after his wife left, he feels elated yet apprehensive. He sees the row of washbasins behind her table, and heads nonchalantly toward them as if to wash his hands. He walks slowly, moving close to her table as he does. Then, when he is about five feet away, the woman stands abruptly, smiles, and extends her hand. "Inspector Mislan. Hi, I'm Rodziah. You can call me Audi, like the car."

Surprised, he mumbles, "Hi." After an embarrassing moment of silence, he notices her extended hand and says, "Sorry, my hands are dirty. Let me wash them first," and hurries toward the wash area. Turning the tap on, he pretends to wash his hands as he watches her in the mirror. Who the hell is she? Do I know her? He wipes his hands and his mouth with several paper towels in exaggerated motions to give himself more time to think, then slowly walks back to her table.

"Audi like the car, right? Do we know each other?"

"Yes, like the car; and, no, you don't know me. I'm from *Astro Awani*. I did the reporting on the late Mr. Robert Tham. I was wondering if you will give me an exclusive."

The words *Astro Awani* places her face as the newslady he saw on television, and his libido instantly plummets. "Damn," he swears. "Sorry, I can't help you. It's an investigation in progress," he says. "By the way, how did you know where to find me?"

"I was trying to meet the pathologist at HUKM when I saw you leaving. I followed you." Audi brims with pride.

"Sorry to tell you, but your effort has been for nothing."

"Inspector, maybe we can work together on this. You know, I'll give you what I've got on the late Mr. and Mrs. Robert Tham, and you give me an exclusive." She gets up and follows him.

Mislan stops in his tracks, and Audi bumps hard into him. "*Ow!* That hurts," she squeals, rubbing her chest.

"What do you mean by 'what you've got on them'?"

"I did some research. Our archive, as you know, is full of unpublished stories. I can share them with you, or you can use me to get access to it. For that privilege, you give me an exclusive. What say you?" Audi is trying hard to sound like a seasoned journalist.

He continues walking, with her in tow. "How about I pick you up for withholding information, or how about me getting a court order to access the archive?"

"Sure you can, but that'll attract attention. I'm sure that's not what you want at this juncture," Audi dares him. "My guess is the police have nothing. Otherwise, your publicity junkie, the OCCI, would've called for a press conference by now." When he doesn't respond, she says, "Off the record, do you have a lead?"

"There's nothing off the record with you people," he sneers, but he's more upset at the fact that she is right. "You give me what you've got, and I'll see what I can do. How's that?"

"That's not fair," Audi protests.

He turns to her with a sarcastic smile, "Who says life is fair?"

"Chill it, okay, no need to get upset. We're both just doing our jobs. It's a deal." Audi pulls a thumb drive from her pocket and holds it out to him. "Do I have your word?" she pulls her hand away as he reaches for the thumb drive. "If you base your investigations on this info, I get the exclusive?"

He smiles. "I thought you don't trust us? What makes you think I'll keep my word?"

"Let's just say, I know you." Audi smirks.

10

When Inspector mislan peeks through the door of his boss's office, she sees him and signals him in, closing the file she is reading. He drops heavily into the chair like a boxer who has just suffered a humiliating round of brutal pounding.

"You look terrible," she says.

"I feel terrible," he admits. "I hate to tell you this, ma'am, but I think the OCCI was right. You should've given this case to someone senior. This case is too much for me."

She crosses her arms, leans forward on her desk, and says softly, "I've worked with you for years. I've never seen you give up on a case yet. Don't you start now! Maybe you're tired of working with me and you want a new boss. Is that it? Do you have any of the OCCI's lapdogs in mind?"

Her low soft tone is scary. He realizes she's getting heat from the top and his giving up could dot the *i*'s and cross the *t*'s on her transfer papers. Superintendent Samsiah Hassan is a professional, never compromises her integrity, and has never played the ass-kissing game. She is respected for her professionalism, yet loathed by some superiors and peers. Given a chance, she could be replaced instantly. He enjoys working with her and knows she will always be there to take the heat for her team. At the same time, she will always be the first to reprimand them, if it came to that.

"I'm going nowhere on this case. It's like a perfect crime," he whines.

"That is not the Inspector Mislan I know, coming in here to throw in his towel. And don't you dare give me the perfect crime crap. There's no such thing. There's always a mistake, a clue, a hint, a lead. You just haven't found it yet. Go back to the crime scene, talk to your witnesses again, review your investigation diary. I'm sure you'll find it. It's always waiting to be uncovered. Get out of here before I take you up on your offer. Go and do some real police work," she hisses, ending the conversation.

"Thanks, ma'am." He knows she is right, and she has just reaffirmed her decision to keep him as the lead.

"You can thank me by solving the Yee Sang Murders, and stop whining."

Back at his desk, he plugs in the thumb drive from Audi into his computer. He sees a folder titled *Unpublished—Robert Tham of RT Fashion* with twenty-two files. He picks one at random and opens it. It is a report called *RT Fashion Accused of Stealing Design* by Tammy Ong. Browsing through the article, he decides it has no relevance to his case. He examines the file list and one titled *Are They More Than Friends?* catches his attention. He clicks it. A picture pops up of the late Mrs. Robert Tham wrapped in the arms of a Hong Kong actor. She holds a drink in her hand and is being hugged from the back, all smiles. The photograph looks like it was taken at a party; small groups of well-dressed men and women hold wineglasses, chatting. The article is about three months old and describes the actor as her new "toy boy," implying the late Mrs. Tham might have had others. It says he is fifteen years younger than she and had recently broken up with his girlfriend because of this latest escapade. According to the story, it's the first time they are posing for the cameras in public. When asked if the two were a couple, the late Mrs. Robert Tham smiled without commenting. The report also said Mr. Robert Tham was abroad on business.

He makes a note to ask Audi about the late Mrs. Robert Tham. He wonders if Mr. Tham wasn't the primary target. Maybe it was Mrs. Tham. He runs through the other file names and decides to read them later. Picking up the phone, he asks the operator for Inspector Song Chee Chin of Petaling Jaya Police. While waiting for his call to be put through, he reviews the case log and sighs. He remembers he has to forward the recordings of his interviews to the district investigator for it to be transcribed and signed off by the witnesses, for inclusion in the investigation paper. As he plugs his digital recorder in to his computer to make a copy of Maria's interview, the phone rings.

"Inspector Song Chee Chin is on the line," the operator tells him, putting him through.

"PJ Police, Inspector Song."

"Hey, Song. Mislan, Major Crimes, KL. How are you?"

"Hey, Lan. Fine, fine. How's KL?"

"Usual. Song, you heard about Robert Tham?"

"Yes, only what's in the news. Are you the lead?"

"Yes, I am. Song, I need to ask you something. You were the case officer for the vic when he was in 21, but his file is not closed but inactive. Any light there?"

"It was long ago, Lan. Seven, eight years?"

"More, but it's not something you'd forget," Mislan prompts him. "Instructions to dormant a file have to come from the top. I'm reaching out here."

"I don't know if I can help you, Lan. I don't have sufficient clearance." Inspector Song is evasive.

"All right, I understand. What if it comes from another source?"

"What do you mean?"

"Four Finger Loo. Can you put me on to him? I'll make sure your name does not come up."

A long silence follows.

"Song, you still there?"

"Let me make some calls and get back to you," Inspector Song finally says.

"Thank you very much. I owe you one, Song."

"Let me make some calls. What's your cell number?" Mislan gives it to him and hangs up. Lighting a cigarette, he turns on the digital recorder to continue copying.

11

THE BOUT WITH HIS boss weighs heavy on Mislan's mind. He calls Chew to ask if he will be in the office working late, then Johan, who is in the canteen having *teh tarik* with a friend who used to be attached to D7. He tells Johan to wait, that he will be down shortly. He signals his assistant from the canteen door before he walks toward the parking lot. Johan arrives just as he starts the engine.

"Where are we headed?"

"Forensics."

"They got something?" Johan is excited.

"No, I just cannot sit around the office doing nothing. Anything from your friend?"

"He said the 21 Immortals was wiped out in the 1995 sweep. Most of them were either sent to Jerejak Island detention or placed under Restricted Residence on the East Coast. By now, many would've settled down." Johan pauses to collect his thoughts. "He heard some of them did make their way back to KL after serving their time. Fatty Mah, the godfather, was never picked up. Some say he got wind of the sweep and scooted off to Thailand, where he still is. My friend says he'll ask around, but he is ex-D7, so he is not promising anything."

"That's good," he tells his assistant. "Are you buying it? Is Fatty Mah back, and did he do this?"

"It is possible."

"I spoke to Song, and he's not saying anything. By the way, the newslady at the restaurant this afternoon gave me some material from their archive. I've not gone through all of them, but there's one article about the wife. There was some gossip surrounding the late Mrs. Tham and a young Hong Kong actor. Maybe we should look into that, maybe she was the primary target. I'll go through the rest tonight and see if there is anything worth following up."

"Juicy, extramarital activities . . . never thought of her as the primary vic. Hmm. She was good looking. Husband always away on business, could be something there."

"You have actor friends, don't you? Why don't you do some sniffing, see if you can verify the rumors?"

"I'll try, but I don't think they know the Hong Kong actors."

The Forensic Department is housed within the Royal Police College complex in Cheras. Making a U-turn under the KL-Kajang overpass immediately after the Police Field Force camp, he turns into the college complex, stops briefly at the guardhouse, and identifies himself. The uniformed guard directs him to the parking lot behind the administrative building. He is familiar with the layout of the complex. He drives to the administrative building, takes a left turn behind it, and parks the car in one of the visitors' lots. Before killing his engine, he calls Chew to ask where he is.

The Forensic building runs parallel to the administrative block, and Chew's office is on the first floor. They climb the stairs and head for the lab, where they find Chew engrossed in studying a bloodstained piece of clothing under a large magnifying glass mounted on the table with lights. A technician at the next table is also examining another piece of clothing that looks like one worn by the victims in his case. The lab smells of stale blood and rotting vegetables.

"Hi, Chew."

"Oh hi, Inspector." Chew is startled. "I'd shake your hand, but I'll have to change gloves, and that would be a waste of taxpayers' money."

Mislan and Johan nod at the technician they recognize as one of the team members at the crime scene. "No, you don't want to do that," he says, playing along. "Got anything for me?"

"Nothing I haven't told you already. Give me the primary scene, and I'll show you what we can do."

"Are you just starting on the clothing?"

"We're doing a second run, to see if we missed anything," Chew replies, defensively.

"And?"

Chew shakes his head, "So far, nothing. Remember when I asked you to smell the vics?"

"Yes."

"After you left, I took samples from their facial skin for trace. I also did my sniff analysis with the perfumes and cosmetics samples taken from the vic's room; they don't match. Unfortunately, my nose is not a certified scientific equipment," Chew says, laughing. "But, if my hunch is right, the trace will give us the same result. Then you might have something to follow up."

"Great. So what're we waiting for?"

"It should be in by now. Why don't you go wait in my office and let me finish here?" Chew motions toward his office. "And, don't touch anything, you hear me!"

"Got it. Do you have coffee in there?"

As Mislan imagined, the office is filled with reports, manuals, miniature models, and reference materials strewn indiscriminately. Almost every available square inch is taken up by one thing or other. How does Chew know where anything is? He sees a small coffee maker in one corner with several mugs. The lingering odor that follows him into the cubicle from the lab stops his yearning for a cup, though. Chew comes in just as they are about to move some material from the chairs.

"Where do we put these?"

Going around the desk to his chair, Chew answers, "Just put them anywhere." He then pulls out his keyboard, saying, "Let's see. Ahh, here it is." He reads whatever is on the screen and says, "You're in luck, Inspector. The samples I took from the daddy and the boy have no match to the mummy's perfumes or cosmetics. An unknown."

"And that translates as?"

"When I was sniffing the vics, I thought I smelled a faint scent of woman's perfume on the daddy and the boy. Then I sniffed mummy. It struck me as strange, because the fragrance did not match hers."

"But what does that mean?"

"I'm not the investigator here, Inspector, but it tells me there was a transfer from an unknown onto daddy and boy. Is there any perfume not collected from the scene? If there isn't, then that's your lead. I know it's not much, but it's still a lead."

"I saw your technicians collecting the perfumes, I'm sure they collected all except the maid's."

"They said they did do hers as well."

"Can you identify the perfume? Any brand or manufacturer?"

"Trace can give you the component, but I don't think they can tell you the brand name."

"So we have the transfer of unknown cosmetic or perfume from an unknown person to the vics. That just sums up the day: unknowns."

"It starts as an unknown before it becomes known. Always has, always does, and always will be. That's what we do, that's what you do, uncover the unknown."

"Can't you match it with existing products on the market?" Johan asks.

"Jo, we're scientists, not magicians. Do you know how many products there are? The big-name products alone run into the thousands, then there are the small players and the homemade stuff. The best bet for a match is still through you, your suspects and leads."

"Sorry, I didn't mean to—"

"Forget it, I know."

Leaving Chew's office, Mislan mulls over his findings. How should he interpret it? An unknown woman at the scene? Who? How was the cosmetic or perfume transferred to the victims? A kiss? Who wears perfume on the lips, or do they? Who would want to kiss a corpse? Maybe the cheek; yes, from cheek to cheek, but why? Chew's information may be crucial in placing the suspect at the scene of the crime, but he has to find the suspect. Until then, the only use he has for the information is to brief the boss and keep the OCCI at bay.

12

INSPECTOR SONG ARRANGES A meeting with Four Finger Loo at eight that night, at the Lock Ann Hotel in Jalan Petaling. He still has about three hours to kill. How he wishes the police offices here had showers, lockers, or changing rooms, like on television. Although he always keeps spare clothes in the trunk of his car, he does not feel like washing in the office toilet cubicle. He tells his assistant investigating officer of the meeting and instructs him to be at the hotel an hour earlier to do some sleuthing.

At 7:30 in the evening he turns off his computer, takes his backpack, catches the elevator to the ground floor, and ambles to the parking lot, wondering if he should drive to the meeting. He speed-dials Johan and asks, "Are you there?"

"Yup. No sign of Four Finger yet."

"He'll be there, just relax and watch your back. I'm on my way."

His assistant sounds edgy, and Mislan does not blame him: a Malay man sitting alone in a Chinese coffee shop is not a normal scene, and in Petaling Street, a.k.a. Chinatown, it is worse. His AIO might as well be wearing a neon sign on his head saying, "I am a cop or immigration officer." By now gangsters, illegal immigrants, petty criminals, and drug thugs are all probably watching him. They are guessing one of two things: a police cleanup operation is coming down, or it's the dirty cop/immigration officer waiting for his kickback. They prefer the latter, of course. He knows it is nearly impossible to get a place to park near Petaling Street. His best option is to drive and park at the Jalan Bandar Traffic Police Station about four hundred yards away and walk. He sees his department detective leaving on a motorcycle and flags him down. "Finished work?" he asks.

"Ya, sir."

"You got a spare helmet?"

"No, but there are always some in the guardhouse."

"Can we go borrow one? I need you to take me to Petaling Street."

The detective makes a U-turn to the guardhouse and comes back with an old helmet. Ten minutes later, they are at their destination. He taps the detective's shoulder, to tell him to stop near the Kuan Yin Temple. He returns the helmet, thanks the detective, and starts walking.

His first case as a rookie investigating officer was in Petaling Street, also known as Chinatown. It was an armed robbery at a fast-food outlet. He had heard of triad activity in the area, and had been advised not to venture there alone under any circumstances. He remembers how he had stepped out of his Land Rover the first time, how shit scared he had been. His assistant then, Sergeant Peng, a seasoned AIO, had to keep nudging him to keep him walking to the fast-food outlet, for his legs refused to move. He remembers having visions of drug-induced machete-wielding gangsters charging out from every door and lane.

The area has not changed much. The streets are still narrow, lined on both sides with prewar shophouses. The area is congested with Chinese restaurants, retailers of Chinese medicinal herbs and prayer items, bed and breakfast outlets, pubs and grills, reflexology centers, betting outlets, and such. As he walks, he watches European and American tourists haggling with street vendors over the price of fake handbags, watches, jeans, shirts, shoes, DVDs, CDs, whatever.

He remembers an in-house seminar several years ago, organized to introduce future crime busters to gang activity. One of the speakers was a chief inspector. "Have you heard of the Malay saying, Where there's water there is fish? Well, it is the same with gangs. Wherever there are night markets, there are gangs. The only question is, are they legal, or illegal?" One of the participants asked, "Are there legal gangsters?" and the chief inspector burst into laughter. After he stopped, he said, "The legal gangsters are people like you and me; dirty cops, dirty City Hall enforcement officers."

Petaling Street is now a tourist destination. The government has declared it so by creating covered pedestrian malls and some cheesy cityscapes. From five in the evening till about two in the morning, the street is closed to vehicles and lined with stalls from end to end. The changes are cosmetic, and the underlying heartbeat is just as dark as before. Although the authorities do not acknowledge it, Petaling Street is still a triad hotbed.

Walking down the street, he notices that, after all the years, his nervousness has not reduced much either. He still feels the rubber in his knees and the tremor in his chest. He senses eyes following him, watching his every move from shadowy corners, alleys, and cracks in darkened windows. His hand creeps instinctively toward his sidearm tucked at his waist under his shirt. The feel of the cold hard steel injects some valor into his stride as he continues into triad land.

The Lock Ann Hotel is a rundown three-story corner shophouse with wooden windows, peeling paint, and a fading signboard; one of the many low-budget ones operating in the area. It is not a hotel he would want to spend a night in. Rooms are probably rented, long-term, to Sri Lankans and Bangladeshi and immigrants of other nationalities working the fake branded goods stalls, he thinks. A Chinese coffee shop on the ground floor has kiosks selling noodles, chicken rice, and *bak kut teh*.

He sees Johan sitting at a corner table, his back against a wall, looking edgy, like a child on a dentist's chair. He picks a spot across the street in the shadow of a pavement pillar and looks over the restaurant and the surroundings slowly, deliberately, more out of habit than with the hope of learning anything. The instant his AIO, the sergeant, had entered the restaurant, word would have flown out that a *sa sun*, meaning three stripes, had entered the premises. By now his own presence would also have been announced, *tua kow*, big dog. Frantic calls had probably already gone out to their stooges in the enforcement agencies inquiring about the presence of officers in their territory. Looking at his watch, he decides it is time to join his sergeant. He takes a last drag from his cigarette, flicks it into the gutter, misses it, and crosses the street.

Johan looks relieved to see him. He sits next to his assistant facing the road and orders an iced coffee. "You all right?" he asks, giving him a friendly pat on the shoulder.

"Fine." His assistant tries to sound nonchalant.

"It must be warm in here, you're sweating," Mislan teases. "Has anyone approached you yet?"

His assistant does not get the taunt. "Just him," he says, pointing to a waiter.

The waiter arrives with the drink and asks if they want anything to eat. Although famished, as he had not touched the *nasi padang* earlier, he is reluctant, as a Muslim, to eat in a non-halal restaurant. He shakes his head and the waiter leaves.

"My friend from D7 called. Rumors are flying about that Fatty Mah is back in town, came back about four months ago. Some say he's trying to revive the 21 Immortals. It is just a rumor, nothing verified."

"Do you think Four Finger Loo can verify that?"

"Worth asking."

Mislan kicks Johan's shin lightly. He gestures, with his eyes, toward a young Chinese man standing near the *bak kut teh* stall. The man is speaking excitedly into his cell phone and casting glances at them. Their shooting hands drop under the table, ready for any danger. The triad members are notorious for attacking targets with meat cleavers, choppers, and iron rods, in full view of the public.

The young man switches off his cell phone, and walks tentatively toward them, saying, "Sorry, Inspector Mislan, right?"

Mislan nods.

"Uncle Loo asked me to come."

He invites the man to sit. "What's your name? Where is Four Finger Loo?"

"Tony. Who's Four Finger Loo?" The man is genuinely baffled.

Mislan apologizes. "Sorry. I mean Loo, where's Uncle Loo?"

"He's coming down. He stays up here," Tony says, nervously pointing to the ceiling.

Mislan hails the waiter, and Tony orders his drink. He tells them that he is Loo's nephew, he is in his early twenties, and is studying accountancy in one of the private colleges in KL. Then, Tony abruptly jumps off his chair, startling both of them, making them reach for their sidearms again. Tony briskly walks to an elderly man standing at the entrance and says, "Hello, Uncle." The older man pats Tony's shoulder, and they walk to their table.

The edginess subsides, and they relax their grips on the sidearms and start breathing normally. After the uncle and nephew sit down, the inspector makes the introductions. However, no hands are shaken. Distrust and caution loom. According to the case file, Four Finger Loo should be about fifty-eight, but the person seated in front of them does not look a day under seventy. He looks feeble, wrinkled, and balding. His sad, hollow eyes reflect defeat. Mislan cannot imagine that this Four Finger Loo was once a fearsome Tiger General commanding hundreds, if not thousands, of warriors.

The old Tiger General orders tea, takes out his cigarettes, and lights one, without offering them any. "Ah Song said you wanted to talk with me?"

"Yes." Nodding at Tony, Mislan asks, "Does he have to be here?"

"Yes. You know we're being watched," Four Finger Loo says, slowly turning his head, indicating the outside. "I need him as my witness, if they decide to call on me. My nephew can be my witness. I'm no snitch. I only do this for Ah Song; he is an honorable *tua kow*."

"We can do this elsewhere if you wish."

"Why? I prefer it here. What do you want to talk to me about?" Four Finger Loo wants to finish the meeting quickly.

"Can I tape this?" Mislan asks, and without waiting for a reply places the digital recorder on the table. "I want to know about Robert Tham."

At the mention of the name, Four Finger Loo turns his head to the side and spits on the floor, his face going red with anger. "That rat," he hisses under his breath. "I hope he rots in hell."

"Tell me what happened in '95?" Mislan says, ignoring the retort.

"Why ask me; you know what happened, what? We got rounded up, thrown in lock-ups. No charges, no trials; put into a truck like cows sent to Jerejak Island for a five-year vacation. I spent five fucking years in Jerejak courtesy of your people and that traitor. Then they throw me in a New Settlement in Kelantan for another five years. You asked me what happened in '95? All I know is that the rat lied to save his skin, betrayed us, and got us sent away for a long time. Look, I don't care what happens anymore; I have done my time, and I'm no longer in the business. Why don't you check your files?" Four Finger Loo shouts, his voice attracting curious stares from the workers, food handlers, and customers. Meanwhile, the sergeant leaves the table and positions himself at the five foot way entrance to the restaurant, where he can monitor both the situation at the table and the surroundings.

"Was it a hit?" Mislan changes the subject.

"What?" Four Finger asks. Suddenly he starts laughing, again a little too loudly, and this begins to annoy the inspector. "You don't know us, do you? We don't do families or children. They're sacred. We're from the old school; we live and die by our oaths, not like the punks you have now. They're not triad, they're just common thugs, punks." He pauses and follows it with another spit. After a few drags on his cigarette, he says, "If we did it, and I'm saying if, it'll not be in his house. He was a diseased dog. Even the gutter would have been too good for his carcass. You think I did it, don't you? I wish I had. I came back a nobody. The young punks, they don't give a shit about me, or who I was. It's not like it used to be: brotherhood, respect, honor. It's *pek hoon* and robbery now. No respect for lives or families." Another glob of spit lands on the floor.

The Chinese word *pek hoon* literally means "white powder" or, in street talk, "drugs."

"What about Fatty Mah?"

"What about him?"

"I heard he's back in town." He watches Four Finger for giveaway expressions.

"I don't know. If he has, he has not contacted me. You got your snitch, what?" Four Finger Loo snaps, then smiling for the first time, he says, "I forgot, your snitch is rotting in hell." Genuine pleasure flashes in his eyes.

"Look, I don't care what happened in '95. I have a murder to solve. Right now, you and Fatty Mah have motives. Maybe you and Fatty didn't do it. Maybe the two of you did, or contracted it out. Either way,

I'm going to find out," the inspector says firmly, having reached the limit of his patience, irritated with Four Finger's attitude.

"You have a hearing problem? I told you it's not our style. We don't do families and children," Four Finger Loo replies, equally irritated.

"As you said, that was how it used to be, but not anymore. Maybe you used non-triad methods to throw us off the track. How's that for a theory? To me, payback is a damn good motive to kill," Mislan replies, watching the retired Tiger General's face closely for giveaway signs. All he can detect is frustration, and the I-don't-give-a-shit look.

"You're the *tua kow*, you figure it out," he replies defiantly.

"You can bet on that. By the way, don't leave town," he says, sounding silly even to himself. He turns off the digital recorder, stands, and asks for the bill.

"I thought they only said that in movies," Four Finger Loo says wryly. "Here is my home, I'm not going anywhere."

The waiter tells him that the drinks are free. He pulls out his wallet and drops a five-ringgit note on the table, retrieves his backpack, and walks away.

They head for Jalan Bandar Traffic Police Station instead of walking all the way back to their office. They are not in the mood to walk more than necessary after the confrontation with the former Tiger General. Maybe they can get a ride from one of the patrol cars.

13

It is close to ten when they are dropped off at the office. The inspector tells his assistant to go home and get some rest. Walking to his car, he feels hungry. Daniel must be asleep, and he's not in the mood to eat alone. Without thinking, he takes out his cell phone and calls Dr. Safia. After two rings, she answers lazily, "Hi."

"Hi, am I disturbing you?"

"No, just watching TV. What's up?"

"Nothing. I'm hungry, thought we could get something to eat."

"Where are you? I've had dinner, but I don't mind having a drink," she replies, sounding wide awake.

"Headquarters. Just got back from a meeting. It's all right, Fie. I'll stop at one of the stalls on my way home and grab something."

"Lan, why don't you come over? There's a place here that makes excellent fried rice. I thought of having it for dinner, but it's too much for me to eat alone. If you come over, I'll share it with you. How about that?"

"Are you sure? It's late. By the time I reach your place, it'll be about 10:30."

"Sure, I'm sure. Call me when you're here. See you," she says, hanging up before he can say anything else.

The prospect of supper with Dr. Safia excites him. The thought of picking up where they left off the night before is invigorating. Traffic is light, so he makes an illegal U-turn and takes the slip road to Loke Yew. He has been to Dr. Safia's place twice, but only to drop her at the guardhouse each time. She rents an apartment in one of the condominiums in Taman Midah, a predominantly Chinese area. Being a liberal Malay, she prefers living in a multiracial community, rather than in a Malay-dominated area: no prying eyes, no sanctimonious judgments of other people's private lives.

He parks his car outside the gate and calls her. While waiting, he telephones home, and his maid tells him that Daniel is asleep. When he sees Dr. Safia coming out from the apartment complex, he flashes his car headlights to attract her attention. She waves and walks toward him. She looks like a college student, dressed casually in dark shorts, white T-shirt, slippers, and a pink Callaway golf cap. He takes his backpack out of the car, locks the vehicle, and meets her halfway.

"Where to?"

"Over there," she says, pointing to a stall across the street. "You look like shit."

He takes her hand and helps her across, a habit he had developed with his ex-wife.

"You're the second woman to say that to me today, but you know what? I'm a happy shit," he says, laughing.

"Who was the first?" she asks.

He detects some jealousy in her voice and smiles. "My boss, Superintendent Samsiah."

"Happy? Did you break the case?"

"I wish."

"A long-lost uncle died and left you a million ringgit. No, make that US dollars," she teases. "Now you can quit your job and enjoy life."

He smiles.

At the stall, they pick a table farthest from the other customers and order a plate of fried rice, one iced tea, and an iced coffee.

"What're you happy about, then?" she asks.

"Happy I'm having an alfresco dinner, or supper, with a beautiful, not to mention intelligent, woman. If that doesn't make a man happy, I don't know what will," he says.

"Who, where?" she teases, looking to her left and right.

"Just enjoy the compliment, Doc."

Just then her cell phone rings. She looks at the screen and slides it back into her pocket where it keeps ringing until it times out. Uncomfortable silence hangs over them as they wait for the ringing to stop.

"Did you mean what you just said?"

Before he can answer, her cell phone rings again. The awkward silence returns. She lets it ring until it dies off again, pulls it out, puts it on silent mode, and slides it back into her pocket. Their orders arrive. That breaks the awkwardness. She moves into the chair next to him from across the table so she can share the fried rice. He uses the spoon and she the fork. The fried rice does indeed taste as good as she had claimed, or perhaps it does because he is starving.

"Did you mean what you said?" she asks again, putting down the fork.

Mislan had thought he had escaped answering the question, but he had thought wrong. "I say many things. What did I say?" He delays his answer to think of a noncommittal response.

"About being happy?" she says, looking him in the eyes.

He lights one cigarette for her and another for himself. He nods, "Yes."

"Me, too," she replies, smiling.

Her answer surprises him. "Really! I mean you, too?"

She laughs, strokes his hand lightly and says, "Yes, Lan. I've always enjoyed your company. You're always, how shall I put it, a gentleman. We've been out, what, five, six times and you've never asked me anything personal, or pushed me into anything. Not like most men. I have wondered if you were gay, or if you didn't find me attractive, though I don't know which is worse."

It is his turn to laugh. "The answers to your questions are 'no,' I'm not gay and 'no,' I don't find you attractive. I find you very attractive."

She squeezes his wrist and slowly pulls her hand away. "Tell me about you, Lan."

"What's there to tell? What do you want to know?"

"Whatever you want to tell me."

The awkward silence returns.

"All right, let's play a game. We each take turns to ask questions that must be answered truthfully. We have only one pass card we can use. Once it is used, the same question cannot be asked again. How about it?"

"Only one pass? I always thought you are given three." He begins to feel a little uneasy.

"Just one. So, use your pass wisely," she says, patting his hand reassuringly.

"It's late, Fie, I've not had my bath and I stink," he says rather lamely, unsure if he is up to a truth game. In his profession, he does all the asking.

"Tell you what, why don't we go back to my place. You can take a shower and we can have coffee out on the balcony. It's nice and breezy, I'm sure you'll like it." Without waiting for his reply, she asks for the bill, which he pays, and they leave. Walking back to her place, she slips her hand into his.

Her two-bedroom unit is on level nine and, as he imagined, is modestly furnished, reflecting her character. A two-seater earth-colored sofa, a wooden coffee table from IKEA littered with women's and medical magazines, a bookshelf overflowing with books, a piano, and a treadmill define her. She disappears into one of the bedrooms. A few seconds later, she calls out to him. When he sees him standing at the door, she says, "It's all right, you can come in. The bathroom is there. There are fresh towels on the rack. I've put a T-shirt and shorts on the bed. I'm sure they fit. Why don't you take a shower and I'll make us some coffee?"

He takes a few hesitant steps into the room as she goes to the kitchen. Dropping his backpack next to the TV, he examines the shorts and T-shirt on the bed and wonders if what he's doing is right. His brain tells him to leave, but his heart tells him to stay.

He showers, passes on the shorts, puts on his own trousers and the T-shirt. He scans the bedroom: more books by the bedside table, no framed photographs. He does not recall seeing any on the bookshelf either. He finds that a bit odd. He goes back to the living room to find her sitting on the sofa with two mugs of hot coffee. From the look on her face, he sees that she has noticed he has not taken up her offer on the shorts, but she does not say anything. Handing him a mug, she points to the balcony.

The view from the balcony is indeed spectacular. It overlooks the city; sadly, it is too dark and cloudy to identify landmarks, except the Twin Towers. He is sure the view is beautiful on a clear night. He sees only one balcony chair, so he remains leaning against the railing while she slides into it. The night air is fresh at the ninth floor, and there is a steady breeze. He struggles to light a cigarette, and his efforts amuse her. After several attempts, he gets it and, using his cigarette, lights one for her.

"Why are you not wearing the shorts?" she finally asks.

"I don't want to seduce you with my sexy legs," he answers evasively. He feels some rain when he stretches his hand over the railing. "It's drizzling."

"Let's sit inside and leave the door open. I like the breeze." She moves to the sofa and rearranges the magazines on the coffee table to make space for their mugs and ashtray. They sit leaning against the arm-rest on either end, facing the balcony.

"Shall we start?" Although she hides behind a smile, there is something in her tone that tells him she is serious about the game.

"Ladies first," he says, uncertain which road the game is going to take.

"Chauvinist," she says, mischievously. "Do you like me?"

"Wow, straight for the jugular. No warm-up question?"

She smiles, shakes her head, and says, "It's late and you're tired."

"Yes," he says, surprised by his answer.

"How much?"

"I thought it is my turn to ask."

"I have changed the rules. I am allowed to ask follow-up questions if the answer is ambiguous. So, 'how much' is a follow-up question." She chuckles.

"Which part of 'yes' is ambiguous? When did this happen? I mean, when did the rules change?"

"When you were in the shower. Okay, that was your question, now it's my turn. How much?" She chuckles again.

"That's not a question. I mean, that was not my intended question. I was seeking clarification over the rules," he rebuts mildly.

"Now, you're getting technical on me."

"Hmm, you're more than just a clever and helpful pathologist," he quips.

"Now, you know," she replies, casually lifting her legs, stretching along the sofa resting them on his thighs. He pretends not to be affected, as if it is something every woman does when playing the truth game, or whatever. Question after question keeps coming from her without him having a chance to ask any. Somewhere during the Q & A, she shifts from the edge of the sofa to lean her head on his shoulder with her legs on the coffee table.

*

His phone alarm jolts him awake. It is the best sleep he has ever had sitting. As gently as he can, he lifts her head, now resting on his numb thighs, and rests it on a cushion. He slowly pushes himself up, holding the sofa's backrest for support. He waits for blood circulation to resume in his legs before attempting his walk to the bedroom. He changes his shirt and gathers his backpack. He looks at her sleeping on the sofa and decides not to wake her. He knows she has two sets of house keys because he had noticed the spare on the holder when he was coming into the house. He kisses her on the forehead, takes the spare set, and tries the front door and grille. It works. He writes a note saying he has taken the spare keys, will return them ASAP, and leaves.

14

MISLAN SENDS A TEXT message to Sarah, his neighbor, asking if she could give Daniel a ride to school. When she agrees, he calls his maid and tells her the arrangement. He then drives to the office and pops his trunk to extract a clean shirt, socks, and his toiletry pouch. It is common for Major Crimes personnel to work overnight, and it made sense to have a mini-wardrobe in the trunk. After being in the same shirt and socks for twenty-four hours, a change is always welcome.

It is seven o'clock in the morning, and the building is not alive yet. Taking the elevator, he gets off at his floor, goes to the toilet, washes up the best he can in the cubicle, changes, stuffs his soiled clothes into the backpack, and slips into his office. The investigator on shift duty and his assistant are discussing something with the front desk officer when he walks in.

"Good morning. How is business?" Mislan asks as he walks to his desk.

"The usual shit. Nothing like the Yee Sang Murders," the shift investigator replies jokingly.

"Good for you," he mumbles, not amused by the insinuation.

He flips through the message slips on his table. Three are from Audi to return her calls. He makes a note to call her later and sticks it on his tiny corkboard with many other slips, long forgotten. Switching on the computer, he takes out his digital recorder, plugs it into one of the USB ports, and slides in a blank CD to make a copy of the three interviews. He ejects the CD, puts it into a plastic holder and labels it, *Report No 21222/08—302 PC— Interviews with Maria, Irene, and Four Finger Loo.* He seals the plastic holder, pastes the red *Confidential* sticker on it, and drops it into the Out tray at the front office. His cell phone beeps; an incoming text message. It is Dr. Safia. She had a wonderful time and not to worry about the keys. She ends it with a smiley face. He replies, saying he too had a good time, and sorry about taking the keys without permission.

He sees Johan coming, his hands empty. "No *nasi lemak* today?"

"Sorry, was in a rush."

"Let's go to the canteen then. My treat."

"You seem happy. Want to share some of it?"

The elevator lobby is crowded now. The door to an elevator going down opens, packed with officers, rank and file, and civilian staff. They squeeze in, ignoring the groans of disapproval. All the passengers get out at Level One where the canteen is, leaving the elevator empty for the rest of its journey to the ground floor.

Mislan hates the canteen during breakfast and lunch, when it festers with internal politics, promotion lobbying, scandalous gossips, backstabbing, ass-kissing, and grumbling. They down a quick wordless breakfast and leave. On the way up to their office, Johan again asks why he looks happy. To shut his AIO up, he tells him that he had a wonderful night without giving any details.

"What's the plan today?"

"I don't know yet. Let's talk about it after morning prayers. I need to put the eyes on Four Finger Loo and see where he leads us. I'll ask ma'am if she can get Special Branch-E3 to lend us a team. Why don't you dig up whatever intelligence you can get on him, say, for the last year?"

"You think he has a hand in this?"

"I doubt it, but let's be sure before we write him off. And don't forget to go through the interviews. It's in the PC titled the Yee Sang Murders. Maybe you'll see something I don't. And Jo, you remember the extortion case we did about a year ago, the Black Dagger gang?"

"Yes. You think they're connected?'

"No, I doubt it. Remember the gang leader, Botak Kim? He was expelled from the secret society, right? I think he's still in prison. Can you have a chat with him? See if he can provide any information on 21, Four Finger Loo, and Fatty Mah."

"I'll arrange for the interview. When do you want me to do it?"

"ASAP, before we write off Four Finger." He then leaves to attend morning prayer.

Investigators are making small talk when he enters. The chair next to the head of Major Crimes, usually reserved for the outgoing shift investigator is empty, with a note, "Reserved for the Yee Sang Murders" on the backrest. The room becomes silent instantly, and all eyes follow him. "Funny, real funny," Mislan scoffs, ripping off the sticker. An investigator seated at the far end remarks, "Touchy!" and immediately regrets opening his mouth. Like a killer laser beam, a vile stare shoots out in his direction. Superintendent Samsiah enters, flanked by two uniformed women officers. Two additional chairs are wheeled in by a civilian staff member. They take their seats, and the head of Major Crimes introduces them as Assistant Superintendent of Police Theresa Yip and Inspector Mahani from Public Relations. To him, the two women look as if they have just stepped out of a beauty saloh after unsuccessful makeovers. Both wear fake PR smiles and look smug and conceited. He wonders if their beauty treatments and cosmetics were paid for by the police force.

"Inspector Mislan, you looked like you have something to say."

"No, ma'am, nothing important."

"Right then, let's start."

The outgoing shift investigator briefs the meeting on the seven cases reported in the last twenty-four hours. One murder between drinking buddies, three armed robberies—all suspected to have been carried out by the same group—and the rest are SDRs, Sudden Death Reports, by the public. All cases are being investigated by district police without the involvement of Major Crimes.

"We believe the robberies are related to my case. We have identified one of their known hangouts, and I've put surveillance on it," interjects ASP Ghani Ishak, Head of Special Projects.

"Good. Anyone attending court today?" Two investigators respond and are released. "Mislan, any update on your case?"

"Now?" he asks, unsure if his findings should be made general knowledge, especially in the presence of the two PR dolls.

"Yes, PR will be organizing a press conference. So, our investigators may as well hear it from the lead, rather than read about it in the papers. Don't you agree?"

"All right, but I think it's premature. Again, who am I to decide?" he responds with as much sarcasm as he can get away with.

ASP Theresa Yip is about to say something, when the head of Major Crimes raises a hand, stopping her. "I have noted your views," she says.

"You're the boss," he murmurs under his breath, expressing his disappointment. "Forensics found traces of perfume and cosmetics on two of the vics, father and son, which didn't match the mother's, or those found at the scene. By the way, 'vic' is 'victim' in investigator's jargon," he explains, looking at ASP Theresa Yip and Inspector Mahani with a cynical smile. Noticing ASP Theresa Yip's raised eyebrows, he pauses, hoping she will say something stupid. She does not disappoint.

"That's a positive lead," ASP Theresa Yip butts in.

He jumps at the opportunity she offers, "And what positive lead might that be?"

"The cosmetics, it tells you that there was a woman present at the scene," ASP Theresa Yip replies, excited.

"Good deduction, but elementary." He gives her one of his many smart-ass smiles, relishing the slow-burning blush on her face. "Unless we can make a match, it tells us nothing. It could be a transfer from an unknown male or female. At present, it's like looking for Nemo in the ocean, so I'm not pursuing your so-called positive lead, unless Forensics can identify the perfume or brand name of the cosmetics." Having appeased his burning indignation at the PR dolls, he continues, "I managed to track down Four Finger Loo, and we had a sit-down last night. He denies the involvement of the SS or himself. Animosity between him and the vic goes back to '95, so he is not grieving over the rat joining his ancestors. They, by that I meant the 21 Immortals, believed the vic had snitched on them in the '95 big sweep that sent most of them to Pulau Jerejak."

"That's motive there."

"I thought so too, but something Four Finger Loo said tells me it's not SS related."

"And that is?"

"The modus operandi. Four Finger Loo is old school and a secret society blue blood. The MO does not fit the SS profile."

"MO changes, you know that. It evolves."

"I agree. What I'm saying is that it was not Four Finger Loo. Even if it were the work of SS, Four Finger Loo is not our man. New players might have been involved, but they don't have any beef with the vic; at least, not that we know. So what was their motive?"

"Makes sense, go on."

"Fatty Mah is rumored to be back in town, but Four Finger Loo is not confirming it. There's another angle I'm looking into. It's an unpublished article by Awani about the vic's wife and a Hong Kong actor. It may be nothing, but it's worth a look. Ma'am, can I brief you later?"

She nods. "All right, anything else?"

"Nope."

"That's it then," she says, ending the morning prayer. She leaves with the PR dolls following close behind, their bums swaying like boats in choppy water.

He sits as other investigators file out, thinking of how to play his cards. One thing is for sure, he needs Superintendent Samsiah in his corner. Holding back information from her is not going to achieve that, but the presence of the PR dolls is not making it easy. He feels it is not the right time to share some things. He needs more time to nail something before they go public. He knows that with that publicity junkie hovering over this case, he has a better chance of winning a lottery than stopping the press conference.

The head of Major Crimes is on the phone, and the two PR dolls are whispering to each other when he knocks on her open door. She points to a chair and continues talking. The PR dolls stop whispering when they see him. He hears her say, "Yes, sir" several times into the telephone before replacing the receiver.

"That was the OCCI. He wants the press conference at 11:00

this morning for the 1:30 news. What's it that you want to tell me?" Superintendent Samsiah asks, looking agitated.

"Ma'am, I'm not sure about this press thing."

"It's a done, Lan. It's out of my hands. I'm not going to debate about it. Let's just drop it," she snaps.

"Yes ma'am. I feel we're moving too quickly here," he says, looking disapprovingly at the PR dolls, determined to get his final say. He continues, "At the moment, we don't have anything solid and we are still chasing soft leads. With the story in the media, we risk losing any chance of getting to the next level."

"Maybe the press conference will spook them into making mistakes." He knows she is trying to sound positive about an impending publicity screwup.

"From what I've seen thus far, they are pros. The crime was painstakingly planned and executed. I won't bet on them getting spooked. The way I figure it, they'll go deeper into cover or start building brick walls around themselves."

"You said earlier that something Four Finger Loo said makes you think the murders were not an SS hit. What did he say?"

"Four Finger Loo is from the old school. You must understand, he is genuine SS, with initiation ceremonies, codes, honor, principles, and all the jazz. The SS code holds family and children sacred. They don't make house calls, and they don't use poison. It's too bland. Their MO is confrontational, with machetes, meat choppers, and samurai swords. It is bloody and always in the open. Their secondary motive is always the education of the relevant parties and public on their turf. Ask any seasoned D7 officers, they'll tell you the same." He pauses, letting them digest what he said. "I know he hated Robert Tham, but I believe him. I don't think Four Finger Loo has anything to do with the case."

"What about Fatty Mah?"

"We're still trying to locate him. After '95, he disappeared. Some say he went to Thailand. Rumors are circulating that he came back about six months ago. If the rumor is correct, he would have had sufficient time to set this up. Again, I don't think he had anything to do with this. The truth is, I don't even believe he is back."

"What are your reasons?"

"For one thing, SS rumors are constantly in the air, it's their way of diverting the attention of the authorities, especially D7. Second, many SS rumors are started by our D7 detectives, to fill their journals that would otherwise be empty."

She smiles. "Not many officers will say what you've just said."

"Look, ma'am, Fatty Mah is no ordinary gangster. Hell, he was a godfather. I don't believe that no one has seen him if he is back here in KL. He is a free man. Why should he hide?"

"All right, I'll buy that. What if it were personal payback? Nothing to do with the SS?"

"Yeah, I have thought of that. But, if we say the motive was revenge, why the charade, what's the message?"

"I know what you mean. The wife, what's the deal with her?"

"As I said, there's this unpublished article by one Tammy Ong, a snoop journalist with Awani. It is a cozy snapshot of her with a young Hong Kong actor at a social event. The vic was out of town at the time. The article suggests there was something more, quoting an undisclosed source. I don't think it's anything more than gossip to sell magazines, but leads are leads, and I'll put in some hours on it just to be sure."

Satisfied with his briefing and reasoning, but more for the benefit of the PR officers, Superintendent Samsiah asks, "Right, anything else?"

"I need a favor. Can you reach out to E3, see if they can lend us a team?"

"What do you need it for?"

"To put the eyes on Four Finger Loo for forty-eight hours. See if the meeting last night stirred up anything."

"Are you expecting him to make a move, or is your instinct telling you something else?"

He laughs, "Neither, just hoping."

"Official or unofficial?"

"Let's go with unofficial. I don't want to alert D7."

"I'll ask a friend and let you know. That's it, then," dismissing him. Standing to leave, he wants to say something but thinks better of it, and leaves the three women to organize the impending press conference.

Johan shuts the interview file as Mislan drops into his chair heavily. "I have read the interviews. I don't see anything new," he says.

The inspector nods, he is not expecting anything.

"I called the prison, and they've arranged for me to meet Botak Kim tomorrow evening. A woman named Audi called twice, didn't want to say what it was about but said you should know."

"Good, at least we can clear up this SS motive shit if it does blow up," Mislan says, still annoyed with the coming press conference.

"Who's Audi?"

"The newslady from Awani. You remember her; I was talking to her at the *nasi padang* place. I'm supposed to call her back, just haven't had the time." He looks for her card and asks the operator to put him through.

"Where the fuck have you been? Are you doing the Houdini on me? We've got a deal, remember!"

"*Woow*, slow down. I was in a meeting, okay. Just came out. I *was* going to call you."

"Duh, and the queen's my aunty. Called you three times last night. Why didn't you return my calls?" Audi demanded.

"I'm not in the office 24/7. I only saw your messages this morning."

"All right, give me your cell phone number then."

"Sure, as if I needed another person calling me every ten minutes. Look, there's going to be a press conference at eleven. Why don't you move your ass over here and ask the OCCI your questions?"

"Inspector, we've got a deal. Remember the word 'exclusive'? I'm sure you know what it means. I don't want any PR shit. I want the inside story, the dirt, the slime, the gory details," Audi snaps.

"Look, there'll be a press conference. Stop bitching about it and come over or you can pass, that's your choice. At this point I can't tell you anything. It's an ongoing investigation. The PC is as good as you'll get for now. I suggest you and your camera crew start moving now and grab the best seats in the house. I'll talk to you again; I'm late for an appointment," he lies. "Bye."

"Okay, give me your cell number. Please." Audi pleads.

"I'll call you. Bye."

15

MISLAN SLINGS HIS BACKPACK over one shoulder and walks briskly toward the door, with Johan running to keep up. He needs to clear his head, focus, and not let things beyond his control distract him. He punches the elevator call button and, while waiting for it, steps to the window that overlooks the city. What has he missed? There is no such thing as a perfect crime. Everything leads to something that leads to someone that leads to the killers. An elevator door opens, and they descend to the ground floor. As he steps out, his cell phone beeps. It is a missed call from his boss. It must have come during his ride in the elevator, where there is no reception. He speed-dials the head of Major Crimes. "Sorry, ma'am, I was in the elevator."

"Are you still in the building?" It sounds urgent.

"Yes, downstairs. What's up, ma'am?"

"Jo with you?"

"Yes."

"We're a bit short, I need you to back up Ghani's team. Briefing in ten."

"Sure, will be right up," he says, relieved.

A team of four detectives is already in the meeting room with ASP Ghani Ishak at the head of the table. A bad sketch on the whiteboard shows a target in Raja Alang. Superintendent Samsiah joins them and nods at ASP Ghani to start.

"Our surveillance team has just reported spotting the Jowo gang entering a house we have been watching," ASP Ghani says, distributing three blurred photographs of the suspects. "They're armed, trigger happy, and will not give up without a fight. They're linked to at least five armed robberies and one murder. As you know, the area is full of illegals, making it impossible for us to use uniformed personnel as backup. So it's going to be entirely our show. Questions?" ASP Ghani pauses. Silence. Looking at the whiteboard, ASP Ghani outlines the plan for the raid. They would be split into two teams. He will lead the raid with four detectives. Mislan and his assistant will be the rear cutoff. Two MPVs will cruise about half a mile away, one around Kampung Baru Mosque and another along Jalan Tuanku Abdul Rahman, ready to provide support on request. The teams will arrive at location in their own vehicles, motorcycles, or cars, at two- to three-minute intervals. Team members are advised to get off at several locations and hang about separately around the designated assembly point. They will remain in sight of one another at the fruit stalls and, on his signal, move casually toward the target. He hands out walkie-talkies, instructing them to switch it on only when the raid starts. He suggests that they suit up here before moving out.

"How sound is the intel?" Mislan asks.

"Positive eyeball. On-site surveillance says the suspects are in the building; must be sleeping after a long night," ASP Ghani says assertively.

"I don't see a twenty-four-hour report connected to them," Superintendent Samsiah remarks.

"Maybe they had an unsuccessful night. We have observed them using this place as one of their safe houses. My source says the house is rented by an illegal who is not living there. That's when I decided to put the eyes on it," ASP Ghani replies confidently.

"Any others inside?"

"Not that we know of."

"All right, I don't want any dead heroes," Superintendent Samsiah reminds them. "Good luck." She leaves the room.

"Lan, Jo, you may want to bring extra clips. I've a feeling they're going to fight their way out," ASP Ghani says, looking at his watch. "Okay, we move out in ten."

Mislan parks his car near the wet market, and they walk the short distance to the designated point. He spots ASP Ghani buying a slice of papaya from the fruit stall and they stop, pretending to examine some mangoes at another shop while Johan keeps an eye out for the signal, which soon comes, and they discreetly move to their target. The sergeant nudges him, and they start walking toward the target, taking separate routes but maintaining sight of the others.

They see the target: a stand-alone, old, nontraditional Malay wooden house. The walls are of red brick and plaster a fourth of the way up. The rest is of timber, finishing with a zinc roof. The doors and its two-leaf casement windows are also made of planks. They see no iron grilles anywhere. The houses are unfenced, separated by narrow dirt footpaths passable only by motorcycles and pedestrians. The target house's backyard, which is also the front yard of the house behind it, is about ten to fifteen feet wide. It is littered with the usual thrown-away junk and an old water tank being used as a garbage dump. It offers little suitable cover should a gunfight break out. He takes his position beside a house behind the target while his assistant tucks himself by the water tank. He gives the thumbs-up to Johan, who acknowledges it, indicating he is settled in and ready. He points to his eyes then to the target's back door and slowly sweeps his arm to the right indicating his arc of fire. He receives a thumbs-up from Johan in return, with a sweeping motion to the left. Satisfied that they will not get caught in each other's line of fire, they draw their sidearms, check the chambers, and wait.

They do not have to wait long before the sound of loud banging and shouts of *"Police"* come from the front of the house. The surrounding area turns into a frenzy of men, women, and children running in all directions, no one taking notice of the two policemen. As abruptly as it starts, the frenzy stops. In seconds, the area becomes deserted; there is not a soul around. "Aliens," Mislan says to himself. He tucks closer behind whatever cover he can get and trains his weapon at the back door.

Mislan hears two bangs, like someone kicking a door in, more shouts of *"Police,"* and gunshots. He makes out at least three types of gunfire, with the sharp sound of rapid fire from the MP5K being the most distinct. More gunshots, loud commands, screams of angry revilement, curses, and cries of anguish in Malay and Indonesian are followed by silence. He hears and feels his heart pounding and takes slow deep breaths to control it. His shooting arm feels the weight of his Beretta. He notices Johan looking at him and jerking his head up, as if inquiring what's going on. Using sign language, he tells his assistant to keep his eyes on the target and wait for his instructions.

The back door bursts open. A shirtless man covered in blood lurches out, clutching his stomach, looking wildly to the right and left. The inspector sees a gun in the suspect's hand, raises his weapon, and shouts "Police! Don't move. Drop your weapons." The suspect looks to his right and takes an agonizing step forward. Another warning to freeze and drop his gun is shouted by Johan. Realizing he is boxed in, the suspect freezes and lowers his gun slowly to his side. Mislan steps out from his cover, his Beretta trained on the suspect, and shouts, "Drop your weapons and raise your hands." The suspect looks at him and remains still. He appears to be considering his next move when a burst of gunshots from inside the house throws him forward, facedown to the ground. Mislan thinks he sees shock and betrayal on the suspect's face as he lies on the ground, gasping his last breath.

ASP Ghani Ishak emerges from the open door, his MP5K pointing at the lifeless body, steps over it, and kicks the Colt away. With his right leg, ASP Ghani rolls the shirtless corpse onto its back, and hisses, "Tronojoyo."

Mislan runs over and shoves ASP Ghani on the chest, "What the fuck did you do that for? We had him covered," he shouts furiously.

"He was going to make a dash for it. Can't let that happen," ASP Ghani answers indifferently.

"Bullshit! We had him covered. He was going to drop his piece!" he cries, their faces inches apart.

His assistant quickly walks over and stands behind his boss while the rest of the team flank ASP Ghani. To anyone watching, it is a standoff between two teams from the same side.

"Back off, this is my raid. I decide how it goes down. You can take off now, I don't need you anymore," ASP Ghani says. Turning to one of the detectives, ASP Ghani instructs him to call the cleanup team and to seal off the area until they arrive.

Mislan feels a tap on his shoulder, "This is not the right time and place," Johan whispers.

He does not move until he feels a grip on his shoulder tugging him. He half cocks his Beretta, locks the safety catch, and holsters it, still staring at ASP Ghani. "Fucking schmuck," he says, loud enough for the rest of the team to hear, before walking away with Johan holding his shoulder.

ASP Ghani Ishak, the head of Major Crimes Special Project, is a product of VAT 69, the Police Field Force version of the commando. He was with VAT 69 until the PFF was downsized. After working in an environment of attack and assault, ASP Ghani was unable to understand rational deduction. Unable to cope with an investigator's duties, and with cases piling up, ASP Ghani was made the head of Special Projects. He has loved every minute of it since. Lacking the necessary brainpower, skill, and patience for proper investigations, he transformed Special Projects into a SWAT team, with him having the highest kill rate in the department. It was not unusual for ASP Ghani's raids to end with all suspects dead.

16

MISLAN DRIVES AIMLESSLY, TROUBLED by what had happened. What if Johan had not pulled him away? Why did it bother him so much? It was a shoot-out, a fair fight, a kill-or-be-killed situation. The suspects' victims, surely, were not given a chance. Was the suspect going to drop his gun or was he just waiting for the opportunity to open fire, taking at least one of them down? Did ASP Ghani see something he did not? It was even possible ASP Ghani's action had saved their lives. Maybe he had overreacted. Maybe ASP Ghani was right. Still, it bothered him.

It is noon when he calls Dr. Safia, reminding her of the appointment with Professor Teh. She tells him that the professor is free at four and is willing to meet with them. She has some downtime and is hoping to come along. He agrees, saying he'll pick her up at 3:30.

He pulls over by the old UMNO building on Jalan Tuanku Abdul Rahman, and they walk across to the restaurant Kudu Abdullah, which sells Penang *nasi kandar*. After queuing for their orders, they carry their plates and sit at a table along the five foot way.

Picking at his food, his assistant asks, "What went on in there? I mean the morning prayer. I saw two skirts going in."

"They're from PR. The OCCI is giving a press conference. It should be over by now."

"You mean on our case! That's premature, isn't it? What's he telling them?"

"I don't know. I told the boss I didn't feel good about it. We have nothing solid yet, and the PC will attract more media attention and make things difficult."

Misfan's cell phone rings, it is Superintendent Samsiah. She tells him E3 can lend him a team but only tomorrow morning. He thanks her, saying it is better than nothing, and will email her the details by tonight.

"Ma'am, how did it go?"

"You know how these things are. Just forget it, okay. How did the raid go?"

"It went. Hasn't ASP Ghani briefed you?"

"He's on his way back. I've arranged for a debriefing at two. The big boss will be attending, as usual," she says matter-of-factly. "You coming?"

"I'll pass, if you don't mind. I have an appointment with Professor Teh later."

"Call me if there's a new development; and, Lan, cool down, okay."

As he was putting the cell phone away, he notices the missed-call sign. The number looks familiar, but he cannot place it. He decides to ignore it. If it's important, the caller will phone again, he decides. The restaurant does not have a television set, so he cannot watch the news. Perhaps it is better this way, he thinks. The news would only infuriate him more. His cell phone rings again. It's Chew.

"Yes, Chew, was it you who called me earlier?"

"Yup."

"Sorry, I was in a raid. What's up?"

"I've got good and bad news. Which do you want first?" Chew asks.

"I'm having a shitty day. I could do with some good news."

"We lifted a partial print, sufficient to run a match. My tech got it from the back of the vic's belt buckle. That's the good news," Chew says with obvious pride.

"That's great. What's the bad news?"

"We cannot find a match for it in our system, or Criminal Records. Sorry, Inspector."

"Damn! Another good lead that's useless."

"Yes and no. Yes, if there is no one to match it to. No, if you find a match. So, go get the killer, and we'll match the print."

"Right. Hey, Chew, good job. Thanks."

"No problem, Inspector."

He has another two hours before picking up Dr. Safia. Two hours of not knowing what to do or where to go. He needs to unwind, clear his head, run over the information again, and plan his next move. He pays for the *nasi kandar* and leaves.

"Have you eaten here before? I think the *nasi kandar* here is better than in Penang," Mislan asks.

"Several times during my MPV days, but I prefer the Penang *nasi kandar*, though. Where are we going?"

"Kill some time. We've got about two hours before we pick Dr. Safia up. I need to unwind; thought we'll go for a reflexology massage."

"Sounds good to me. Anywhere in particular?"

"Sungai Wang."

Leaving the restaurant Mislan makes a left onto Jalan Tun Perak heading for Bukit Bintang. The New Shu Jin Reflexology is on the second floor of Sungei Wang Plaza.

"Have you been here before?" Johan asks as they climb the stairs.

"Only once, it's clean."

"You sure? I don't want our pictures in the newspapers, arrested with underaged girls by the Religious Department. It's not beyond them to set us up, you know."

Mislan joins in the joke, "You mean the OCCI and D7? Your mind is more screwed than mine." It has been in the news lately, about reflexology centers offering more than just foot massages. They reach the floor they want and look for New Shu Jin Reflexology. They see the signboard and stroll toward it.

It's early, and the place is deserted. Noticing the look of concern on his assistant's face, Mislan explains, "These type of places, the business usually picks up after office hours up till closing time at midnight." They pick a seat next to each other. Two women reflexologists, or whatever they called themselves, appear with a basin of warm water and towels. Mislan and Jo lean back on the reclining chairs, similar to poolside recliners. The therapists remove their shoes and socks, roll up the legs of their trousers to the knees, and wash their feet in the warm antiseptic water. Once cleaned, the feet are towel-dried before being massaged.

As his reflexologist presses and pokes the soles of his feet, his tension eases. Perhaps it is due to the pressing of the right nerves in his feet, or perhaps it is the combination of soft instrumental music, dim lights, and aroma. He doesn't know and doesn't care. He closes his eyes and thinks of the partial print that Chew has found. He cannot understand why the police don't have a computerized database of DNA, ballistic, fibers, knives, and shoe prints like one sees on CSI shows on TV. Fingerprint-matching is still done manually by D6. The process of digitizing is in progress, but it is not online and available to the districts. Fingerprint information and other databases are not shared between government agencies like Immigration, Police, and National Registration, limiting the chances of finding a match.

His mind drifts to when he played the truth game with Dr. Safia. He tried to recall the questions and his answers, but he cannot. Then someone calls him, "Sir . . . sir." Opening his eyes, he sees Johan sitting where the reflexologist was. "It's three, we should make a move."

"Sorry." He sits up and asks for the bill as he puts on his socks and shoes.

As they drive out from the parking lot, his cell phone rings again. He plugs in the headphone and answers, "Mislan."

"Are you avoiding me again?" Audi is clearly angry.

"How did you get my number?"

"Reporters have sources, too. It doesn't matter how I got it. Is it true, what they said at the PC? We have an understanding, but I heard it with twenty other reporters."

"What did they say at the PC?"

"The triads, damnit," Audi says angrily.

"If you don't believe what they said, why didn't you ask them? I was not the one saying it. You should be asking them, not me. I'm driving, talk to you later."

"So you're saying it's not true then, and don't give me the excuse that you are driving. Who's going to give you a summons? Is it true, or just PC bullshit?"

"No comments, it's an ongoing investigation." He is disturbed by what Audi said about the PC.

"Come on, Inspector, don't brush me off. Look, I'll talk to my station manager to hang back with the PC bullshit, but you have to promise me. I get the exclusive on the Yee Sang Murders. How's that?" Audi says.

"Let's talk later. I'm not promising you anything, but we can talk about it."

"Promise?"

"I'll call you."

Mislan calls Dr. Safia when they arrive. He drives around the complex to the parking lot at the morgue, where she is already waiting. Johan moves to the back, and she slides into the front seat, freshening up the car with the sweet scent of her fragrance.

"Hi," she says.

"How are you, Doc?" Johan greets her.

"Hi, sure you're okay about coming along?" Mislan asks.

"Yup. It's a slow day. Told my boss I'm going to UM to do some research on embalming." She makes a call, and has an exchange of a few words, then says, "Professor Teh will be in his office at the Faculty of Science."

With his mind in a mess, he just cannot figure out the best route to the University of Malaya. "Which is the quickest route, Doc?"

"Don't you police guys know all the streets? Aren't you trained to respond to calls fast?" Safia jests.

"I knew all the roads when I was on duty in the MPV. Inspector Mislan was never in MPV." Johan says, coming to his boss's defense.

"Oh, all right then. Hit Jalan Bangsar, we will go through Pantai," Dr. Safia says.

As they turn in at the university, Mislan notices Dr. Safia's silence. She looks out the window, lost in thought. "What's on your mind?"

"I was just thinking about the old days," she answers without taking her eyes away from the window. "You know," she says to no one in particular, "it's the oldest university in the country and was once among the best in Asia. Now it struggles to make the top five hundred," and her voice trails off.

The two policemen don't know whether they are supposed to respond.

Mislan has been to the university several times, but that was more than ten years ago when he played field hockey. Sometimes he went to the bookshop. The university used to have the best library in the country. But not anymore.

He tells Dr. Safia he isn't familiar with the roads and needs her to direct him.

"First of all, slow down, Lan," Dr. Safia says.

He slows to an agonizing speed of twenty-five kilometers an hour as he avoids running down some motorcyclists and pedestrians.

"It's not my speed, it's those idiots," he hisses.

"I used to be one of those idiots," Dr. Safia snaps.

"Sorry, I didn't mean that."

The sergeant taps Dr. Safia's shoulder and shakes his head when she looks at him to tell her not to make it a big thing. She nods. She understands.

"Take a left up there," Dr. Safia navigates. "See that building? That's where Professor Teh's office is."

The professor's office is on the second floor of an old square building that is in dire need of a fresh coat of paint. The building doesn't have an elevator, so they take the stairs, navigating through clusters of students who are either shortsighted or just oblivious of other people's right to use the corridor. At the end of the corridor, she knocks lightly on Professor David Teh's door, and pokes her head in. Mislan hears a hearty "Come on in," and she pushes the door open.

The professor is in his mid-forties, well-built, and does not, in the least, look like a nerd. He is good-looking, casually dressed in jeans, a light-blue polo shirt, and track shoes—more like a TV talk-show host than an academic, Mislan thinks. Safia makes the introductions, and Professor Teh insists they call him by his first name.

"So Safia, how have you been keeping?" David says non-professorially.

"Couldn't be better," she answers. The inspector notices that her usual smile has disappeared.

"I've read your report. Your mortician has used the method known as Waterless Embalming, an effective method, but expensive and not used commercially."

"Is it unique?"

"No, not unique, but not used commercially."

"Is that because it's expensive?" Mislan asks.

The professor nods. "You see, embalming is a process of replacing the blood with a variety of preservatives and disinfecting agents. In modern embalming, additives are used to prevent decomposition and restore natural appearance. Commonly, the mixture is five to twenty-nine percent formaldehyde, nine to fifty-six percent ethanol, plus other solvents. The chemicals and additives form the arterial solution." The professor pauses. He looks amused by their perplexed faces. Folding his arms, he continues, "Arterial solution is a diluted mixture of chemicals made to order for each body, also known as 'accessories chemicals.'"

"Do you know which funeral house provides waterless embalming?" Dr. Safia asks.

"I'm sure all funeral houses can perform it if the clients are willing to pay."

"So the technique isn't unique and won't lead us to anyone," Mislan says, disappointed.

"No, I'm afraid not. I'd suggest you look at how the embalming was done. That'll give you a better chance of finding who the embalmer is."

"I don't understand," Dr. Safia says.

"You see, the chemicals tell you nothing of the embalmer. Chemical mixtures used are standard; there is nothing unique about them. However, the techniques used are unique. You see, in this country, embalmers learn from a mentor. It is a hand-me-down skill, so he or she uses similar techniques. Embalmers use an embalming machine that acts as the artificial heart to pump out blood from the body. To use the machine, the embalmer has to make two insertions, one to pump the embalming fluid in, and one to pump out the blood. Several known methods of doing it exist. Some prefer the radial from the hands, others the carotid from the neck, or jugular, or subclavian from the shoulder. If you check with funeral houses, you can identify the technique used by them that might lead you to the embalmer. It's a long shot, I know, but that's the only possibility I can see," David explains.

"And the most common techniques used are?" Dr. Safia asks.

"I would say the carotid artery and vein."

"How difficult is it to do embalming? I mean, can I do it at home, or would I need a special room?" Mislan asks.

"The machine is small, about the size of a microwave. I suppose if you want to, and don't mind the mess, you can do it in your house. If it's done in a house, the most sensible place would be the bathroom. Much easier to clean up than the dining room or the kitchen," the professor says.

"Is the machine readily available on the market?"

"Could be, but I think not. Who would have any need for it? It's not a household item. I assume it's available through medical or funeral suppliers. I'm sure there can't be too many of them."

"How long does it take to embalm a corpse?" Mislan inquires.

"About four hours, depending on the condition of the corpse. If death is by natural causes, it may take less time. A corpse of a violent death may take longer due to the repair work necessary. It also depends on the machine used, its speed; but modern machines are fast." David's eyes rest on Safia.

"Thank you, Professor, it's been educational." Mislan tries to hide his disappointment.

"Educational, but not helpful," the professor remarks.

"Not now, but that could change as we go further with our investigations," the inspector replies, not wanting to sound ungrateful.

"I understand. It has been my pleasure," David replies graciously.

They shake hands, and as they leave David asks Dr. Safia if she's still using her old number, to which she hesitates before answering, "Yes."

17

Hitting pantai baru after leaving the campus, they are caught in the evening rush hour. Dr. Safia suggests they find a coffee shop nearby and wait it out. She directs him to an Indian Muslim restaurant she frequented as a student. They choose a table on the pavement farthest from a group of bantering students laughing loudly. They order some drinks and pass on the food.

"What are you thinking?" Dr. Safia looks at him.

"Another dead end," Mislan says, in frustration. "What was the technique used in this case, the insertion method, or whatever he calls it?"

"Subclavian. It's at the collarbone. That's why Chew didn't find it when he examined the bodies at the scene. It was concealed by their clothing."

"Jo, why don't you work the Internet tonight? See if morticians or funeral houses have associations, or something. Maybe we can visit them, learn who is offering 'waterless embalming' and the names of embalming machine suppliers. I want to know whether anyone bought one recently."

"Are you thinking it was not done at a funeral house?" Johan asks.

"I don't know. Just want to check everything. Try KL and Selangor. I don't think it was done outside Klang Valley."

"What makes you think that?" This time it's Dr. Safia who is curious.

"Timing. Maria left Friday night and found them Sunday morning. That gave the killers plus or minus thirty-six hours, not enough to have it done out of KL or Selangor. I don't think they would have taken the risk of driving three stiffs on a long haul. They could have been stopped by a roadblock, a routine check by the Highway Patrol, or had an accident. It would have been too risky."

"You're saying it was done in thirty-six hours, the killing, embalming, and the staging? *Wow*, that's efficient," Dr. Safia is amazed. "Could use them at the morgue."

Everyone seizes the opportunity for a good laugh.

"The operation was well planned, based on good information, and precisely executed." He lights a cigarette and hands it to Dr. Safia.

"It must have been someone close to them," Johan says.

"Could be. The thing is, who was close to them? Irene, the manager at RT, says the vic was private. She says he didn't speak about his family, or meet any of them at the office. I need to talk to her again." Mislan lights another cigarette.

Loud laughter from the students, whose group seems to have grown bigger, distracts them.

"They're having fun."

"They should." Dr. Safia smiles.

"Miss your uni days, eh?"

"Sometimes. Only sometimes."

"We should make a move. Shall we?"

In the car, Johan suggests that he be dropped off at the Bangsar LRT Station to take the train back to the office, and Mislan can send Dr. Safia back.

After dropping his assistant off, he decides to take the Brickfields route to HUKM.

"What's with you and the professor?"

"Ancient history."

"Sorry."

"For what?"

"Making you revisit ancient history on my account."

"No fuss. He's the best. I need to learn, too. Let's drop it, okay?"

After the Brickfield's Police Station, he turns right and heads for the KL-Seremban Expressway. It is a much longer route through Bandar

Tasik Selatan and Tun Razak, but it would avoid the evening rush. He lights a cigarette, hands it to her, and lights another for himself. Reaching down to the bottom of his gearshift, he picks up her bunch of keys and hands it to her.

"Sorry about taking your keys."

"Don't you want to keep them?"

"You sure?"

She nods, pushing his hand down.

"Thanks."

"Are you coming over tonight?"

"Love to, but I have to go home and spend time with Daniel. I also need to listen to the interviews, see if I missed anything."

"We can listen to it together. Four ears are better than two, right?"

"Let's play it by ear." He is noncommittal. "How long before you can embalm a corpse?"

"Lan, don't you ever think of anything else?"

"Sorry," he says and laughs at his insensitivity.

"Forget it," she says, looking away. "Oh, I don't think there is a waiting period."

"Immediately?"

"Soon as the body stops wiggling. It would be difficult to do it if the body is still wiggling, don't you think?" she says, chuckling.

"Doctor! I'm serious."

"Yes, Inspector. Sorry, Inspector."

"Death was instant. How long does it take to do one corpse, four hours? Let's say embalming took twelve hours, that is, if it was done one at a time. Dressing them another three hours, max. That will make it fifteen hours to get them ready."

"How about the table setting?"

"It could have been done while they were being readied."

"So you're saying there were others?"

"It was not a one-man job, that I'm sure. Fifteen hours. That would have left them with an eleven-hour window for transport and staging."

"So, as you said earlier, you don't think the embalming was done away from KL or Selangor?"

"The window is too tight, apart from the risk being too high."

It is almost 6:30 in the evening when he drops her at the morgue and promises to call her later.

18

As MISLAN OPENS THE front door, Daniel comes running out of his room with a string of questions. Passing the third degree by Daniel the Inquisitor, it is the father's turn to ask how his son's day was. Daniel answers all questions with "good."

"Do you have homework?"

"No," Daniel answers casually.

"Can I see your communications book?"

"You don't believe me," Daniel says, running behind his father.

"That's because you always trick me." He is careful not to use the word *lie*. "Let me see it, please."

Daniel leaves the room, repeating, "You don't believe me," and comes back with his communications book. "See, I told you,"

"I believed you. I want to see if your teacher has written anything in it." Returning the book, he says, "Why don't you get ready for Quran lessons?"

"Okay."

When he comes out of the shower, he sees Daniel all dressed up in his *baju Melayu*, watching a cartoon. He tells his son he might have to go out on work later in the night and receives a disapproving stare from his six-year-old. As Daniel prepares to leave for Quran lessons, Mislan asks for a hug and tells his son to have fun.

He makes a mug of strong black coffee, and plants himself at the work desk. He turns on the television for the TV3 prime-time news at eight, lights a cigarette, and switches on the digital recorder. It starts with Maria's interview. It is brief and contains nothing of significance except for the chronology. He stops the recording and asks himself: Who knew Maria would be away on Friday instead of her usual Saturday? Was it a coincidence? Did she, by chance, mention it to anyone in an innocent conversation? It may not even be she who mentioned it but one of the victims.

The news starts with the day's headlines, one of which is the murder of Robert Tham and his family. Then it kicks off with news of the political turmoil in Perak before it moves on to his case. After that is a brief account of the victim's profile, leading up to the press conference by the city's crime chief.

He cannot believe what he hears. According to SAC Burhanuddin, the police strongly believe it is secret society related, and they are working on the theory that it is a payback for some cooperation rendered by one of the victims to the police several years ago. The police also believe the killing is intended to warn would-be police informers. The OCCI then delivers a killer blow: Loo Ah Kau, a.k.a. Four Finger Loo, a former secret society member, has come forward to assist in their investigations.

As the news segment ends, his phone rings. Without looking at the display, he presses the answer button and says, "Mislan."

"Lan, what the fuck were you thinking? You are going to get him killed," Inspector Song fumes.

"*Woow*, Song. I just heard it, too. Look—"

"You reached out to me saying you needed to talk. I arranged the meeting for you to talk, not to use him as bait. You know the SS have nothing to do with your case. It's not their style," Inspector Song barks, cutting him off.

"Look, Song, I know. I told them, I don't think it's SS, either." He tells Song what transpired that morning, the PR dolls, and the OCCI's insistence on having the press conference. "I'm sorry, man. Nothing I could do."

"If anything happens to him, it's on you, Lan," Song says, and the phone goes dead.

He wants to call Superintendent Samsiah for an explanation, feeling he deserves one. Who is he kidding? Since when did a boss owe a subordinate an explanation, especially in the police force? His conscience is clear; whatever happens to Four Finger Loo will not be his doing. It is a vicious world with publicity junkies like the OCCI, playing right into the hands of the media and its infinite craving for sensation, real or made-up.

Mislan needs to be with someone. He calls Dr. Safia, asking if her offer of another pair of ears is still open. He throws a pair of fresh pants and shirt into his backpack, puts on a pair of shorts and a crew-neck T-shirt, and leaves. He knows Daniel will be upset with him for being away two nights in a row with only the maid to keep him company. He feels sorry for Daniel, but he really needs adult company. On the way, he stops at the Ampang McDonald's drive-in and buys two quarter-pounder cheeseburgers.

As he takes the elevator to the ninth floor, he wonders if he should use the spare keys or ring the bell. He chooses the latter, and when the door opens, Dr. Safia teases him for not using the keys. They sit in the living room facing the balcony and stuff their bodies with the fatty fast food.

"What?"

"What's with the long face? Somebody died?"

He ignores her.

"Something bothering you?"

"Only the usual crap," he answers, unsure if he should be telling her his work frustrations.

"Told you, I've got good ears, if you want to talk," she offers.

"Good, let's test it," he says, eager to avoid the subject and getting all worked up. He gathers the McDonald's paper wrappings, cups, and bags, and walks to the kitchen to dispose of them in the rubbish bin.

"You want coffee?" She follows him.

"Thought you'd never ask."

Leaning against the cabinet, he marvels as Dr. Safia, the forensic pathologist, methodically prepares two mugs of coffee. She arranges all the utensils, cutlery, and ingredients neatly, within easy reach, before she begins. Two teaspoons of instant coffee into one mug and one teaspoon into the other, a teaspoon of sugar in each, fills them with hot water, and stirs with deliberate circular motions. He thinks she even counts the number of stirs for each mug. She returns the ingredients to their original places, washes the spoon, wipes it dry, and puts it back in the drawer. Mislan has never seen her perform an autopsy, but having just seen her make coffee, he is sure she is well-organized. Does she even think about it?

"You like yours strong, right?" She hands him his mug.

He nods. "Thanks."

They amble toward the living room. He gets the digital recorder, a notepad, and a pen from the backpack as she turns the music down. Sitting on the sofa, he tells her there are three interviews recorded and suggests they listen to them sequentially, starting with Maria. He switches on the recorder, lights two cigarettes, hands her one, and leans back. She fiddles with the recorder to turn up the volume and leans against him, a position that now seems natural. He closes his eyes, calmed by the fresh fragrance of her hair and warm body. He feels her moving, the recorder is silent, then something jabs his stomach.

"Are you sleeping?"

"Almost."

"Remember your thirty-six-hour theory? You based it on Maria's statement. Maria said she left Friday evening and came back Sunday morning, that's how you got the thirty-six hours, right?"

He nods.

"You're assuming they were killed on Friday evening, immediately after Maria left. Are you thinking she was involved?"

"Her story checks out. She may be involved without knowing. I mean, she might have told someone she'd be away Friday evening, innocently, and that info was used."

"What makes you think they were killed on Friday night and not Saturday?"

"The timing window. I don't think they would have wanted to shorten it. With only one chance at execution, I figure they would have wanted the biggest window they could have. Time would have been crucial in their planning."

"What about Saturday morning or afternoon, then?"

"I think not. When I did the house, everything was in order: the air conditioners, lights, except the bedroom curtains. They were drawn. I read that as something the killers overlooked because it was night, and the curtains would not have mattered."

"I'm impressed, Inspector Mislan."

"Elementary, my dear Dr. Safia."

"Who's next?"

"Irene, the RT manager."

She switches on the recorder, placing it on her chest, and reassumes her position. He observes the recorder moving up and down on her chest, like it was riding the humps of a camel, in sync with her steady breathing. She tilts her face up, kisses him on the chin, and tells him, "I know what you're staring at." He blushes and looks away. Then his cell phone rings, startling them.

"Ma'am."

"Lan, have you heard?" Supintendent Samsiah asks.

"Heard what?"

"Four Finger Loo, he was killed an hour ago." Her voice is calm.

"What?" He is shocked.

"He was assaulted by a group of men with machetes as he was having his meal at a coffee shop in Petaling Street. Jalan Bandar received the call. When the MPVs arrived the assailants were gone, and Four Finger Loo was dead. D7 believes it was the SS, they're handling the case. They're conducting a roundup operation in the area. Sorry Lan, thought you should know."

Mislan wants to scream at her but does not. Instead, he says, "Thanks."

"Lan, you okay?"

"Fine, ma'am," he says, turning off the cell phone.

He does not realize he is pacing the living room, monitored by a concerned Dr. Safia. He staggers to the balcony, grips the railing tightly with both hands, tilts his head up, and sucks in the fresh air fiercely. Anger burns through his being. For someone's few minutes of personal glory on TV, an innocent man pays with his life. It had to be the most expensive few minutes of airtime. Was it worth it? "Fool, stupid fool," he swears softly. His body stiffens as Dr. Safia hugs him from behind. Her calm and warmth are comforting. He turns around and hugs her back, resigned to the fact that there is nothing he could have done to prevent Four Finger Loo's death. No way is he taking the blame. His anger subsides and is replaced by emptiness.

"Hey, you want to take a break? Watch a DVD, or something?" Dr. Safia whispers in his ears.

"No. Let's just stay here a while."

"Sure."

19

MISLAN DELICATELY LIFTS DR. Safia's arm, moving it from his chest, careful not to wake her. Untangling himself, he gropes for his shorts in the dark and wanders to the living room. It is 2:17 in the morning, according to the digital clock on the bookshelf. He takes a sip of his cold coffee, lights a cigarette, and shivers as a sudden gust of wind from the open balcony hits his bare body. He braves the chill to stand on the balcony, looking out at the city lights. After a few minutes of shivering and rubbing of arms, he is awake. He thinks of what happened. They were in one another's arms, she comforting him, telling him it was not his fault, and that he should not blame himself. He remembers kissing her, and how she responded. Then they moved from the balcony to the bedroom, where they made love. No words were spoken, none were necessary. He desperately needed to feel alive again, to have a relationship, to share, to care and be cared for. As for her, he doesn't know what her reasons were. Perhaps she feels the same needs and shows it by being there for him. He probes his conscience, trying to understand what happened. Was it a need, a want, or lust?

He flings his cigarette butt over the balcony and follows the path of its red glow to the ground. Returning to the living room, Mislan starts when he sees Dr. Safia stretched on the sofa, wrapped in a blanket, smiling at him.

Recovering his composure, he says, "Did I wake you? Sorry."

She shakes her head and smiles. "Just missed you in there."

He sits next to her; he notices she is wearing his T-shirt under the blanket. She rests her head on his lap.

"You want to talk?"

He tells her about the press conference, his boss's phone call, the senseless death of Four Finger Loo, and his resentment of the OCCI's inanities and obsession with publicity. She listens without saying a word, but an occasional squeeze of his hand tells him she understands. He remembers her telling him she is a good listener; she has just proved it.

She raises her head and kisses him lightly on the lips. "You did all you could to stop them. No one can pin this on you."

He nods and holds her head to his chest.

20

It is 6:15 in the morning when Mislan leaves. Dr. Safia is still sound asleep on the sofa. On the way down, he turns on the recorder and listens to the interviews from where they stopped. At the end of Irene's interview, he rewinds the recorder and listens again. He switches off the recorder and speed-dials his assistant.

"Jo, meet me at the office ASAP."

"Why? What's wrong?" Johan asks, half awake.

"I think I know what the primary scene was."

"What! You said 'what' the primary scene was. I don't get you."

"I'll explain when we meet. Get me *nasi lemak* with cuttlefish and fried egg."

He turns off the cell phone before his assistant can ask more questions. He presses Dr. Safia's speed-dial number, and it is answered immediately. He tells her he had a wonderful time and apologizes for sneaking off.

He reaches the house as the maid is getting Daniel ready for school. After answering Daniel's questions: about his whereabouts last night, why he is just coming home, and if he is sending him to school, permission is granted for a hug and kiss. He hurriedly washes, changes, gives his son a bottle of Vitagen, and drives him to school.

"Daddy, are you going to be late again?" Daniel asks as they reach his school.

"I don't know, kiddo. Why?"

"Nothing," Daniel says.

"What's wrong, kiddo?"

Instead, Daniel responds with, "Knock, knock."

"Who's there?"

"Bumble."

"Bumble, who?"

"Bumblebee, that cries because he cannot follow Sam," Daniel says, laughing.

He too laughs, guiltily.

After dropping Daniel at school, Mislan drives to his office.

The parking lot is nearly full, the lobby crowded, and the elevators are packed with noisy staff reporting for work. He squeezes into one that is full, amid snarls and protests. Johan is already at the pantry making coffee when he drops his backpack on his desk.

"Morning. Made you coffee," he says

"Morning. Thanks, I'm starving. Did you buy the *nasi lemak*?"

"Just as you ordered, with cuttlefish and fried egg." He hands his boss the packet. "Where or what is the primary scene?" he asks, unable to contain his curiosity.

Mislan unwraps his packet of *nasi lemak*, sips his coffee to wet his throat before spooning his first mouthful, and enjoys his breakfast of caffeine, carbohydrates, fat, and nicotine.

"Remember my interview with Irene, the RT manager? After the interview, I forgot to turn the recorder off. When she walked me to the door, I asked her about the vehicles in the parking lot. She told me two of them belong to the vic. She was surprised the Cayenne was still in the lot because she thought the vic was using it for his vacation."

"So you're thinking the Cayenne is the primary scene?"

"Dr. Safia said they were gassed. She saw no defensive wounds or signs of struggle. She also said that the gas kills fast, is colorless, odorless, and dilutes easily in open space."

His assistant nods.

"Luxury cars are designed to be airtight so you don't hear the noise made by the tires or the wind. What if the gas was discharged when they were inside the car? They wouldn't know what hit them, and seconds later they'd be dead. The question is, how was the gas discharged?"

"Makes sense."

"I'm going to run it by ma'am to see if she buys it. If she does, I'll get excused from morning prayer and we'll go to RT. Why don't you get some blank copies of the search lists and put Chew on notice. If the Cayenne is still there, and I'm sure it will be, we'll get Chew and his boys over. Did you get anything on the Net search?"

"I have found two suppliers, but there are no records of sales made to individuals. They supply the full range of morticians' equipment, complete with installation, testing, and commissioning. They also provide maintenance and chemicals. They don't make much money on equipment, but they do when they provide maintenance and chemicals. I couldn't find a morticians' association. I made some calls. Morticians are usually registered as members of their clan associations, like the Hokkien or Hakka."

The inspector shakes his head, and sighs. "Another dead lead. Let's try to find a friendly mortician that we can talk to. Maybe they're superstitious, or *suey* to be on the Net, or to advertise."

He finishes the *nasi lemak*, gulps down the coffee, and lights a cigarette, ignoring the government policy of no smoking in the office. He is a police officer and needs to smoke to melt his brain cells so he can think.

Putting out his cigarette, Mislan goes to the office of the head of Major Crimes. She beckons him in before he can knock.

"Sorry about Four Finger Loo," she says in a manner indicating no discussion was welcomed on the subject. "I was about to call you. D7 has been calling me all morning, insisting they take over the Yee Sang Murders. What are your thoughts on it?"

"What's the reason given?"

"They believe your case may be related to Four Finger Loo's death," she calmly explains, letting his rudeness slide.

"It's not," he says harshly, inciting a watch-it expression from his boss. "Sorry. It's not SS related. If it were, they would've asked for the case when I filed the twenty-four-hour report. Four Finger Loo's death may be SS related, but not my case. I mean, any officer who has done murder can tell the difference between the two," he argues, lowering his tone.

"Does this mean you're not willing to let them have a crack at the Yee Sang Murders?"

"Not the way they intend. Ma'am, is this one of his instructions to prove himself right?" He jerks his thumb upward. "If it is, this case could be buried." His hand reaches for the pack of cigarettes in his pocket.

"Don't you dare smoke in my office," she cautions him. "You think they intend to bury the case?"

"I know you don't want to discuss it, but Four Finger Loo's death may be a result of —"

"Okay, let's not go there. I hear you, and let's just leave it at that unless it's proved otherwise," she says firmly.

"I'm sorry, that's the basis of my objection. I've a feeling that's what they'll do," he insists. "You see, the PC might have caused Four Finger Loo's death. If Four Finger Loo's death is investigated by a district investigator, it may be revealed that he was killed because of the PC. If my case is solved with the accused having no links to SS, they, I mean the OCCI, will look bad. Ma'am, you gave me till Sunday, it's still four days away. Let me have the four days," he pleads.

"And?"

"And," he pauses, "If I can't close it, you give it to D7. They're going to bury it anyway."

"Thought you were going to tell me you would have solved it by then," she says smiling.

"I'm not Lieutenant Horatio. I don't make promises. I don't wear shades, or talk standing sideways. Ma'am, you should stop watching the CSI shows. It doesn't work that way," he saying with a smile, more at ease.

"Okay, let's see what they say. I think I can hold things off for a few days before the heat goes up."

"Ma'am, can I be excused from morning prayer?"

"Why, what have you got?" She is curious.

"I think I know what the primary scene is. I want to seize it before it's moved or used."

"I don't get you."

"I think it's the vic's car, more precisely, the SUV. I think the Porsche Cayenne was the primary scene. The gas chamber. It was at RT House when I went to interview the manager. She told me the vic was supposed to use the Cayenne for his vacation and was surprised to see it at the office parking lot. At first, it didn't strike me as odd that there was only one car, a BMW 3-series, at the vic's house until I went over the interview recordings again this morning."

"All right, keep me updated," Superintendent Samsiah says, gathering her files for morning prayer.

"Thanks, ma'am."

"You should get some shades. You are already thinking like Horatio," she says as they walk out.

21

MISLAN CALLS RT. IRENE's secretary tells him that she will be coming to the office at 9:30 for about fifteen minutes, before she goes off to a meeting. He says he needs a few minutes of her time to clarify one or two matters.

At 9:20 he drives into RT's compound. As he expects, the Cayenne is still in the lot where he last saw it. He thinks of two possibilities. First, it hasn't been driven by anyone since it was last parked there, and all the evidence it may hold is intact. Second, that parking space is reserved for the Cayenne, and it could have been driven after he last saw it but parked back in the space reserved for it, in which case whatever potential evidence may be either contaminated or removed. He hopes for the former. He does not see Irene's Bimmer in the lot. He decides to wait in his car and walk in with her when she arrives. His cell phone rings; it's Irene telling him she'll be a few minutes late.

He notes Johan watching the Cayenne, like it's a tranquilized monster that's going to awake and run off at any moment.

"Relax, it's not going to run away," he jokes.

Johan chuckles. "That's obvious! If you're right, that car could be the break we need. I'm not letting it out of my sight until it's under our care."

"Don't get too excited. Even if I'm right, it may still not reveal anything. These people are good. Let's just hope Chew and his boys are better, and we're smarter."

A blue Bimmer Z4 arrives with its tires screeching and makes a sharp drifting turn into a parking lot. Irene Rijanti steps out of the car to Johan's low whistle. Both the Bimmer and she, on their own merits, deserve admiration. They get out of their car to Irene's greetings and apologies. They shake hands and he introduces her to Johan, who seems to have forgotten about the Cayenne coming to life and taking off. They follow Irene to the front door, and she punches in some numbers on the keypad, opening the door. He hears the voice greeting her from behind the Plexiglas, to which she responds with a wave. As he expects, there is no need to register. He hears a click, and she pushes a door open and goes in, with them close behind. As they make their way to her office, he wonders if his assistant, too, is drooling over Irene's swaying rear.

The secretary greets them when they reach the office and comes around from her desk and follows them in. Irene waves them to the sofa and deposits her handbag on her table while asking if she can get them coffee. Mislan declines, saying they will not be taking too much of her time as she has another appointment. She tells the secretary to call her next appointment to tell them she is running a little late, and to bring an ashtray. He takes the cue, lights a cigarette, and hands it to her. She then sits on a single-seater across from them and crosses her legs, exposing acres of smooth creamy thigh. She is good, he thinks.

"You said you have a few matters to clarify," she says, pulling the edge of her skirt over her knees, to the sergeant's disappointment.

"In our last meeting, you told me you thought Mr. Tham was taking the Cayenne for his vacation."

She nods, "That's what he said."

"You also told me Mr. Tham does not have a driver."

"Yes, he drives himself."

"Do you know which car he left in, on Friday evening?"

"I don't, but I can find out." She asks her secretary. "May I know why?"

"We were wondering why both of Mr. Tham's cars are here. How did he leave the office? We noticed only one car, a BMW 3-series, at his house."

"That's his wife's car. He might have left with a friend. He did that sometimes when he felt like a night of drinking."

The secretary returns and hands her a piece of paper.

"He left in the Cayenne at about 4:30," Irene says.

"I notice you have CCTV. What's your storage turnaround?"

"I'm not sure, but I think it's fourteen days, unless there is an incident. Then we make copies and store them for reference."

"Do you have a security guard here?"

"Only at night, on weekends, or on public holidays."

"Who has the keys to the Cayenne, apart from Mr. Tham?"

"I think he kept a spare in his office. Why?" Irene looks puzzled.

"We have reasons to believe the Cayenne is the primary crime scene, and we need to take possession of it, together with all documents related to it. I'll also need a copy of the CCTV recording from Thursday, when Mr. Tham left, up to midnight on Monday."

"I'll get Esther to help you. I have to leave now, or I'll be late for my appointment," Irene apologizes. She calls her secretary, instructing her to help them in any way they need, except on design drawings or financial statements. She snatches her handbag, apologizes again, says her goodbyes, and leaves.

Esther, the secretary, is in her early thirties. She is a short woman, thin as a pencil, wearing designer jeans, T-shirt, and open-toe slippers. She has a charming personality but is nothing like her boss. Johan's cell phone rings, and he steps out to answer it. Coming back in, he says Chew and his team are outside. Mislan asks Esther if she can allow them in. She hesitates, not sure if she should leave them in her boss's office by themselves, unmonitored. The inspector tells her they will not touch anything, and will wait for her. Only then does she leave, but not before scanning the room to see if there is anything she should lock up. He makes a mental note of her loyalty and decides not to waste his time asking her anything about her boss's activities. A few minutes later, Chew and two of his technicians enter, led by Esther.

"Hey, Chew. Did you see the Cayenne out front?"

"Yup, a beauty."

"I think it's the primary scene." He then turns to Esther. "Irene said the spare keys are in Mr. Tham's office. Can you show us?"

She nods, leads them across the general office to another room that's bigger, but not as elegant. She is about to walk around the table when Mislan tells her to stop.

"Is it in there?" he asks, pointing to the drawers.

"Yes, Mr. Tham keeps the spare keys in the lowest drawer," Esther replies nervously.

"Okay, thanks. Can you step aside, please?"

He asks Chew if he wants to handle it from here. The Forensics team members put their bags on the floor, pull out surgical gloves from their pockets, and slip them on to a chorus of snapping rubber. One of the technicians dusts the drawer, shakes his head, pulls it open, fishes out two sets of keys, dust them, shakes his head, and hands them to Chew. Chew takes a closer look at the two sets of keys, shakes his head, and hands them to the inspector, who is getting increasingly frustrated with every shake of a head.

"What?"

"No legible prints. You want to log that in your search list?" Chew says.

"All right. Let's check out the Cayenne. Esther, can you get us the file for the car, with the insurance, registration, lease agreement, servicing records, repairs, everything, and give it to"—looking around, he notices one of the technicians holding up his hand—"him? Please don't touch the documents inside the file. Before I forget, can you get the CCTV recordings from last Thursday to Monday, the security company's telephone number, and give it to Sergeant Johan?"

They approach the Cayenne like it really is a tranquilized beast, expecting it to regain consciousness at any moment. Mislan presses the unlock button on the remote but nothing happens, no blinking signal lights, no beeping sound normally associated with remote devices. He moves closer and tries again. Still, nothing happens. He thinks the battery in the remore control is flat and swears under his breath. He is about to turn around and go into the building to ask Esther if she has a spare battery, when he sees Chew pointing to the SUV's interior.

"What's it?" he mutters, expecting more complication.

"The key's inside," Chew says, pulling the driver's door and opening it. "It's not locked."

"Shit! A million ringgit SUV parked here for days unlocked, with the key inside, and no one notices it? Jo, can you call the security company?

Find out who was deployed here from Friday to Sunday. When I came on Monday, the Cayenne was already here. Get a duty detective to bring him in for questioning."

Johan nods and disappears into the building.

"Chew, are you doing it here?"

"Just the cursory. I've called for a flatbed truck to take it back to the garage. Before they move this baby, I need to do the external and bag loose items so we don't damage or contaminate evidence."

"You still need the spare key?"

"Yup."

"Can you do an overnighter on this? I need something urgently to hold on to this case."

"Someone's snatching it away?" Chew asks, surprised.

"It was hinted. D7."

"It's true, then?"

"What's true?

"The news, saying it's SS related."

"Just between us, that's crap. You heard of the killing in Petaling Street last night? That is SS style. Me and the vic, we had a talk the night before. The OCCI gave a PC yesterday morning and the vic got whacked. Now D7 wants to take my case and bury it to save someone's ass."

"Wow, you guys do that?" Chew is appalled.

"We guys don't. Just him. Now you know why I need something ASAP."

"Okay, Inspector. I'll do what I can."

22

ON THE WAY BACK to the office, Johan tells him the security guard has left the company. The guard had not come to work since Tuesday, and a detective is trying to locate him at his last known address. The news disappoints but does not surprise Mislan. Guard turnover is high in the security industry, and it is common for guards not to show up for work after payday. It is a cutthroat industry, with price wars being the main marketing strategy.

Walking into the office, he runs into several unfamiliar faces around the detectives' area, engrossed in small talk. The front desk officer tells him that the big boss and D7 are in the meeting room with Superintendent Samsiah. He has a feeling it has something to do with his case and feels blood rushing to his head. He wants to barge into the meeting, dump the case on the fools, and tell them to do whatever they want with it.

Instead, he says to his assistant, "Jo, you want to run through the CCTV to see if you can make out the Cayenne coming in? I figure it'll be Sunday night or early Monday."

"Sure. What's going on in there?" Johan asks, thumbing toward the meeting room.

He shrugs.

"It's about our case, isn't it?"

"Maybe. I don't know. You've got the Cayenne file?"

The sergeant gives him the file. "We're going to lose it, aren't we? Shit! It'll be my first."

No investigator likes losing his case to another investigator, for whatever reason. It is a humiliation, with all the innuendo, stigmas, and fabricated stories that come with it. It's worse if the case is later solved by the other team.

Flipping through the file, a service requisition catches his eye. It was for a sixty-thousand-kilometer routine checkup, dated a few days before the victims' intended trip. The order was made to Pro Care Service Centre in Sungai Besi. Several other requisitions went back three years. Picking up the phone, he calls Esther and she confirms Pro Care Service Centre as the contractor who repairs the company's cars. She also confirms that the Cayenne was sent to the workshop on Wednesday evening and returned on Thursday afternoon at Mr. Tham's request. According to their agreement with the garage, Ricky, the supervisor, came for the pickup. She tells him that as far as she knows, it is the only workshop they used, but if Mr. Tham has sent it elsewhere, it was not paid for by the company.

When he puts down the receiver, the phone rings instantly. It is the front desk officer telling him that his presence is required in the meeting room. He slams the receiver down hard, startling Johan and the others in the room. "Here we go," he sneers.

"Come in, take a seat."

Mislan nods to his boss, who greets him with a warm smile.

"I understand you have not made any progress." The OCCI says it more as a statement than a question.

He squeezes his way to a seat at the end of the table. ASP Theresa Yip and Inspector Mahani, the two PR dolls, are seated next to their current boss, again looking as if they've just stepped out of a beauty salon. Superintendent Henry Lau from D7 is flanked by two of his officers. The others are his boss and ASP Ghani, Head of Special Projects. The seat reserved for him is a chair directly facing the OCCI.

"I'm sure Superintendent Samsiah has told you D7 will be taking over your case. Henry feels it's related to last night's murder of a known SS leader," he continues.

"An old ex-SS that you got killed, you fool," he wants to answer, but does not. He looks at his boss, hopeful of a sign permitting him to have a go at the fool. None is given.

"As you know, Four Finger Loo was assaulted and killed by those we believed to be SS gangbangers. We managed to round up eight known SS members immediately after the incident. The info we got from them, and collaborated by our CI, was that the order for Four Finger Loo's hit came from the top. We've good reasons to believe it came from Fatty Mah, to cover his involvement in your case," Superintendent Henry says without conviction. "We feel it's best if we treat both cases as one and take the lead, with you as secondary, of course."

"Of course," the OCCI butts in.

"May I ask what good reasons make you to believe the orders came from Fatty Mah?" Mislan asks, unable to contain himself any longer.

"Well, none of those rounded up knew who gave the order, but they said it came from the top. Our internal sources are telling us the same thing," Superintendent Henry mumbles, avoiding eye contact with him. "We hear rumors of Fatty Mah being in town."

"Sorry, I didn't hear what you said," he says, wanting Superintendent Henry to repeat himself, hoping the rest, or at least his boss, will see through the bullshit.

"I said, we don't know who gave the order for the hit, but our info indicates it came from the top. We have heard rumors that Fatty Mah is in town."

"That's your good reasons to believe? If Fatty Mah is in town, your internal sources will surely know where he is. We're talking about Fatty Mah here, okay, not some lowlife gangster. It's just a rumor. Even if he is in town, he wouldn't do Four Finger Loo; they're close. Fatty Mah knows Four Finger Loo would never snitch on him. Your files will tell you that."

"Things change, friends turn into enemies," the OCCI says, coming to the defense of his D7 lapdog.

Superintendent Henry Lau Tuck Meng is legendary, not for his fights against organized crimes but for his closeness to vice and gambling operators. If there is a need for a fun-filled night of forbidden pleasure by visiting brass, local or foreign, Henry is your man. He can arrange it in minutes, 24/7. Whenever a district's Crime Prevention Unit does a gaming raid, Henry would show up like the mystical black mist, well before the raiding party's report is filed. In the gaming and vice world, everybody knows Henry, the longest-serving D7 officer in the country.

"I don't buy that. Not these guys; these are old SS, true SS," he says, daring Superintendent Henry to say otherwise.

"I've discussed this with Inspector Mislan; he has given me his word. If he still has no strong leads by this Sunday, he'll hand over the case to D7. I think that's fair. D7, meanwhile, can pursue its theory so there is no time wasted," the head of Major Crimes steps in, mitigating the building discord.

"That sounds fair," says Superintendent Henry, jumping at the face-saving way out, aware he has just been slam-dunked by an inspector in his own field.

Everyone looks at Henry, surprised by what they hear. Smugness and smiles vanish fast.

"Henry, you sure you're okay with the arrangement?"

Henry nods, leans towards the OCCI and whispers something. The latter nods several times, then looks at the inspector and asks, "What new leads do you have?"

"We're working on some leads, but it's too early to discuss them. I'll update Superintendent Samsiah once we get confirmations."

"I'm the OCCI, I outrank your boss."

"I'm aware of who you are," Mislan answers audaciously. "The last I checked, she is my direct supervisor, and I report to her. Until you change the protocol, I'll continue reporting to her."

"When do you expect these confirmations?" Henry asks harshly.

"Before Sunday, I hope. We're still chasing leads. The fewer people who know what we're chasing, the better chance we have of nailing them. Isn't that true, sir?" Mislan replies in a mocking voice, staring at Superintendent Henry.

"Are you implying something, Inspector?" the OCCI snaps.

"No. I'm only repeating what we were taught at crime school." Mislan grins.

"Right, I think we're done here," Supterintendent Samsiah says, standing, killing the potential altercation between the two, and risking her butt for him again. "I'll update you daily when I get it from Inspector Mislan. Henry, if you require anything, please contact me. I'll be happy to accommodate."

23

AFTER THE OCCI'S ENTOURAGE leaves, Mislan follows Superintendent Samsiah to her office. She closes the door behind them, walks to the file cabinet, pours herself a cup of coffee, looks out the window, and sips it. Her deliberateness, the absence of gestures, and her silence unnerves him. It seems to him she is going to stand and sip her coffee forever. Finally, she walks to her desk and puts the cup down gently. "Here it comes," he says to himself. He wants to say sorry but isn't sure if he is allowed to speak. He craves a cigarette, and knows it will only ignite the keg of powder on the chair in front of him. When she speaks, her words are calm and unrelated to what happened in the meeting room. "How was this morning's hunt?"

Relieved, he jumps at the question. "I think we might have something. The SUV was driven out by the vic on Thursday evening. Jo is reviewing the CCTV recordings to see when it was returned, and by whom. I think it would be Sunday night or Monday morning, and I'm hoping we'll get a look at the person bringing it back. RT had a night security guard, but he has absconded. A standby detective is trying to track him down. Chew has taken the SUV back to the lab. He says he'll do an overnighter on it. The key was in the vehicle all the while. But it's clean. The same goes for the SUV. The manager said the vic was going to use the SUV for his vacation, and I found a service request dated a few days before that. I'll be checking the workshop to see if it leads us anywhere." He pauses to catch his breath.

"Good. When will Chew come back to you?"

"He didn't say, but I'll see him later today, once Jo has finished viewing the CCTV recordings. We may need his help to enhance foot-ages Jo identifies. I have a good feeling about the SUV being the primary scene."

"This may be the break we need. Good job."

"Ma'am, I'm sorry about—"

"Don't be. You did what you felt was right. I should be the one saying sorry to you for not being firm sooner. One thing, Lan; if there's to be a face-off between Major Crimes and other departments, please remember I'll do the fighting. That's my shit; yours is to solve crimes."

"Yes, ma'am. I can't promise it won't happen again, but thanks."

"I bet you Henry is in the office planning how to bring you down instead of looking for Four Finger Loo's killers." She gestures toward the meeting room by turning her head in that direction and says, "That is not the end of it. You watch your step, Lan."

"Always, and I have you as my extra pair of eyes. You take care, ma'am. I don't want a new boss, not unless my present boss goes on a promotion," he says with a smile.

His assistant is still reviewing the CCTV recordings and taking notes when Mislan comes back to his desk. He asks how much longer it would take, and his assistant asks for another half an hour. He calls Chew, but the office tells him the latter has gone out for a late lunch and will be back soon. The word "lunch" reminds him he has not had any, and neither has his assistant. With the adrenaline rush of possibly discovering the primary crime scene, and the live-wire tango with the OCCI and Superintendent Henry, he has forgotten food. Now that things have settled, his bodily needs have moved up the hierarchy.

While he waits, he examines the victim's cell phone, switching it on and scrolling through the incoming calls. One number keeps coming up. He jots down the number and scrolls through the outgoing calls. He sees none made to that number. The incoming and outgoing text message listings are empty. He writes the service provider a letter requesting details of the number and stamps it urgent. He calls a standby detective and instructs him to go to the Maxis Centre at KLCC and wait there until he gets a reply.

He redials Chew. The Forensic Department supervisor tells him they have struck gold with the Cayenne. It is, definitely, the primary crime scene. They have not finished with the vehicle yet, and it will be some time before they're done. He asks if Chew can make a video technician available to do some CCTV footage enhancement, and says he will be there in about an hour. Once Johan signals he's done, they pack the DVD and are off to Forensics. In the car, he asks Johan if he wants to get something to eat.

They stop at a *nasi campur* stall in Taman Segar. Mislan decides on a fried fish, salted egg, some bean sprouts fried with tofu, a dollop of *sambal belacan*, some *lemak* gravy on rice, and iced lemon tea. Sitting at a table under a tree, they start eating with their fingers. Famished, they clean their plates in five minutes.

"You're quiet. Something on your mind?"

"I might have overdone it with the OCCI."

"What do you mean?"

"I told him I'm not giving any information directly to him."

"You're serious? What did he say?"

"I didn't say that exactly, but that was the message. I think I stepped on Superintendent Henry's toes, too. He was pissed off, and I might have endangered ma'am. I don't know, Jo. I feel it's best if D7 takes over this case. If they want to bury it, let them. What do you think?"

"Are you having second thoughts?" He looks at his boss' face. "Remember what you said to me when I was assigned to you? You said there were two types of investigators, one works hard to close a case and the other works hard to get closures. You asked me which I was. I didn't know then, but after working with you, I know."

"Well, that was before we landed this case, before I participated in the death of an innocent man. Before—"

"Don't go there. You didn't contribute to Four Finger's death, you were following orders. You did all you could to stop the PC. Don't hang that around your neck. After this case is over, maybe you should take a break. Go away with Daniel. Better still, take Dr. Safia along," his assistant says, smiling.

"There's nothing between us."

"Yah, right. I can see the way she looks at you and you look at her.

What's stopping you? How long has it been now, a year? Some guys won't even wait a month."

"It's complicated, Jo. I saw the way you were looking at Irene. You were almost drooling on her office carpet."

"She's hot."

"She is older than you."

"Wise men say, age is only a number."

"It is, until she hits fifty, but your libido is still on full throttle. Let's go."

In the car, Johan briefs his boss. According to the CCTV recordings, the victim left alone at 1631 hours on Thursday in the Cayenne. The security guard came to work between 1955 and 2010 hours. The guard left the premises every morning between 0400 and 0430 hours and came back thirty or forty minutes later. The Cayenne entered the compound at 0412 hours on Monday morning. The person coming out of the Cayenne was wearing a baseball cap, dark pants, T-shirt, and a dark jacket. He did not go into the building but walked out of the compound. No frontal images of his face are on the recording, only his side and back. The guard left at 0800 hours.

"So the guard was not at his station when the Cayenne was returned to the compound. You think the guard was compromised?"

"Possibly, but I think not. He went out at the same time every morning, maybe for coffee or something. The killers could have observed the routine."

"Is there no clear shot of the person delivering the Cayenne?"

"Nope. He was careful to avoid the cameras. As you said, it was well planned and executed."

"Shit! I thought it was too easy; the CCTV, I mean. These guys are good, too good to be merely good."

"What do you mean?"

"They are too good, and for them to be that good they need intelligence or knowledge. My money is on knowledge."

"And?"

"Someone inside was feeding them info. First about the vics going for a vacation, then the maid taking Friday off, now the guard taking time off for a coffee break."

"Are you thinking it's the sexy manager? Oh, boy!" Johan exclaims.

"What's her motive, though? That's what we need to figure out. We learn the motive, and we nail the bastards."

24

THE POLICE COLLEGE STAFF are already leaving for the day when they approach the guardhouse. Mislan flashes his identification, and the guard waves them through. He drives around the block, parks at the emptying lot, and climbs the stairs. A technician tells him that Chew is in the garage on the ground floor at the end of the block.

The facility comes with a hydraulic lift and dug-out floor for undercarriage examination. The difference between a normal workshop and the lab's garage is the presence of equipment for tearing up vehicles. The garage is enclosed and dimly lit except where vehicles are being inspected. It smells of exhaust smoke and hot lubricant. Apart from the Cayenne, there is another car with its four doors, trunk, and hood removed. Chew is bent over the Cayenne, shouting instructions to two technicians when they enter unnoticed.

"Hey, Chew," he says, startling him.

"Hi, Inspector. Can you guys wait in the discussion room?" Chew says, pointing to a row of cubicles at the corner. "There are too many parts on the floor. Can't have you stepping on them. I'll be with you in a minute."

"Sure, no problem."

"Go into the first room. It has coffee, and you can smoke there," Chew shouts.

Mislan lights a cigarette as he watches Johan pour coffee into two paper cups. Chew comes in with a technician in a white lab gown, whom he introduces as Kalinathan, the video technician. Nathan, as he wishes to be called, looks as if he has been dragged out of a geek convention and given the lab gown to cover his odorful clothes. His hair is drowning in gel.

"Where is the CCTV recording? Nathan can work at it while we discuss other things. If there is anything worth extracting, we can go up and view it later. How's that?" Chew suggests.

"Fine by me. Jo, why don't you and Nathan go on ahead? I'll join you when I'm finished here."

The sergeant nods and leaves with the video technician.

"Right, the crime scene: we've done swabs of the interior and found traces of hydrogen cyanide. We believe it was released through the air-conditioning vents. We are taking off the compressor, the piping, and the vent to run more tests. My guess is the hydrogen cyanide would've been disposed of and the system refilled with normal refrigerant." Noticing the discomfort on his face, Chew quickly adds, "No worries, there'll still be traces. The SUV was wiped and vacuumed clean inside out. We'll be stripping it down, see if there's something they missed in between the seats, paneling, or grooves. That's going to take some doing, so don't expect anything soon." He pauses, sounding exhausted.

"Do you have a theory about how it was done?"

"My first thoughts were the gas was released using a remote device, but we have found nothing so far to support that."

"I don't understand."

"I mean, we havent found any remote-control devices fitted in the vehicle," Chew explains.

"Aren't these high-end cars computer controlled?"

"Yes, by the Electronic Control Unit, the ECU."

"What does it control, exactly?

"All the automation, data, GPS. I'm not sure what else. Why?" Chew realizes he is being led somewhere.

"I'm thinking: if I can manipulate the ECU, I should be able to control the electronic systems of the vehicle, right? Like the locking mechanism, air-conditioning, and the engine."

"I suppose so, but how do you manipulate them? I may be wrong, but I have heard you can't hack into the ECU. The source codes are well protected."

"These are electronic devices, and electronics can and do go bonkers, right? When it does, it needs to be reprogrammed. So, someone must know how to do it. Is it possible to open the ECU and see if it has been tampered with?"

"I'll check with my IT guys. You think the killer took control of the SUV?"

"Since you haven't found any foreign devices fixed, it's possible they did it through the ECU."

"It makes sense."

"Is there anything else?"

"Not now."

They walk up to the visual room at level two, where they find Nathan and Johan glued to a computer screen. Chew leaves them, disappears into the inner office, and comes back with a strange-looking woman with her hair streaked in red, blue, green, and yellow. She, too, wears a lab gown. She is dressed in slacks with a thousand creases, a black crew-neck T-shirt with the words "Love Me or Hate Me—I Don't Give A Shit" in bright orange. She wears three earrings on one ear and many more on the other. All her fingers have a ring each, including her thumbs. Mislan suspects there are probably several more on other parts of her body. She is introduced as Fadillah Hanum the IT technician. She insists on being called Di.

Mislan's cell phone rings. It is the detective he sent to the Maxis Centre. The number obtained from the victim's cell phone is a prepaid number listed to one Wong Peng Soon, a sixty-year-old man from Kepong. According to Maxis records, the SIM card was sold by an agent in the Kuala Lumpur International Airport about three years ago. Calls made to the number by Maxis were not answered. A check with the National Registration Department revealed that the identity card number used was phony and belongs to a Malay man named Kamaruddin Abdul Majid living in Melaka. The detective has asked for the help of Melaka Police to locate the subject. Mislan is sure nothing is going to come out of the inquiries by the Melaka police.

"Inspector, can you tell Di what you told me?" Chew says, pulling out a chair.

"Okay, the Cayenne is fitted with an ECU, right? Can someone manipulate it so he can remotely take control of the car's functions, like doors, air conditioners, and the engine?"

"Technically, yes. Realistically, I'm not sure. First, you'll have to gain access to the ECUs, meaning you've got to have the access code or protocol. Second, you'll need the source code to be able to manipulate the programs." Di sounds like she knows what she is talking about.

"You said ECUs, are there many of them?" He is surprised. He always thought there is only one ECU, like a master computer, that controlled everything in the car.

"There are, depending on the car model. Some models may have as many as twenty or thirty. Each ECU controls a specific electronic function of the car."

"What about the workshop? I'm sure the workshop would have the access codes and source code."

"I don't know about the source code, but I'm sure they have the access codes. It comes with the diagnostic system."

"Can you manipulate the ECUs with the access code?"

"You mean hack into it? Possibly, if you know how to get around firewalls. Anything can be hacked," Di answers with a mischievous smile.

"Once you hack into it, can you control the car's functions?"

"Depends. If you hack and install a virus, you're just screwing up the system. If you plant a sleeper program to take control, then you can take control of the car."

"How difficult is it?"

"What? To hack or to plant the program?"

"Both."

"Hacking, it can be quite difficult depending on the built-in security. Writing a control program is easy, depending on what you want to control. Hacking and planting it may take some doing. I have no experience with car ECUs, don't have reasons to," Di says, with a sly smile. "If you want, I'll chat up a friend; get some insight, as you guys say it."

"What friend?"

"A guy from our chat group. He's cool. Does plenty of 'anti-capitalism' crap, nothing illegal."

"Stop there, I don't want to know what your friend is into, okay. How good is he?"

"Quite good. And when we say 'quite good,' by normal standards, it's ass-kicking-good," Di says, smirking.

"What do you think, Chew?"

"I don't know; it's your case. Maybe it's worth a try. It'll prove or disprove your theory," Chew responds.

"Can you trust him?" Mislan asks Di, unsure if he should solicit the services of an anti-capitalist radical.

"As much as you can trust me. Look, I don't need to tell him about the case, I just need his expertise. If he says it can be done, I'll get Chew's permission to show him the real thing and see where it takes us. How's that?" Di says.

"All right, but nothing moves until I give the okay. When can you come back on this?"

"I'll chat with him tonight and let you know." With that, Di leaves.

Johan looks discouraged when asked if the CCTV recording has yielded anything. He says there is not a single frontal shot of the man parking the Cayenne. The man has made sure he has his back to the cameras constantly, and there is nothing significant on his clothing to give him away. He asks Nathan to zoom into some footage, focusing on the head. All they can make out is the back and top of a baseball cap.

"Nathan, is that the best we can do?"

"You see, Inspector, the system only enhances what is captured. If it's not there, the system cannot do anything. Very sorry."

"Don't be, it's not your fault," he says, regretting letting out his frustration on Nathan.

After they zoom in and zoom out on other footage several times, they leave.

25

THEY DRIVE BACK TO the office in silence. The excitement of discovering the primary crime scene, closing in on the killer or killers, is fast fading. It is mentally tiring and emotionally unsettling. Perhaps it is possible to commit a perfect crime, Mislan mulls. Were all the unsolved cases perfect crimes or sloppy investigation? He has the primary crime scene, he has the CCTV recording, he has a partial fingerprint, he knows what the murder weapon is, yet he has nothing. Maybe he is sniffing round the wrong bush, maybe he is not sniffing hard enough, or maybe he is just not the investigator he thinks he is.

Mislan parks the car and asks Johan if he wants to knock off for the day. His assistant says he wants to hang around a little, listen to some detective gossip.

"Any news on the security guard?"

"According to the detective, one of the guard's former coworkers said he has joined another company and might be working at Central Market. They'll bring him in as soon as they locate him."

"I want to go over the CCTV recordings again. Do you have the DVD with you?"

Johan digs into his bag and hands it to him. "You think we've missed something?"

"Maybe not. I just need to do something."

When he walks into his office, the desk officer tells him that the head of Major Crimes wants him in her office as soon as he is back. He asks his assistant if he wants to tag along and update the boss.

Superintendent Samsiah Hassan is a tall Malay woman in her

mid-forties, short hair, handsome features, elegant in uniform, and does not wear the headscarf. She is soft-spoken. A Kelantanese, she was a teacher before she joined the police force as a probationary inspector. She was posted to Melaka as an investigator, then transferred to the Federal Police Headquarters in Bukit Aman as head of Criminal Records, before becoming head of Major Crimes in Kuala Lumpur. She is leaning back in her chair, gazing out of the window when he knocks. She swivels around, straightens herself, and invites them in.

"Trouble, ma'am?" Mislan asks with apprehension.

"Hi, Jo," she greets his assistant. Turning to face Mislan she says, "Nothing more than the usual. How's your case coming along?"

Mislan sighs.

"Not good, eh! Want to kick it about?"

"You up to it?"

"Let's hear it. Maybe a fresh mind can see a new angle."

"We've got the primary scene nailed, but so far Chew's not getting much from it. The CCTV recording is another dead end. No frontal images. The phone number is that of a prepaid card with a false identity card number. Looks like we are back where we started."

The sergeant nods in agreement.

"Sounds like a pro job."

"It's definitely not an impulse crime. The knowledge, planning, preparations, and execution are detailed and painstaking. It's intriguing, like nothing I've worked on before; and the risks they took were crazy."

"Maybe there were no risks. Knowledge eliminates risks."

"They still had to reckon with the uncontrollable factors, like someone dropping in when they were staging the vics, the police stopping the SUV while the bodies were being transferred, or the maid deciding to come home early. I just can't figure out why they were willing to take such risks with the elaborate display. The motive's a mystery," he says, standing and walking to the window. "Revenge? If it were revenge, it would've been bloody, to satisfy the bad blood. But why do the wife and kid?" Walking back to his chair, he continues, "Teach them a lesson? They are dead, what lesson can they learn?"

"Someone else?"

"Who? What's the lesson? You screw us, we wipe you and your family out, and oh, one more thing, after that we put you guys on display? Is that the lesson?" Mislan pauses, rubbing his forehead. "Unless we have a motive, we don't have an angle."

"The staging; have you considered ritual?"

"You mean hocus-pocus stuff, like black magic?"

She nods.

"No."

"Why not?"

"Nothing found at the secondary scene indicates ritual. No incense, prayer items, or utensils related to ritual."

"*Hmm.* I'm going to bend the rules here. You may smoke if you wish," she says, opening the file cabinet, pulling out a crystal ashtray with a police logo on it.

Taking a drag, Mislan starts, "The way I think of it, the killers hacked into the Cayenne's ECUs and—"

"What are ECUs?"

"Electronic Control Units that regulate the vehicle's functions. That way, the killers could take control of the vehicle remotely. When the vics were in the SUV, the killers disabled it and released the gas. Once the vics were dead, they were driven to an unknown location, embalmed, and driven back to the house for the staging. The SUV was then cleaned and returned to the RT office."

"Jo, do you agree with the theory?"

Johan nods, saying, "I believe we're on the right track."

"All right; why park the SUV at RT? Why not leave it at the house?"

"The killers needed to do the cleaning. Doing it at the house was too risky. They, possibly, needed special equipment that was not available at the house."

"What might that be? The special equipment."

"I don't know; maybe a machine to discharge the hydrogen cyanide. This part is still guesswork."

"Oh, okay, sound reasoning."

"Anyway, by doing it elsewhere, they minimized the risk of being seen. Sending the SUV back to the house after the cleanup was also risky, so parking it at RT makes sense."

"Why was it more risky to park it at the house than RT?"

"The vics. Someone might have already found the vics by the time they finished, so going back to the house was an unnecessary risk. The neighbors might see them. Once was bad enough, but repeated goings and comings was too much." He shakes his head.

"That makes sense," she says, writing something on her notepad. "And to support your theory?"

"Chew found traces of hydrogen cyanide in the Cayenne, confirming it as the primary scene. Chew's failure to lift any prints from it proves the cleanup. The CCTV recording confirmed the Cayenne was sent back to RT. My guess is, the ECUs were hacked during the Cayenne's routine maintenance service a few days before the intended vacation, or at one of the many times it was sent for repairs. The IT tech, what's her name, Fadillah Hanum, Di as she insists on being called, says technically ECUs can be hacked if you know the protocol, and control programs are easy to write and install."

"That could well be your break. What makes you think the hacking was done during the servicing?"

"It's the most sensible time to do it. Who is going to question what you're doing when the SUV is in the garage? The workshop working on the SUV must have a diagnostic system to communicate with the ECUs," he says, killing his cigarette. "And because we don't have any other lead."

They laugh.

"What do you think, Jo?"

"I'll go with Inspector Mislan, he's dialed in on this."

"I'm waiting for Di to come back with her findings before I go for the workshop. I don't want to spook them." He then hesitates before adding, "Di is not sure if you can hack a Porsche's ECUs, so she's consulting a friend."

"What does 'a friend' mean?" she asks, brows rising.

"Someone from her circle of friends who, how shall I term it, is a 'vigilante' hacker. I know it's against procedure, but it's the only way of determining whether the ECUs can be hacked, or was hacked. I'm sorry, I should've consulted you before agreeing to it."

"When is this going to take place?"

"In her words, she'll chat him up tonight. If he says it's possible, I seek your permission for him to check out the ECUs. The way I figure it, the killers needed to control the locking, engine, and air-conditioning systems."

"Why those three?"

"To disable the locking system so the vics can't can't escape, kill the engine so the vics can't engage the gear and ram the vehicle, allowing them to break out or attract attention, and disable the air conditioner's control so it cannot be turned off."

Smiling, Superintendent Samsiah says, "There you go. You have it solved. Good work. Going by what you've just told me, your best bet is the workshop. I know motive is crucial. Sometimes the motive becomes evident only after you peel off all the layers. About this vigilante hacker, exercise the need-to-know policy strictly," she cautions him.

He nods. "Thanks. If it leaks, I'll take the heat for it. You don't have to say you knew. This meeting never happened."

"Told you. Everything that happens in this department is my responsibility. If there's heat to take, I'll do the taking. Next time, if you even think about breaking the rules, let me know first so I'm not caught with my skirt up. That'll be it. Good job, both of you," she says, dismissing them.

After leaving the boss's office, Johan goes into the detective room and comes back with some fried banana. He asks Mislan if he is going to work late. The latter shrugs, "I'll hang around for a while. I'm hoping Di will call, I want to meet her friend in person."

"I'll be in the detectives' room then,' Johan says. "Call if you need me."

26

It is ten past seven in the evening, and the office is deserted except for the shift investigator, his assistant, and the standby detective. Going through his in tray, Mislan pulls out a few messages with his name on it. Three are from Audi, one from Melaka Major Crimes with the message "Kamaruddin Abdul Majid checks out. Retired government servant. He knows nothing about the SIM card—Inspector Tay, D9, IPK Melaka." Mislan is not surprised.

Mislan drops his backpack next to his desk, lights a cigarette, and calls home to check on Daniel. His son has just taken his bath and is having dinner.

"Hey, kiddo, how was school?"

"Good. Can you call me later? I'm eating now."

"What're you eating?"

"Rice with egg. Daddy, can you call me later?"

"Okay, I'll call later. Love you, kiddo."

When Daniel doesn't respond, Mislan teases his son with, "Love you too, Daddy," and terminates the call.

Turning on the computer, he loads in the DVD and waits for the Windows Media Player to play it. He drags the time to the 03:50 Monday morning frame and lets it run. An image of the parking lot and the gate appears and, except for the running timer counter at the bottom, there is no other movement. At eleven seconds after 03:57 he notices something move. It is the security guard coming out from the side of the building, pushing a motorcycle, probably from his "snooze zone," a hideaway somewhere by the side of the building out of the camera's view. The guard stands the motorcycle, walks to the entrance, and opens a previously unnoticed side gate. The guard kicks back the stand, pushes the motorcycle through the side gate, and disappears out of camera range. The gate closes, and the image becomes still again. Occasionally, the image brightens a little from headlights of passing vehicles.

At 04:12:21 the image becomes very bright. The gate slowly opens, the Cayenne rolls in and turns right to the parking lot. The gate remains open. The brightness goes back to normal as the Cayenne's headlights are turned off. After a lapse of fifteen seconds, the driver door opens; a figure steps out, reaches into the Cayenne as if looking for something, stands upright, closes the door, and casually walks toward the gate. The figure's back is constantly toward the camera mounted on the wall. He notices the gate starts closing as the figure closes the Cayenne's door and walks toward it. He thinks the driver must have closed the gate using the remote control in the Cayenne. The unhurried walk is another indication of a sound knowledge of the gate's speed and timing. At 04:13:33 the gate is completely closed and the image is still again.

Mislan continues looking at the monitor for a moment longer but is not rewarded with anything else. He fast-forwards it to 04:30 and lets it run. At 04:32:44 the image brightens again, the side gate opens, and the guard rides his motorcycle in and disappears. A moment later the guard reappears, locks the side gate, and disappears. He rewinds the video to 04:12 and replays it until 04:14.

The inspector replays the segment a few times until he is sure of what he has seen. Satisfied, he calls Forensics asking for Nathan, but they tell him he has left for the day. He calls Johan, who says he is out for *teh tarik* with some detectives and he will come over soon. Just as he puts down the phone, Superintendent Samsiah pops in for a last look before she goes home. He waves her over, eager for a fresh pair of eyes. She comes over and he invites her to view the segment.

"What exactly are you looking for?"

"See if you can spot anything peculiar. I don't want to influence you."

She pulls a chair from the next desk, sits next to him as he restarts the segment. At the end of the recording, she asks him to run it again.

"There," she says, pointing to the screen. "Bring it back." As he drags the frame control back, she guides him saying, "A bit more, a bit more, pause! You see that, the way she gets off the car. That's a woman."

"What makes you say it's a woman?"

"Go back a little, there, pause. See the way she got off the driver's seat with two legs closed, slanting out toward the door? That's how a woman slides off a car seat. They don't want to expose their panties to watching weirdos. She may be in pants, but habits are habits. Men don't have such habits."

"You still have it, don't you?" he smiles at her. "If it's a woman, it's a new lead."

"Yes, I still have it. Once you've got it, you'll never lose it," she says, laughing, pleased with herself. "What's next?"

"I want to get the IT guys to confirm what we think. Maybe they've some system, or software, or scientific method to measure the figure and confirm if it's a man or woman."

The head of Major Crimes nods. "Does this mean the target has now shifted to the vic's wife? We know she's been fooling around. Jealousy can be a strong motive."

"You think so?"

"Yes. Jealousy can drive people to do things you cannot imagine. It's like love, but in reverse."

"Hmm."

Johan comes with some *teh tarik* for him. He runs the video segment again, and after the second viewing, his assistant says, "What?" much to the amusement of his bosses. She points out the way in which the figure steps out of the Cayenne, and only then does the sergeant notice it. "You guys are good," he says with a laugh.

"We're not good, we are experienced," she says.

Superintendent Samsiah bids them goodnight and good luck, and leaves. Mislan calls Chew. He asks if the Forensics supervisor can arrange for the video tech to come back in for a short while to verify something on the video. Chew says he will do it within the hour. He then asks if he can have Di's cell phone number and Chew texts it to him. He calls the number and after several rings, the messaging system announces, "If it's important leave a message after the beep, otherwise try again later." He leaves a message for her to return his call.

A detective comes into the office escorting an Indian man. It's the security guard who was stationed at RT.

"Do you want to interview him?"

The sergeant nods, and, turning to the detective, instructs him, "Put him in room one and get the detective to check with D6 if he has any previous convictions. I'll join you in a minute."

The security guard, K. Kuppusamy, is in his late fifties. He has bloodshot eyes probably from lack of sleep, and a five-day stubble. His disodored uniform smells of dried curry, sweat, and alcohol. He wears no socks and a pair of shoes that should have been replaced months ago. Kuppusamy's eyes dart wildly, as if looking for some hidden danger. He is so jittery he almost jumps out of the chair when Johan enters the room, and as the sergeant takes the seat facing him, he leans as far back as he can without tipping over. The inspector joins them, lights a cigarette, leans against the door, and signals for the interview to begin.

"Kuppusamy son of Kulasingam, is that your name?"

The guard nods.

"You were working at RT Fashion House in Bukit Bintang last Sunday?"

He nods again, his eyes shifting to the inspector leaning against the door.

"Why did you run away?"

"I don't like the place. I asked to be posted somewhere else, but they still put me there," Kuppusamy answers without taking his eyes off the cigarette in the inspector's hand. The nicotine craving overcomes his fear and he pleads, "Hey, can you spare a cigarette?"

Mislan shakes his head, not because he is insensitive to a smoker's needs, but for fear that his goodwill would be misrepresented by the suspect as inducement, should the suspect be charged.

"Did anyone ask you to leave at four on Monday morning?" Johan draws the detainee's attention back to the interview.

"No, I always leave about that time for a drink. That place does not have any drinks or food. I go to the stalls behind KL Plaza," Kuppusamy answers, his eyes straying toward the cigarette.

"When you left on Monday morning, did you see anybody or any car waiting outside RT?"

"No."

"What about when you came back?"

Kuppusamy shakes his head.

"Did you notice the Cayenne in the parking lot when you came back?"

"What's a Cayenne?" He looks genuinely blank.

"A four-wheel drive, a jeep."

"That is the company's jeep. It's always there. I've seen it parked there many times before."

"It was not there before you left at four. How did the jeep get inside the compound?"

"I don't know. The gate is automatic. I only have the key to the small gate. I returned it to the office before I left. You can ask my officer."

"How long have you worked for this security company?"

"Three months."

A detective enters, passes a note to the sergeant, and leaves. He studies the note and asks, "Do you have a criminal record?"

"A loooong time ago. I stole a motorcycle and was sent to jail for six months. That's why I cannot work very long in one company. When they find out, they fire me, and I don't get any pay."

Johan smiles at his boss, receives the signal to end the interview, and releases Kuppusamy. It is a waste of time to continue with the questioning. They know there is no chance in hell the killers would have used him as a coconspirator.

27

When Mislan's cell rings, it is Di returning his call. He asks her if she has managed to chat with her friend, and she tells him she is on her way to the McDonald's in Bukit Bintang in front of Sungai Wang Plaza to meet him. He asks if they could come along. Di says it is fine with her, so long as he's buying. They hitch a ride on an MPV going out on patrol.

The patrol car drops them off at a bus stop near the Bukit Bintang–Sultan Ismail junction, just after the McDonald's outlet, attracting curious stares from people who are waiting for their bus or taxis. Just as they are getting off, two men at the bus stop suddenly take off and run around the corner, into the back alley. The MPV leaps forward into action even before all the doors are closed; it takes a sharp left, narrowly missing a motorcyclist, and disappears into the alley leaving those watching in awe. Johan grins and shakes his head.

"Brings back memories?"

"Sure does."

They stand at the entrance to the McDonald's outlet trying to spot Di. Many in the crowd have red, orange, blue, green streaked hair. Giving up, they chose the alternative; making themselves obvious. Dressed the way they are, they stand out like two lions among the zebras. As they move slowly toward the ordering counter, the inspector is stunned by a slap on his butt and a female voice, "You owe me 29.55." Feeling red in his face, Mislan asks, "Where are you sitting?" Di points to a table near the entrance where a large young man seems to be trying to devour a Big Mac in one mouthful. Mislan says they will get their orders and join them. He watches her go and instantly has second thoughts about wanting to meet her friend. After nearly fifteen minutes, they get their order of a Quarter Pounder, a Filet-O-Fish, two fries, and two Cokes.

When they join Di and her large friend, the two IT geeks have already finished eating. She introduces her large friend as Hubble, adding, "Like the Hubble telescope, probing deep into space without leaving any trace."

"Di tells me you know something about ECUs used in cars," Mislan said, wasting no time. "I want to know if it's possible to hack into a car's ECU and upload a control program?"

"Anything is possible, man, if you know how," Hubble replies, eyeing the fries on the inspector's tray.

"What do you need to hack into one?"

"*Duh*, obviously the ECU itself."

Di laughs. "Dude, talk straight, okay? These guys are cool."

Looking at Di doubtfully, Hubble says, "If you say so."

Di pats Hubble's big shoulder and nods.

"Okay. All ECUs have protocols that are recognized for data input and output. You get the protocol, and you can do anything you want; download, upload, delete, and other stuff."

"How can you get hold of the protocols?"

"I'd say, easiest: the diagnostic system; hardest: the manufacturer's system. All car manufacturers have diagnostic systems that they make available to appointed workshops that repair their cars. In the case of luxury cars, like Mercs, Bimmers, I suppose only their appointed workshop will have it. You have the diagnostic system, you have the protocols. Simple," Hubble explains.

"Is it possible to get it from the Internet, or elsewhere?"

"No way, man. These babies are religiously controlled by manufacturers to safeguard their interests in parts, accessories, and repairs. I guess the diagnostic systems are easier to get for the mid-range cars, because the workshops are not specialized. But, for the big boys, it will not be easy to lay your hands on one."

A brief pause follows as Mislan considers what Hubble has just said, during which the geek's hand reaches for his fries. Four rapid extensions of the hand, and the fries are gone. The inspector ponders if he should take another step across the line without checking with his boss. He has just been warned by his boss about this, but the maverick in him wants to take control. "If I give you the ECUs, can you get hold of a diagnostic system to probe it?" He decides to walk on the side of caution and consult her first thing in the morning before making any moves.

"Don't think so, man. Why don't you flash your badge and get one from an authorized workshop? Let me have it for half a day and I'll tell you whatever you want to know," Hubble says.

"Okay, how do I contact you?"

"I'm not giving you my number. Di can contact me when you have the item," Hubble replies, shaking his head.

"No problem, I'll take care of him."

"Right. That's it then, thanks." Mislan takes out a RM50 note and hands it to Di. "Get Hubble another round of fries; he has earned it."

28

Once outside, he calls Chew to ask how much longer he will be at the office, and if he has finished with the ECUs. Chew tells him that they have removed all the ECUs and the technicians are dusting them for prints. They should finish soon. He tells Chew to call him once they're done, then asks for Nathan.

"Nathan, Inspector Mislan. Sorry for dragging you in so late. I need to check if you have any system that can differentiate between a man and a woman in a video footage?"

"No problem, sir, I wasn't doing anything. As for specifically identifying whether a person is male or female from a video, the answer is no."

"Shit. How about image measurement; you know, like what they do in hospitals when they measure babies in the womb or the size of a tumor?"

"You mean like ultrasound scanning? We have software that can do something similar, but not ultrasound. Why?" Nathan sounds baffled.

"Okay, I need you to do this for me. Take precise measurements of the figure from the video this morning. The height, shoulder width, chest, waist, head, legs, hands, fingers, whatever that can be measured in three dimensions. Once you have the measurements, call me."

"Sure, it'll take a while. Give me an hour or so."

"Don't worry; take the time you need to be as accurate as you can. Call me, no matter what time you finish. Thanks."

Mislan tells Johan to hail a cab or an MPV while he makes another call, this time to Dr. Safia. As he waits for her to answer, Di and Hubble come out of McDonald's. He waves them over, switching off the phone.

"Di, if I were to provide you with three-dimensional measurements, is there any way you can create an image from it?"

"Measurements of what?" Di inquires, excited.

"Human."

"Human," Di repeats, closing her eyes, "Sure. But I can't give you a face, just a figure."

His cell phone rings, he signals for Di to hang on. It is Dr. Safia. He tells her he will call back shortly and turns off the phone.

"That's fine. How long will you need?"

"Depends. How good and complex the measurements are. About two hours."

"You need to do it at the lab?"

"Nay, it's my software; I mean, it's not the lab's software. I'll do it at home."

"Great, I'll call you once I get the measurements. Thanks, Di."

He watches them walking away.

Johan manages to flag down a cab. Getting in, Mislan returns Dr. Safia's call. He asks if she can tell from a three-dimensional image of a figure if it's male or female. She says she can make an informed guess, but that wouldn't stand up in court. He tells her that's good enough and will send them to her once he has the 3-D images.

It is 9:40 when they walk into his office. He remembers his promise to Audi and calls her. It is answered on the first ring with, "You sure take your time calling. I hope you've something good for me," Audi says, without asking who it is.

"It has been a busy day. Off the record, we've nailed down the primary crime scene and the Forensics guys are going over it. That's all I can give you now. I should be able to give you more by tomorrow. It's off the record, so don't you dare run it yet."

"Oh, my God! Where? Give me some details," she yaps excitedly. "Okay, okay, I promise, I won't print it," she agrees.

"Look, Audi, we're still working on possibilities and long shots. I hope we'll get something by tomorrow. You'll be the first to know."

"Come on, Inspector; you can at least tell me where, what you discovered, and why you think it's the primary scene."

"You know I can't do that. As I said, you'll be the first to know when we have something."

"I'll hold you to that."

"You do that. Good night."

Waiting is not one of Mislan's strong points, but that is all he can do for the moment. He has been pumped up since the discovery of the primary crime scene, and now with the prospect of finally getting a much-needed break, he finds it impossible to sit still. He switches on the computer and starts searching for local Porsche dealers, authorized workshops, and diagnostic systems. The Web search isn't fruitful. He finds some write-ups on diagnostic systems but nothing about authorized workshops. He manages to obtain information on the local Porsche dealer, Auto Eurokars Sdn Bhd, though. He notes down the address and contact number, and decides to call tomorrow. He switches off the computer and thinks of calling Superintendent Samsiah to ask if she knows anyone who owns a Porsche he can talk to, but discards the thought as silly.

He calls home, tells Daniel who has just returned from his religious class that he will be late. He asks Daniel not to stay up too late and promises he will carry him to his room to sleep in his bed when he gets home. That puts some cheer in Daniel's voice. How easy it is to make a six-year-old happy, he thinks. After his ex-wife left, he has been plagued with guilt every time he has to work late, doing things he is passionate about, while Daniel stays home with no one to play with except the maid.

Nathan calls to inform him that the measurements are ready. He gives Nathan his e-mail address and thanks him. Then, he calls Di to ask for hers. He informs her he is e-mailing the measurements over and to revert once she is done.

He tells Johan to get some intelligence on Pro Care Service Centre, and to arrange for a stakeout first thing in the morning. Realizing there is nothing else he can do, he decides to go home.

29

ON THE WAY HOME, he remembers Daniel asking for *satay* about a week ago and stops to buy some. When he reaches home, Daniel wants to know why he is back early, what is that he is carrying, and their sleeping arrangement. He answers all the queries, tells the maid to set the table while he takes a much-needed shower. After the *satay*, Daniel follows him into his bedroom, switches the TV to his favorite channel, and jumps on the bed.

"Turn the volume down and get some sleep, kiddo, it's late."

"A little more, please?" Daniel pleads.

"Okay, a little." He switches off the light, gets into bed, and hugs his son. Kissing his head, he says to him, "Night, kiddo, Daddy loves you."

"Love you, too," Daniel replies without looking away from the TV screen.

Stroking Daniel's head, he reviews the day's discovery. If the figure is that of a woman, who can she be? Irene? She said she was away in Hong Kong; that can easily be verified. If it was her, he doesn't think she will be stupid enough to lie to him. Furthermore, what motive would she have? According to her, Robert Tham gave her a job she loves. Money, greed, or anger for not making her a full partner? Maybe she is more than just an employee. It is not unknown for a married man to start a business with the woman he is having an affair with. Mislan makes a note to check her alibi with immigration.

He picks up the cell phone and dials Chew's number. When Chew answers, he says, "Hey, you still at the office?"

"About to leave. Why?"

"Something just came to me; the Cayenne driver's seat is electronically controlled, right?"

"Yes, and?"

"Did you move the seat?"

"Nope, why?"

"Can you do me a favor? Measure the distance of the seat to the steering, and the pedals. If my guess is right, it will be short. Can you do that the first thing tomorrow?"

"Sure, no problem. Since you're on the line, I might as well tell you: we found a hydrogen cyanide canister attached to the air-conditioner piping, with an electronic release valve and a remote-control receiver. We have solved the mystery of how the gas was discharged. Did you manage to speak to Nathan?"

"Yes, thanks. Good work, Chew, appreciate it. You done with the ECUs?"

"Yup. They're ready for pickup whenever you want them."

"Thanks, again. Have a good rest, night."

"You too, Inspector, night."

After Daniel falls asleep, he removes the TV remote from his hand, pulls the blanket over him, and kisses his forehead. He then gets up and sits at his desk. Although he's exhausted, his mind is too restless to sleep. It is 10:47. He speed-dials Johan, who is still in the office detailing some detectives for tomorrow's stakeout. His assistant asks if he has any specific instructions. Mislan tells him to take snapshots of the employees and customers, especially women. He asks Johan to call Maria in for an interview at 0900 hours before telling his sergeant to get some rest, and to expect a long day tomorrow.

Recalling Superintendent Samsiah's little talk on the jealousy motive for murder, he switches on his notebook computer, navigates to the Yahoo search engine and keys in the words "jealousy homicide." 877,000 search results show up. He tries a new search: "murder with jealousy as motive" and gets 864,000 results. He browses through a few sites and is shocked at how far a jealous killer will go. His attention is drawn to a case of a man convicted of killing a woman he friended on Facebook. The motive: the killer was jealous because the woman was also chatting online with other men. After two hours of reading, he turns off his notebook computer and joins Daniel under the blanket.

Lying with his eyes closed, eager for daybreak, he thinks of Lionel. He was only ten. He has never been involved in a murder case involving a minor, and with a six-year-old son of his own, the case is becoming personal. What were the sins of Lionel's parents? Seeing death is never easy. They said you'll get used to it. Just don't get attached. How can one get used to it? How can one not get attached? You dig into their lives, businesses, relationships, finances, activities, loves, fears; you begin to know them completely, even better than their coworkers, friends, relatives, and families. How can you not get attached? Forensic pathologists have it easy; they do whatever they need to do, and move on to the next case. Investigators do not have that luxury. They carried it with them from the moment the case is reported through the investigation, court proceedings, and convictions or acquittal. Often, they live their cases. Sometimes even when they win, they lose.

If only this was an episode of *CSI*, he would have found something he could use to nail the killers by now.

Exhaustion finally takes its toll, and sleep mercifully overcomes him.

30

HIS CELL PHONE HAS been ringing for a while before he realizes it. Turning to his side, he reaches out and answers sleepily, "Mislan."

It is Di. "Are you sleeping? Sorry. You said to call you when I was done."

"Hey, Di, no problem, thanks. Sorry to make you work so late," He's instantly wide awake, in anticipation.

"Don't fret. I'm used to staying up late, doing my thing." She laughs.

"Nothing illegal, I hope."

She laughs louder. "I've mailed the 3-D images to you."

"All right, I don't want to know why you're staying up so late. Thanks, Di. Really appreciate it." Before replacing his phone, he looks at the time display. It is 02:56. Daniel stirs, turns away, pulling the blanket with him. He pats him lightly until he hears Daniel's smooth rhythmic breathing. Di's call excites him, and the urge to get dressed and drive off to the office keeps him awake, and restless.

He sends Daniel to school at seven. Then, he drives as fast as he can in the morning traffic to the office, parks the car, and squeezes into the first available elevator. Dropping his backpack on the floor, he switches on the computer, lights a cigarette, and waits for the system to boot up. Johan appears at the door, greets him, and heads straight for the pantry to make two mugs of coffee.

"You're in early."

"Wanted to check the stakeout team. They were a man short last night. I'm trying to get one of the standby detectives to join them, and I need to follow up on Maria after I spoke to her last night. She sounded hesitant about coming, so I thought I'd give her a friendly reminder," Johan says.

"Careful, we don't need her running to the embassy and attracting more attention."

Carrying the two mugs, Johan puts them on his desk and asks, "Any developments?" Just then, the computer comes to life. He keys in his password and extracts Di's e-mail. The text reads, *"m i gud or wat."* He clicks the attachment and is impressed with what pops up. He signals Johan to come over to look.

"What's that?" Johan asks.

"3-D image of the person who returned the Cayenne to RT. Nathan did the measurements from the video recording, and Di has come up with this. What do you think?"

"Hard to say, but small men exist." Taking a closer look, Johan says. "The height is four feet eleven inches; that's a girl height."

"Look at the waist and chest measurements. The chest is too big for the waist. I think it's a woman. Here, look at the side angle," he says, clicking the right and left arrows to rotate the image.

"I'm not very sure about the measurements. The waist is okay, but the chest? The figure is wearing a jacket with a waist garter, that usually makes the stomach and chest look big," Johan argues.

"Good point. Here, look at the head's measurements. It's too big at the top. It's not proportional to the length of the head, like there's something under the cap. Curled up hair?"

"Possible."

"Let's look at the video." Mislan loads the DVD and waits for the Media Player to come up. He moves the timer to 04:12 and presses Play. He stops the player, brings it back to the best footage of the figure he can find, and pauses. He sends an image of his screen to the printer. Mislan studies the printout and makes a note to ask Nathan how he got the measurements.

The front desk officer signals that morning prayer is starting. The meeting is brief: two cases of armed robberies; shots were fired in both cases but no casualties reported. Throughout the briefing, ASP Ghani begs the head of Major Crimes for the project, to track down the suspects, claiming they were involved in several other reported robberies. The boss is not convinced, asks ASP Ghani to produce evidence of his claim, and until such time, the cases will remain in the hands of the district investigating officer.

"Lan, please see me after this," she says, ending the meeting.

On his way to her office, Johan tells him that Maria has arrived and is waiting in interview room one. He tells Johan to make her comfortable, to get her some coffee and he will be with her in ten minutes. He updates Superintendent Samsiah about his meeting with Di and her friend, Hubble the telescope, Chew's discovery, the 3-D images constructed by Di, his research on local Porsche dealers, and the diagnostic system.

"You look as if you've not slept for days," she says, making a circular motion around her eyes with her finger. "I heard Johan has asked for a stakeout team?"

Ignoring her comments, he says, "Yes, my feelings say the service center, or the mechanics, are involved. Thought I'll put some eyes on it, just in case. Hubble says he needs, at the most, half a day to go through the ECUs. That is, if I can produce the diagnostic system. Meanwhile, I need to keep an eye on the service center."

"Can you get hold of the diagnostic system?"

He smiles. "I was hoping you'll help, maybe persuade Auto Eurokars to lend us one for a day or two. At the same time, maybe they can also provide you with a list of workshops supplied with Porsche's diagnostic system."

"I'm open this morning, I'll pay them a visit and charm them into lending us one," she laughs.

"Ask for their latest, the Durametric Diagnostic Software, and I need your approval to work with Hubble on the ECUs."

"How do you spell it, D-u-r-a . . . metric?" she asks, scribbling on her notepad. "Talk to Chew, get Di to be the case technician, with Hubble as an independent consultant. That way we won't need him to testify. Do you need a backup team for your raid?"

"I'll use the stakeout team; I don't expect resistance. It would help if I can get general duty personnel for the transfer. I prefer to detain them here instead of the district lockup. Gives us better control. The shift investigator and his assistant can help with the interviews, if need be."

"Looks like you have it all worked out. The killers are good, so watch your step," the head of Major Crimes reminds him.

"Thanks. Let me know when you have the diagnostic system."

Maria is on the cell phone phone, talking rapidly in Tagalog, when they enter the interview room. She quickly ends the call and smiles nervously. Mislan takes a seat in front of her as Johan sits by the door.

"Maria, how have you been?"

"Okay," she answers tensely.

"Are you still living at the house?"

"No, I stay with my agent. I'll go back to Philippines next week."

"Maria, did you prepare dinner for the family on Friday?"

"Ma'am said they were going out. She told me not to cook. Why?"

"When you came back on Sunday morning, did you notice what was served?"

"The first time I did not but, when I went closer, I noticed it was *yee sang*."

"You know *yee sang*?"

"Yes, Mr. Tham would take the family and me for *yee sang* during Chinese New Year."

"Where did you normally go?"

"The Palace of Golden Horses."

"What about at home: did Mr. Tham serve his friends or relatives *yee sang* at home?

"No."

"Did Mr. Tham or ma'am bring friends to the house?"

"Mr. Tham, no; ma'am, yes."

"How about relatives?"

"No. Ma'am only brings friends. Always only for a little while, for ma'am to change her clothes. Sometimes, ma'am's friends wait in car."

"What about Lionel; did he ever talk about his uncles, aunts, or grandparents?"

"Not to me. Lionel only talked about his friends at school." Tears well in her eyes when she talks about Lionel.

"Did Lionel ever bring his friends to the house? School friends?"

"No, he only talked about them."

"Right. When did you talk to Mr. Tham about taking Friday off?"

"Not Mr. Tham. I asked ma'am. Maybe one month before. Ma'am was strict. I always had to tell her early because she sometimes went out and I had to take care of Lionel. So I told her early."

"Did Mr. Tham know you were taking Friday off?"

"I think so, because one night at dinner he asked me where I was going. I told him, to my friend's birthday party."

"Can you remember when he asked you that?"

"I think, the night after I told ma'am."

"That's about a month before you took your Friday off, right?"

"Yes."

"Ma'am; did she always go out?"

"Every day."

"Was she working?"

"I don't know. Sometimes ma'am left at ten in the morning, sometimes in the evening."

"Did she go out at night, or come home late?"

"Yes, ma'am went out at night. Sometimes ma'am came home very late."

"With Mr. Tham?"

"Sometimes. Sometimes alone."

"How about vacations? Did she go away on vacations often?"

"Every month."

"With Mr. Tham?"

"Sometimes, but always with Lionel."

"After they moved into this new house, did ma'am go away?"

"Two times."

"Where did you stay when ma'am went away?"

"In the old house, I stayed home. But this new house, I was afraid because there is no alarm and I didn't know anyone. So Mr. Tham let me stay with my friend. I come back early on the same day ma'am came back."

"Do you know where ma'am went?"

"Ma'am never told me, but Lionel always did. They go to Singapore."

"Did Lionel ever tell you who ma'am meets in Singapore?"

"He told me, they only went shopping."

"Do you know whether ma'am had a boyfriend?"

"No."

"How about Mr. Tham, did he have a girlfriend?"

"No, I don't know."

"Did you bring any friends to the house?"

"No, ma'am warned me when I started working. No friends were allowed to come to the house."

"Did you ever hear Mr. Tham and ma'am fighting or arguing?"

"No."

"Okay, Maria. Thank you for coming."

31

LEAVING THE INTERVIEW ROOM, he calls Dr. Safia to ask for her e-mail address, telling her that he will be sending the 3-D images. He asks if she can give her professional opinion on the gender of the figure.

He makes another call. "Nathan, Inspector Mislan."

"Hi, Inspector."

"Nathan, thanks for the measurements. I was wondering how you got the chest measurements, the width and depth."

"I took the width from the back. As for the depth, there were three frames where the figure was standing by the driver's door before and after bending into the vehicle. I got the measurements from these frames."

"I must have missed that. Good eyes. Thanks."

He slides in the DVD and runs the video. Nathan is right.

He sends the three frames he wants to the printer. He picks them up, walks to the pantry, makes a fresh mug of coffee, and slumps wearily into his chair. He takes out the notepad and starts writing what he has so far:

- *Primary crime scene—Cayenne,*
- *Serviced by Pro Care a few days before vacation,*
- *Returned to RT by an unknown woman,*
- *Hydrogen cyanide canister fixed into air-con vent, remotely controlled,*
- *ECUs possibly compromised,*
- *Partial fingerprint under belt buckle,*
- *Motives—unknown,*

- *Suspects—none.*

After four days, he still has nothing: no motive, no suspect, and is no nearer to solving the case.

In his experience, most murders are committed by someone known to the victims. The general exceptions are murders that are a result of other crimes. These murders were premeditated. The killers knew the victim; but which victim? Mr. or Mrs. Tham?

His cell phone rings. "Hi, Fie."

"Hi, Lan. Sorry for the delay. I managed to look at the images you mailed me. From the measurements, the probabilities are it's a woman. How accurate are the measurements?" asks Dr. Safia.

"Spoke to the video tech; he says it's accurate. He made some adjustments for the thickness and flabbiness of the jacket. Why?"

"If he's confident of the measurements, I'd say it's a woman, based on the chest and hip measurements."

"Can I use that in court?"

"Any physician can come to the same conclusion based on the measurements. The challenge will be the measurements and how accurate they are, especially when they're taken from a video."

"Yes, you're right. Let me show it to my boss and see what she has to say. Thanks, Fie."

"No problem. How's the case coming?"

"It's not coming. Many discoveries, but no leads," he answers dejectedly.

"You'll crack it. I know you will. If you need to talk, I'm free later. Maybe we can have dinner. Have to go. Call me, okay? Bye."

Johan walks in red faced, as if he has just gulped down a couple jugs of beer.

"What's with you?" he says, as Johan drops heavily into his chair.

"Just heard, ASP Ghani has been given this morning's robbery case. It came from the top, bypassing Superintendent Samsiah. His assistant wants the stakeout team back, immediately. I told him to talk to you. I may just lose it one day and deck that geezer right here in the office."

"Cool down, let me handle it."

No sooner has Mislan finished his sentence than ASP Ghani and his assistant march in, heading straight for his desk. He notices Johan tensing and gives him the stay-out-of-this look.

"You've some *detectives* on stakeout. I need them back here, ASAP," ASP Ghani says, even before reaching his desk.

"I'll send them back when the stakeout is done," he answers calmly.

"I need them now. I've just got intelligence on the suspects," ASP Ghani retorts, raising his voice. "You've got nothing there, so call them in, stand them down, and return to base."

Mislan notices the desk officer and a detective standing at the outer doorway, observing the scene. They are probably betting on who will win this round. He is aware the head of Major Crimes is away, probably charming her way to a diagnostic system. Standing slowly, he points to the emergency door and moves toward it. The emergency staircase landing area is enclosed and rarely used, ideal for holding very private, personal discussions. He is waiting at the staircase landing when the door is forcefully pushed open by ASP Ghani, missing him by inches. Mislan takes that as an act of aggression, and, before the door even closes, he grabs ASP Ghani by his shirt, pulling him away from the door, and throws a right hand into his stomach. Surprised, ASP Ghani buckles. Mislan jerks his limp body up and presses him against the wall. ASP Ghani groans in pain with both hands holding his belly, eyes blinking rapidly to hold back tears, mouth gasping for air.

He holds ASP Ghani's jaw tightly with the right hand, the thumb and index finger pressing hard into the soft cheeks, stopping him from speaking. "You listen well. I'm not going to say it again. If you ever challenge me in front of my men or cross my path again, it will be your last. Do you understand?" he says, calmly.

Unable to speak, ASP Ghani nods.

"Good. Now, if you want to take this up with the boss, you go ahead. You want to take this further, just tell me where and when," he hisses, easing his grip on the jaw but still holding ASP Ghani pinned against the door. He can hear soft voices and footsteps on the other side of the door, but ignores them.

Soon as he eases his grip, ASP Ghani shouts, "Fuck—" and is rewarded with a sharp right jab on the same spot in his stomach. "Shit

. . . *Aghh*," is all that escapes from ASP Ghani's mouth. The inspector grabs ASP Ghani by the hair, shoves him against the door, blocking any potential intruder from joining them, saying, "No shouting, we're officers. We settle our difference in a civilized manner. We don't shout. Got it?" He smiles.

ASP Ghani nods.

Releasing his hair, he says, "Good. Do you want to say something?"

ASP Ghani shakes his head.

"Does this end here?"

ASP Ghani nods.

He releases his grip, and ASP Ghani bends forward clutching his belly. He pats ASP Ghani's back and helps him sit on the landing leaning against the door. Mislan sits next to him, keeping a close watch on his every move, ready for some more. He pulls out a cigarette, lights one, passes it to ASP Ghani, and lights another for himself.

"You okay?"

"Fuck you," ASP Ghani snarls.

"I take that to mean you're fine. So, I heard you got the project on this morning's robberies; what intelligence have you got?"

"None of your fucking business."

"It's my business when you're trying to screw my case, and can you drop the f-word. You should stop watching so many American movies. Stop trying to be them. You sound stupid."

"Go fuck yourself."

He hears loud banging on the door, followed by the voice of the head of Major Crimes asking what is going on in there. Turning to ASP Ghani, he asks, "Do we have an understanding?"

ASP Ghani nods.

"Good." Standing, he helps ASP Ghani up, giving him a cold stare before opening the door.

"What's going on here?" Superintendent Samsiah gives them the once-over.

"Ma'am, we were just having a private discussion. Weren't we?" he says, turning to ASP Ghani.

ASP Ghani nods.

32

STEPPING BACK INTO THE office, Superintendent Samsiah points to the diagnostic system on his table and says it is a goodwill loan from Auto Eurokars. It is a Durametric Diagnostic System that runs on Windows with USB adapters to communicate with Porsche ECUs.

"Your charm worked. Thanks, ma'am."

"Don't mention it. I have to return it by Friday evening. Whatever you do, make sure you don't damage or corrupt the system. It's the latest in the market and there are only two units in the country."

"I'll take good care of it," he says, teasingly. "Anything on the workshops that have this diagnostic system?"

"According to the master technician, they don't give it out to every workshop. They are provided only to authorized garages in the country, but he said that doesn't mean other workshops can't get hold of one." Pressing some buttons on her cell phone she says, "Let's see, ah, here it is. The earlier system, KTS 500 or KTS 650, also known as Porsche System Tester 2, is available in the secondhand market. Unauthorized workshops can buy them from Hong Kong or Singapore."

"It means, even if Pro Care is not an authorized Porsche workshop, they could still own a Porsche diagnostic system."

"Yes, and they may also get their parts and accessories from Hong Kong or Singapore apart from secondhand dealers; through the Internet, or through many Porsche Clubs worldwide."

"Okay, thanks. I appreciate your help, ma'am," he says, eager to get moving.

When he looks around, ASP Ghani is nowhere. He figures his nemesis must have taken the stairs up or down to avoid curious stares. He shoves the incident aside, pulls out his cell, and dials Di. After several rings, she answers.

"Di, this is Inspector Mislan. Can you get Hubble to the lab? I'll be talking to Chew to get him cleared. How long will it take?"

"It's 11:10. He should be up. I can get him in here by 12:30."

"All right, I'll see you then."

He makes another call, this time to Chew. He tells him he has discussed bringing outside help with the boss, and has her blessings, provided a Forensic Department technician is the primary.

"You okay with it?"

"Yah, sure, if it helps solve the case."

"Great, I need you to clear Hubble and prepare the ECUs for testing. Di says they'll be in at 12:30. I'll be there, too."

"Done."

"Thanks, man. See you later."

Johan, who is listening quietly from his desk, rolls his chair up next to his. "What went on back there?" he jerks his head toward the emergency door.

"We had a private conversation."

"I caught a glimpse of him; he didn't look too good. Looked as if he knocked against something," Johan says knowingly. He had heard small talk about officers working out their differences amicably, but this is the first time he has encountered one.

"Yah, said he wasn't feeling too good, stomach cramp. Probably something he ate for breakfast."

"You're not going to tell, right?"

"Nope," he says, laughing. "Jo, I need you to run a check on the vics' credit cards, just Mr. Tham first. Go back two months. All his credit cards. Get hold of the tech who bagged the vic's personal items."

"You're on to something?"

"A small chance, maybe it's nothing. Let's see how our vic spent his money. I'm going to see Di and Hubble." Pointing to the diagnostic system, he says, "I'm hoping Hubble can work his magic and get something out of the ECUs. Keep the stakeout team in place. If Hubble delivers, I want to hit the workshop before it closes today."

"You want me to join you later?"

"Can you come on a bike? That way, if we have to hit the workshop, you can go there first and brief the stakeout team."

"Sure, I'll borrow one from a detective."

Driving to the Forensic Laboratory in Cheras, he reflects on the staircase confrontation he had with the head of Special Projects. ASP Ghani Ishak outranked him and one day may become his boss. When that happens, he guesses it would be time to retire his badge. What drove him to do it? What made him lose it? He wondered what would have happened if ASP Ghani had fought back. Well, ASP Ghani did not, and he would never know. He is sure the entire office is talking about their private conversation by now, probably with wildly exaggerated versions. Superintendent Henry and possibly even the OCCI would have heard it. Whatever comes, he is ready.

He arrives at 12:05 and heads straight for the office. Chew stops working on his computer, pushes his chair back, and walks out to meet him. Chew leads him to a table where several small boxes the size of cigarette packs, with wires sticking out, some copper tubes, and one six-by-three cylinder are neatly laid out.

"Is Di here yet?"

"Nope. Here are the items you probably want to run some diagnostics on," he says, pointing to the small boxes. "These are ECUs, all labeled so you know which is which, and here is the remote-control valve with the receiver. I don't know if you can run a diagnostic on it, because it's third party. We've examined it. It's just a standard industrial remote-controlled valve, locally made."

"Can you trace it?"

"Sure, but don't see how it'll help you; it's retailed. You can get them from any vehicle and machine-parts shop. My guess, it's a vehicle part. You don't need any registration to buy it."

"What's this?"

"That's the canister that contained the hydrogen cyanide. We nearly missed it. We thought they had used the air conditioner's compressor for the gas, but it registered only a low-level trace. So we tore up the SUV and found the canister hidden in the dashboard. Clever. The valve was attached to its nozzle. The gas ran through this copper pipe into the air conditioner vents. We did a swab of the canister, and it showed a high concentration of the gas. Same with the copper pipes. We managed to lift a few sets of clear prints from it, but have found no match in the records."

"Damn," Mislan swears. "Just hang on to it, maybe we'll get a match from the workshop mechanics. What do you make of it? Why the elaborate design?"

"It's ingenious."

"What is?"

"By controlling the gas independently, the killers could determine when to discharge the gas. You said the Cayenne was sent for servicing, right? It was delivered to the RT Fashion House before the vic drove it home. If the gas control had been in the air-conditioning, the person delivering the car would have been the first to die when it was switched on. So, designing it separately was ingenious. They had full control; they could wait until all their victims were in place before releasing the gas."

"Good planning, good thinking."

33

SOUNDS OF GIGGLING AND heavy panting announce the arrival of Di and Hubble. The latter leans his large flabby body against the door frame as Di pushes him from the back, "Come on, just a little more." The two flights of stairs must have taken a heavy toll on Hubble's legs, heart, and lungs. He struggles through the few remaining feet and slumps on the first chair he reaches, stretches his legs, lolls his head all the way back, pants, and sweats like a horse. Di disappears and comes back with a bottle of Coke. Hubble empties half of it in one gulp. Pulling a face towel from his pocket, he wipes the sweat dripping from his face and neck. Chew is dumbfounded by what he sees. "That's Hubble?"

"Yup, big as they come." The inspector laughs softly. When he feels Hubble has recovered sufficiently from his ordeal of climbing two flights of stairs, he gestures for Chew to follow him.

"Hubble, how are you? This is Chew, Di's supervisor."

Chew smiles, hesitates before extending his hand.

"Hi, nice to meet you," Chew says. "Are you okay?"

"Don't you have elevators here?" Hubble wipes more sweat from his face. "By the way, I think you should give Di a parking space near the office. She had to park her car so far away. Crazy, man." Hubble takes another long gulp of the Coke, emptying the bottle, and asks if he can have another. Di disappears and comes back with another.

"You ready to go?" the inspector asks Hubble.

"Sure," Hubble says, pushing himself up laboriously. "Do you have anything to eat around here? I'm starving."

"Chew, can we eat here?"

"Yah, in the pantry or the discussion room," Chew replies.

"Tell you what," Mislan says, addressing Hubble, "you take a look at the items first. Tell me what you think, and I'll arrange for lunch. Okay?"

"Sounds like a plan." Hubble follows him to the table where the ECUs and other items are laid out.

At the table, Chew hands Hubble a pair of latex gloves, which the latter tries to put on, but all he can manage is to run his fingers halfway through the sheaths. Giving up, Hubble stops trying to put the gloves on and starts handling the ECUs. He closely examines all the items, like a jeweler examining gemstones, and for such a large person Hubble is surprisingly delicate.

"Do you have the diagnostic system?"

"Yes, the latest," he says, reaching into his backpack. "It's a Durametric Diagnostic System, and it runs on Windows."

Taking the casing from the inspector, Hubble says, "Great, let me check it out. See what this baby can do."

Chew tells the hacker to use one of the discussion rooms, and Di says she will get her notebook. The inspector asks if the Forensics supervisor can organize lunch from the canteen.

After another bottle of Coke, Hubble heads off to the discussion room. Mislan's cell phone rings. It's Johan telling his boss that he has the credit card listings and is on his way to Forensics. Mislan tells him to bring four large bottles of Coke for Hubble.

"He's huge, isn't he?" Chew whispers. "Did you see him try to put the gloves on? I have to check with procurement to see if they have bigger ones, just in case we need his help in the future. Boy, I just can't imagine being that big."

"Not easy," the inspector smiles, "but you'd get used to it if you were. For now, that large man is the best hope we have of cracking this case. If he doesn't come through, I don't know what else to do."

"Just keep at it, something will come up. If not today, one day," Chew says encouragingly. "I did some research on hydrogen cyanide and found out you can buy it in a can. Zyklon B is the trade name. I saw no mention of the supplier, and I don't think you can get it locally. The manufacturer is in Germany; it's supplied for pest fumigation and military use."

"That's useful info. One could've easily been brought in from overseas."

"I know what you mean."

Di pokes her head out, signaling them to come to the discussion room, just as the technician arrives with the lunch packets. They sit around the discussion table as the technician distributes the Styrofoam boxes, the biggest pack being for Hubble, who immediately opens the cover and examines its contents.

Satisfied, he leans back saying, "Okay, I've got a handle on this baby," tapping the Durametric Diagnostic System. "What do you want me to check?"

"Why don't we eat as we talk?"

Di and Hubble nod and start attacking their lunch, while Chew watches, amused. Soon, Johan comes in carrying a plastic bag containing four large bottles of Coke.

"Here are the Cokes you asked for."

"Jo, have you had lunch?"

"You can have mine, if you want," Chew offers.

"No, thanks. I had something to eat while waiting for the credit-card listings. You go ahead. What are you looking for from the listings, anyway?"

"Let's see. How many cards did the vic have?" Mislan inquires, leafing through the report.

"Four."

"Here, you take these," he says, passing several sheets to the other two. "Run through them and circle any charge exceeding two hundred ringgit. Then run through it again and put an asterisk against it if it's charged at a restaurant or hotel."

"What are you looking for?" asks Hubble. "I can visit their system and get what you want."

The inspector gives Hubble an admonishing stare.

Di elbows Hubble and says, "These guys are cops, okay?"

"I was just trying to help," Hubble squeaks, disappointed.

"It's okay, just forget it. So, the diagnostic system; what can it tell us?"

"All you need to know of the car's electronics. What do you want me to check?" Hubble is excited, now that the conversation is more in his territory.

"You saw the ECUs on the table back there? I want to know if they have had their programs modified. I don't know how to put it. Something that overrides the system, or allows it to be controlled remotely by another party. Anything that is not supposed to be there. You know what I mean?"

"Sure, but there is one problem. I don't know what is supposed to be in the ECUs."

"Check for sleepers and worms," Di butts in.

"That, I can do. Tell you what, I'll run a diagnostic and see if any of these suckers have third-party programs in them," Hubble lights up.

"Do that, but don't go changing or adding anything."

"Okeydokey, you got it, boss," Hubble answers.

"Good. How long will you need?"

"It's straightforward. An hour, max."

"Great. Let me know when you're done. Di will help you."

"No problemo."

The other three leave for the second discussion room to go through the listings.

"I am done, now what?" Johan asks.

"What do you have?"

"Three charges of more than two hundred ringgit, one at Boutique D'Gala, one at Mandarin Oriental, and one at Shangri-La," Johan answers.

"I've got two, one at Four Seasons Restaurant and the other at the Grand Millennium Hotel," Chew says.

"I've got two, one at Grand Millennium Hotel and one at China Treasures," Mislan announces. "Chew, the Grand Millennium charge, when was it and how much?"

"Tenth of last month, 722.43 ringgit," Chew answers.

"Mine is for second of this month, 1,220.89 ringgit. Jo, reach out to the chief security officer and learn about the hotel's CCTV: locations, storage periods. We may need to get copies."

"What are you looking for?" his assistant asks.

"The mystery woman. It's a slim chance, but it's the only thing I can think of."

"You're saying the mystery woman is the vic's girl?"

"I don't know if she is the vic's girl, but her confidence when she returned the Cayenne was remarkable. I mean, the way she drove the Cayenne, her knowledge of the speed of the gate, keeping her back toward the camera all the time, and the casual manner in which she walked. Anyway, the amounts spent are too much for one person, even at a five-star hotel. Either the vic was entertaining a large group or was paying for rooms. If we're lucky, we'll discover who the vic ran with."

"Okay, I'll make some calls."

Thursday. Four days gone, another four days to convince the boss he is making progress. Four days to give her enough ammunition to keep the OCCI and Superintendent Henry at bay. Yet all he has, and is sure of, is the modus operandi. He desperately needs some leads or, at least, one sure lead. He is convinced the OCCI is keeping close tabs on his progress through his lapdog Henry and the PR dolls. Perhaps even striking off dates on his calendar, eagerly waiting for Monday when he, his lapdogs, and PR dolls will burst in during morning prayer claiming victory, at the same time ridiculing the head of Major Crimes and ripping into Mislan in his victory speech in front of all the other investigators. He's surprised he hasn't heard whispers around the office of anyone taking bets or starting a pool against him keeping the case. He'll have to ask Johan about it, perhaps make some easy money by placing a bet against himself, he thinks, smiling.

What is it about this case that keeps him awake at night, constantly nags him, fouls his moods, and shortens his fuse? It's not like this is his first murder case. Yes, the others did keep him awake and nag him, but they were not like this. Was it the frustration, and the feeling of hopelessness? He handles crap daily; it came with the job. "Three quarters of a policeman's salary is for taking all the crap, and the rest is for doing his job," he always says.

Perhaps, it was Lionel, his eyes. He was only three years older than Daniel, with so much living ahead. What went through Lionel's mind just before his heart stopped and the lights went out? Was he afraid? Did he cry? Did he feel any pain? Lionel must have been the first to die because he was the smallest. He must have called out for his mother, and she might have heard him. Only she was dying, too. Lionel kept him awake at night with those questioning eyes and innocent face.

"What're you thinking about?" Chew asks.

"The case," Mislan says, whispering.

"What about the case?"

"Everything. The killers planned, prepared, and executed it with surgical precision. Nothing was left to chance, nothing to lead us back to them. All of it, for what? Unless I can understand the purpose of their death, I cannot crack this nut."

"It'll all come, in due time. Just keep chiseling at it, and it will be revealed."

"My chisel is getting blunt and my mallet is broken. I'm scraping with my fingernails now. You know the forty-eight-hour theory about solving cases? I'm way past it. Criminologist say the chances of success drop with every hour. If what they say is true, my chance of cracking this case is below zero."

"What do they know? They just make up theories to sell books, appear on TV and make plenty of money. It's what people like you do that matters."

"I suppose, you're right. Let's go see what the geeks have uncovered."

Everything depends on Hubble, a 330-pound hacker whose fingers can't even fit into standard latex gloves. The two geeks don't even look up when he and Chew enter the room. Amazingly, Hubble's huge fingers are lightning fast and graceful on the keyboard. Not once does he stop talking, either at something on the notebook computer or to Di. They watch him with fascination as he works. "I see you . . . you can't hide from me . . . here we go . . . closer . . . closer . . . got you!" He punches more commands saying, "Now tell me what your evil master ordered you to do."

"There, there, you see that," exclaims Di.

"Yeah, baby. Spill it." Without taking his eyes off his notebook computer, his hand reaches out for the Coke, from which he takes a big swig.

Hubble then says, "Got them all," pointing to the screen of his notebook computer.

"What did you get?" Mislan asks eagerly.

"Viruses," Hubble announces. Pointing to the ECUs, he continues, "All of them have worms, I mean sleeper programs, which, when activated, will override the ECU's original programs. See this one?" Hubble points to an ECU marked "Door." "Its original function is to unlock doors when the engine is killed or the release button is pressed. The sleeper overrides the original program and disables the locking devices."

"But, you can still unlock the doors manually, can't you?"

"Nope. The sleeper program disables the locking mechanism; even if you pull the knob it won't budge. It will be stuck. This one," pointing to the ECU marked "Ignition," "is the same thing. The virus kills the engine, you know, like an anti-theft system. It will immobilize the car. It was popular once, but dangerous."

"What do you mean by 'dangerous'?"

"I remember one car company trying to promote a device like this some years ago, but they didn't have GPS tracking then to monitor the vehicle's position. The operator could cut off the engine while the vehicle was still moving and cause serious accidents. You see, most cars now are electronically controlled. When you kill the engine, everything stops: steering, brake, so the driver loses control of the car."

"Okay, what about that?"

"The air conditioner sleeper. The valve only has a release and shut command. Fairly straightforward," Hubble explains.

"How do you plant the sleepers? I mean, can you plant the programs wirelessly?"

"You mean like through Wi-Fi or Bluetooth? Not in these babies. You need direct access. They are hardwired."

"So the person must have the ECUs?"

"Yup, and the device to communicate with them. Like this baby here," tapping the Durametic Diagnostic System.

"Then how did they control it remotely?"

"The immobilizer. Remember, I told you," he answers as if he was talking to someone who is slow. "You can then send a signal by satellite to kill the engine. They use the same method to activate the sleeper."

"What else can you tell me?" Mislan ignores Hubble's sarcasm.

"I think I know who the programmer is. You see, people like us, we like to think of ourselves as painters, artists, or sculptors. Like all great works of art, ours have the creators' signatures on them." Hubble smiles, winking at Di. "The sleeper's programmer, too, has signed his work of art, and I think I've seen it before. I don't know who the dude is, but we have chatted online a few times. He goes by the handle 'Deepseeder.'"

"A guy? Where? When?"

"A guy, a girl, I don't know. Hackerchat.com chat room. This was a few months ago, though I can't remember exactly. There was this dude asking for help with a program he was working on, and Deepseeder put up his program as a sample. A real show-off, he was." He asks Di, "Do you have another computer I can use?"

Di nods and leaves the room.

"Hubble, are you sure the sleeper programs can only be planted directly into the ECUs?" He has to be absolutely certain before he makes a move.

"Yes, on these suckers. The immobilizer is designed to receive command signals, not for downloading programs. For uploads and downloads, you'll need the diagnostic system and the ECUs."

"Great job."

34

MISLAN SIGNALS HIS ASSISTANT, who is working the phone at one of the workstations, to join him as he walks toward Chew's office. Lighting a cigarette, he takes a long drag, letting out the smoke slowly. Chew raises his brows but doesn't say anything. He sees a big "No Smoking" sign on the glass pane in clear view. He flicks the ash into the wastepaper basket, kills his cigarette, and then smiles apologetically at Chew. "Sorry, old habit." Johan comes in, saying he managed to speak to the chief security officer of the hotel, an ex-police officer, and that he needs a request letter before he can release the recording. Hotel procedures.

"I think it would be better for us to pay him a visit later. We will view the recording and pick out what we want. You got his number?"

"Yep." He gives him a piece of paper.

"I want you to call the station and ask for two MPVs with on-call backup duty. Don't give them the address. I'm not taking any chances. You go down to Pro Care and organize the stakeout team. Break them into two groups, one to cover all escape routes, and one for the raid. Tell the blockers to get into position soon as you finish briefing them, and the raiding team to move in when they see my car at the main gate."

"And the MPV backup?"

"Call them only after we have entered the building. I don't expect any resistance, but remind the boys to be careful. Especially the blockers."

"Okay, what time will you be there?"

"I'll leave as soon as I finish this call to the hotel security chief. You're riding a bike, right? You'll have enough time. Jo, no one slips off."

"Right."

He dials the number and waits. "Hello," says the person answering it.

"Mr. Rajan, hi, I'm Inspector Mislan, Major Crimes. I believe Sergeant Johan, my assistant, spoke to you."

"Yes. I told him I need a letter from the police. It's procedure, you know," Rajan apologizes.

"Sure, no problem. I'm thinking there must be hours of recording, and we don't want all of it. So I'm wondering if we can view the recordings first. Tonight. One of your staff can help us. If there is something we need, I'll send you the letter. Otherwise, there'll be no reason to."

"That sounds okay. Sure, I'll make the arrangements. What time will you be here?"

"I've got some errands to run now. Let's make it at nine. I'll call you if there is any change in the time."

"I'll inform the shift super. His name is Kamil. But I'll try to swing by when you're here."

"Great. Looking forward to meeting you, thanks."

He picks up his backpack, thanks Chew, pops his head into the discussion room where Hubble and Di are still working the notebook computers with their occasional yelps of "There!," "Run, baby!," "Shit!," "Damn!" He thanks them and tells them he's leaving and to call him should they learn anything about Deepseeder.

The road is busy with the evening rush hour. He turns off at Salak South and goes toward Sungai Besi. It has been thirty-seven minutes since his assistant left, and he's sure everything would be organized by now. He calls Johan, "All set?"

"Yup, waiting for you."

"See you in three."

Pro Care Service Centre is one of the many stand-alone two-story light industry buildings along Jalan Sungai Besi. As he approaches, he sees two luxury cars on the shop floor with hoods lifted and five others parked in the compound. Business must be slow, he thinks. He drives up and parks his car across the gate, blocking it. The raid team appears from both sides of the entrance before he is out of the car. They walk in together, with him leading.

"Police! Stop everything now," the announcement sounds. Heads peek out from under the hoods, and there are sounds of tools dropping. The detectives start rounding them up, all five mechanics, before searching the toilets and the backyard. Once satisfied there are no others, one of the detectives barks for them to produce their identity cards.

A Chinese woman comes down the stairs to ask what is going on. The inspector introduces himself and tells her that it's a police raid. She immediately calls someone on her cell phone and talks rapidly in Chinese, to the owner of the workshop, he presumes. He hears his sergeant calling the blocker team and the MPV backup. He then walks toward the Chinese woman, who is still frantically speaking on the phone. She stops speaking and gives the phone to him, saying, "My boss."

He says, "Inspector Mislan, who is this?"

"Inspector, hi, I'm Lai. What's going on there?"

"Mr. Lai, are you the owner of this workshop?"

"Yes. Why are you raiding my workshop and stopping my workers?"

"I have reasons to believe that your workshop was involved in a case I'm investigating. I'm taking your workers in for questioning."

"Are you crazy? What case? I know Supintendent Henry, D7. You want me to call him?" Lai threatens.

"You can call anyone you wish," he says, handing the phone back to the woman. She says something in Chinese, nods several times, and rings off.

"Your name is?"

"Ms. Winnie."

"Okay, Winnie. I need you to get me the records on the Cayenne that belonged to Mr. Robert Tham."

"Cannot. My boss said not to do anything. He'll be angry with me," she says nervously.

"You can make thing easy and do what I ask, or difficult. Which is it?"

"I don't know. My boss say wait, I wait," she says, sounding even more nervous.

"Look, Winnie, I'll wait until the patrol cars arrive, that's all. If you do not produce the file, I will go up to the office and take the entire cabinet," he says, pointing upstairs.

His cell phone rings. "Mislan," he answers.

"Mislan, this is Henry. I just got a call from a friend saying you're raiding his workshop. What's going on?"

"Doing my job, that's what's going on. Nothing to do with D7."

"Look, he has friends. They are not going to like what you're doing," Superintendent Henry says menacingly.

"It that a threat?"

"Take it any way you wish." The line goes dead.

He instructs Winnie to follow him to the office, where he asks for the file again. She hesitates. He walks toward the filing cabinets lining the wall and pulls one of the steel drawers. He takes out a few files and deposits them on the nearest table. Winnie says something in Chinese that he cannot understand. She then takes a file with the Cayenne registration number from one of the cabinets and hands it to him. "That wasn't hard, was it?" Winnie gathers the files on the table and starts putting them back, mumbling continuously, probably swearing at him.

He had noticed several CCTV cameras trained at the entrance and the shop floor when he came in. He scans the office for the camera monitors. Failing to spot any, he asks Winnie. She points to a desktop computer at the corner. He calls Chew to ask for a video technician to be dispatched to the location. He tells him that he needs copies of CCTV recordings made. Chew promises to send Nathan over ASAP. He tells Johan to get the mechanics to lock up the garage and take them back to the station. He will wait for Nathan from Forensics and join him once the technician is done here.

His cell phone rings. It's his boss. "Ma'am."

"Just received a call from OCCI," she says. "What's going on?"

"Superintendent Henry just called me. We're at Pro Care picking them up for questioning. Jo is about to take them back, but I've to wait here for Forensics to make copies of the CCTV recording."

"You want to fill me in?"

"Hubble has confirmed that there are sleeper programs in the ECUs. He also confirmed the only way to install the sleepers is into the ECUs directly. That makes Pro Care a prime suspect."

"Good. You need any help?"

"I'm okay down here, but I can use some back in the office. We have five mechanics and one clerk to interview. It'll be good if someone can do a prelim to screen them. Jo can coordinate. I'll be stuck here a while."

"I'll get the shift investigator and his assistant to do the prelim. I'll be in late. Stop by my office when you're done, and, Lan, do it right."

"Thanks, ma'am."

Loud honking coming from the front of the building attracts his attention, and he walks to the window to check what is going on. A Chinese man is standing by a car parked next to his, looking into the shop floor with his hands on his horn through the open car window. He sees Johan walking up to the man, but the man's hand remains on the horn. He is shouting angrily above the honking, attracting curious onlookers from the surrounding buildings. Mislan signals Winnie over to ask her who the man is. It is the owner, Lai. He speed-dials his assistant, tells him to get Lai to stop pressing the horn and if he refuses, to arrest him for disturbing the peace and obstructing the police from discharging their duties. The honking magically stops, and he watches as Lai marches into the shop floor.

The office door is flung open, and Lai storms in, red faced, swearing in Chinese. He heads straight for his desk and throws himself into a chair, picks up the phone, and calls someone. Mislan does not understand what the owner of the workshop is saying in Chinese but understands the tone and the expletives. He continues shouting at the person on the other end, makes a few more calls, and then calms, probably realizing there is nothing his powerful friends can or are willing to do, and that it is best for him to cooperate.

"What's your name, again?" Lai says arrogantly.

"Inspector Mislan, Major Crimes."

"My lawyer asked if you've a warrant."

"Who's your lawyer? You may want to consider getting a new lawyer," he answers, smiling. "Look, the quicker we finish here, the sooner you can restart your operations. I'm sure your friends have told you to cooperate, right? You should listen to them."

Lai fishes out a pack of cigarettes and offers one to him, which the inspector refuses, politely. He lights one himself, and says, "Okay, what do you want?"

"Winnie has given me the file. I'm waiting for Forensics to make copies of your CCTV recording, so I don't have to take your computer and shut down your CCTV. After that, I'm out of here."

"What about my mechanics?"

"They'll be taken to headquarters for questioning, and, if they're clean, they'll be released."

"You said something about a case. What case?"

"Robert Tham," Mislan says, watching for any giveaway sign from Lai or Winnie. He sees nothing, no expression of shock, neither at the mention of the victim's name, nor that the workshop is being raided in connection with it.

"The papers said they were killed in their house, robbery or something. What has it got to do with my workshop?" Lai asks.

"Sorry, no can say. It's an ongoing investigation."

Johan appears at the doorway followed by Nathan, holding an evidence bag. "We're ready to transfer," he says.

"What's that?" he asks Nathan, pointing to the evidence bag.

"It is the diagnostic system I took from downstairs. Where is the computer?" Nathan asks, placing the evidence bag on the table.

"Over there. Copy its entire memory; I don't know how far back the storage goes."

"No problem, I brought a terabyte disk, just in case," Nathan says, already working on the computer.

35

He pulls into his office parking lot at 7:20 p.m. and escorts Winnie up. He peeks into his boss's office. It's empty. He logs Winnie in at the front desk and gives instructions for her to be kept there until he finds a more suitable place. He asks if the boss is still around, and the front desk officer tells him she is in interview room two. He finds her and the shift assistant interviewing one of the mechanics. Johan comes out from room one.

"Where are the rest?" Mislan asks his assistant.

"One is in there with Chief Inspector Krishnan," pointing to the room he came from, "and the rest are in holding."

"I've got the Pro Care clerk at the front desk. I'll use the meeting room."

Superintendent Samsiah steps out from interview room two. "You got a minute?"

He nods, and she points to his desk. He and Johan follow her. He drops his backpack on the desk, pulls a chair for her, and takes his seat while the sergeant remains standing.

She smiles. "I hope you're right on this," jerking her head toward the interview rooms. "The brass are breathing fire, and Henry is in a trance doing his lion dance." She breaks into a genuine laugh. "It's been a long— No, let me rephrase that, it's been too long since an inspector created such a storm for the brass. I can't remember the last time my phone rang this much."

"You are enjoying this, aren't you?"

"In a way, I am. Okay, what have you got?"

"Hubble ran diagnostics on the ECUs and confirms that sleepers have been planted in them. According to him, it can only be done by direct access. So, whoever planted the sleeper had to have the ECUs. The Cayenne's records taken from RT contain invoices from Pro Care from the last three years."

"Could it have been done elsewhere?"

"It could have, but I've only Pro Care on record. If it was done elsewhere, then I'm back to where I started. Nowhere. Nathan from Forensics has taken the diagnostic system from the workshop to dust for prints, and for Hubble to run some tests on it."

"What are you expecting?"

"Don't know, but I'm sure if there is anything, Hubble will find it."

"The mechanic I interviewed, Tan, said Ricky and Ah Meng are the mechanics for Porsche. He and the other two don't do Porsche. They repair other models: Mercs, BMWs, Audis, and Jags. He says he knows Robert Tham. He has seen him at the workshop many times, but Robert only talked to Ricky, Winnie, or the boss."

"In that case, let's do the three first and release them. We'll keep Ricky and Ah Meng. I'll do Winnie and let her go. Jo, why don't you do one, let Krishnan and Ahmad do the other two? Ma'am, I'm going to the Grand Millennium to see the chief security officer, a former police officer named Rajan. You know him?"

"Maybe. Why are you going there?"

"To view some CCTV recordings. I want to see if I can spot the vic with some people he ran with. I'm hoping to put a face on our mystery woman."

"Why the Millennium?"

"I see several heavy expenses on the vic's credit card there. I figure it was more than a meal for one. As I said, I'm desperate," he says.

"Good. Let's go work on them," she says.

Mislan calls the front desk and asks for Winnie to be sent to the meeting room. Once Winnie is seated, he switches on the recorder, lights a cigarette, and starts flipping through the Cayenne's records. Winnie shifts several times in her chair, watching him, but does not say anything.

"Can you state your full name for the record?" he says, casually pushing the recorder closer to her.

"Winnie Wong Swee Ling." Her voice is barely audible.

He reaches for the recorder, presses the rewind button, then Play. He can hardly hear her on the recorder. "Can you speak louder, please," he says, pushing the recorder closer to her. "Please state your full name for the record."

"Winnie Wong Swee Ling," she says, a little louder.

"What's your position at Pro Care Service Centre?"

"Finance and admin."

"Okay, which mechanic was assigned to service or repair this Cayenne?" he asks, tapping the file.

"Ricky. He takes care of Mr. Tham's car. You can see the service report; it's all Ricky's name and signature."

He flips through the service reports and notes that it has been Ricky for the last twenty visits. "Okay, Ricky. And what about Ah Meng?"

"Ah Meng also do Porsche, Mr. Tham's car only by Ricky."

"Why is that?"

"He knows the car well. Ricky started servicing the car since the first time Mr. Tham sent to us."

"What is this?" he asks, pushing the file toward her, pointing to a column in the service report.

"Outside work. Mrs. Tham called, told me Porsche is sending people to check the electronic. The car engine keeps stalling, and she has arranged for a Porsche technician to check it."

"Do you know Mrs. Tham?"

"Yes, she sends her BMW to us."

"Did she call you, or the workshop?"

"The workshop."

"How did you know it was Mrs. Tham?"

"She said she is Mrs. Tham. So it's Mrs. Tham."

"Did she speak in English or Chinese?"

"Mixed. She's not Mrs. Tham, *meh*?"

"Is that normal, I mean for Mrs. Tham to call about the Cayenne?"

"I think so, she's Mrs. Tham. She cannot, *meh*?"

"Has she called you before about the Cayenne?"

"Me, first time. My boss or Ricky, I don't know."

"Did the technician come, I mean the Porsche's technician?"

"I did not see him. I told Ricky, he's the mechanic."

"Is it normal for an outside technician to come, to do work at the workshop?"

"No, but if the owner wants outside technician or mechanic to check his car, we cannot say anything. If we say 'no,' we'll lose business."

"So you don't know who this technician was? Did you pay him for his work?"

"Customer call, customer pay. My boss say income tax problem."

"Did Ricky tell you anything about the technician's work?"

"No, he only write on the service report."

"So you don't know if he was Malay, Chinese, or Indian?"

"No."

"Did you recognize Mrs. Tham's voice?"

"No. She said she was Mr. Tham's wife, so to me she was Mr. Tham's wife *loh*."

"Are your office phone calls recorded?"

"*Huh?*"

"Forget it. I'm going to let you go home. Do you need someone to send you home?"

"What about my mechanics?"

"Apart from Ricky and Ah Meng, the rest can go home once we're done."

"I'll wait. I'll go with them. My car is in the workshop."

"Sure. Can you sit outside in the waiting area? Thanks for your cooperation."

Johan comes into the meeting room just as Mislan is about to leave and tells him that they're done with the three mechanics. He leaves instructions for them to be logged into the diary and released. He calls Chew, asks if there are any prints they lifted from the diagnostic device brought in by Nathan. Chew tells him there are several sets of prints, but none that matched criminal records. He tells Chew to e-mail him the prints and he will try to match them with the two mechanics he has in custody. He then asks to speak with Nathan, who answers after a few seconds.

"Nathan, Mislan. Can you view the recording for Wednesday from eleven onward? See if you can spot a guy coming in to work with the workshop's mechanics on the Cayenne."

"Sure, I'll have to run through and make out the mechanics first. The shop floor cameras are good. You can see what the mechanics were doing with every car. I suppose they have it to stop their employees from cheating."

"Good, let me know once you've picked out the outsider. E-mail me his photos. Nathan, can you send it to my private e-mail?"

"No problem. What's the address?"

Superintendent Samsiah, Chief Inspector Krishnan, and Johan gather around his desk.

"What?"

"You look like a guy who has just received a Dear John letter." Superintendent Samsiah laughs.

"That bad, eh?" Mislan says, joining in the laughter. "What did they say?"

"Mine said he didn't work on the Cayenne. He only did Merc. He said Ricky and Ah Meng do Porsche," Chief Inspector Krishnan says. "Here," he says, passing the notes of the interview to him.

"Same here."

Superintendent Samsiah nods, indicating hers, too. Looking at the clock on the wall, she asks, "You going to the Millennium?"

He looks at the clock and notes that it is almost 20:31. "Yah, we should get going. Krish, can you do me a favor? Can you help me do the remand diary for Ricky and Ah Meng? I expect it's going to take a while to view the recording."

"How many days?" Krishnan asks.

"Ask for seven, you'll probably get three. Thanks."

"Are you not talking to them later?" Superintendent Samsiah asks.

"I don't know what time I'll finish at the Millennium. If it's not too late, I'll do them tonight."

"Okay, I'll see you tomorrow. Good night."

36

THE DIGITAL CLOCK ON his car dashboard shows nine o'clock as Mislan drives into the hotel's basement parking. Grand Millennium Hotel, once the Regent Hotel, is in Bukit Bintang, surrounded by many shopping malls, and is one of the many five-star hotels in the area known as the Golden Triangle, catering to tourists and business travelers.

Johan approaches a security guard in the lobby to inquire. The guard points to the waiting lounge, saying, "The officer will be up shortly." Mislan lights a cigarette and slides into one of the comfortable singles and admires the lobby, the grand staircase, polished marble floor, chandeliers, and fresh flowers. After about ten minutes, a man in a suit approaches them, introduces himself as Kamil, the shift supervisor, and invites them to follow him. They walk in silence through the lobby to a side door past the bank of elevators, down the stairs, and into the parking lot. They come to a door labeled Security, which Kamil unlocks and invites them in. It is a small room with scarcely enough space to accommodate the three of them, but is well furnished with a modern office table, chairs, a cabinet, a flat-screen computer, and a CCTV monitor. Kamil says, "CSO Rajan said you wanted to view the CCTV recording."

"Yes, of the following dates," Mislan says, giving him a piece of paper. "Do you have cameras in the outlets?"

"The lobby, all the outlets, elevators, and concourses. Who're you looking for? Maybe I can help?" Kamil offers.

"Robert Tham, you know him?"

"Not the name, maybe if I see his face. . . . Okay, let me get these DVD recordings up on the monitor." Kamil pulls out the keyboard from a shelf beneath his desk and punches some keys. "Which part of the hotel do you want to view? We have 177 cameras, and I can pull them out by sections; the lobby, outlets, parking lot, floors, or perimeter," he says with obvious pride.

"Let's start with the lobby."

Kamil punches a few keys, and a matrix of images appears on the monitor, but too small to see the faces in it.

"It's too small. Is there a bigger monitor or can you make the image bigger?"

"This is a twenty-four-camera matrix. I can make it sixteen, twelve, eight, four, or one. The less it is, the longer it will take to view because I have to run the other cameras for the same period." He punches some keys, and the matrix is down to twelve. "How's that?" he asks.

"Better, but still too small to identify him."

Kamil nods, picks up the phone, calls someone and says, "Nori, do you know a guest, a regular, one Mr. Robert Tham? Great . . . When? . . . You remember the date and time? Okay." He is silent for a while, then he says, "Thanks," and replaces the receiver. Kamil again punches several keys on the keyboard and asks, "Is that him?"

"Can you make it full-screen?"

Kamil nods, punches several more keys, and the monitor displays a side profile of Robert Tham at the check-in counter.

"Yes, that's him. Is he checking in?"

"Yes. The front office staff, Nori, knows Mr. Robert Tham. He is a regular at our outlets. She says he checked in for two nights."

"Was he alone?"

"The check-in record states single occupancy," Kamil answers.

"All right, I'll need you to spot him through the two days. Everywhere, lobby, outlets, floor corridors, parking lot. Can you do that?"

"I can, but it'll take time," Kamil answers with a slight note of bother.

"Don't you have a facial recognition system, or something, that you can use to get the system to track him?" Mislan asks.

"Our system is high-tech but not that high," Kamil answers follow by a grin.

"Why don't you and Sergeant Johan get started on it while I go talk to, what's-her-name, Nori, and see if I can get something from her?"

Leaving the office, Mislan lights a cigarette in the parking lot. Why was the victim checking in to a hotel in the city? He is sure it was not the victim who stayed in the room. It had to be someone else. A client? A friend? A mistress?

The inspector walks to the lobby and heads straight for the check-in counter. He identifies Nori by her name tag. He introduces himself and asks if he can have a word with her. She signals to another staff, probably the supervisor, whispers something. Nori disappears through the door behind her and reappears from a side door. She beckons him over and they go into what looks like a tiny discussion room.

"Kamil tells me you knew Robert Tham, and he was a regular here?"

"Yes, we know him. He likes to go to Zing, our Chinese outlet. He sometimes checks in to the hotel for one or two nights. Why, has something happened to him?" Nori asks, concerned.

"No, just routine," he lies. "When you say he checked in, did he stay here or did he just pay for the room for someone else?"

"I guess he did, because he always checked in, and out, alone. I've seen him with friends at the lobby or at the outlets, but I don't know about upstairs."

"Male or female friends?"

"Men and women."

"Always the same male or female?"

"The woman, yes, always the same one. I thought it was his wife. They seemed so loving," she says.

"Did he ever introduce the woman to you, or to any of your colleagues?"

"Not to me. You should ask the staff at Zing, maybe they'd know more."

"I will. What room was he in the last time he checked in?"

"Room 1212."

"Thank you. You have been helpful."

Stepping out into the lobby, he looks for the house phone, asks the operator to put him through to Kamil's office, and asks Kamil to check out the recording for cameras focusing on the corridor of room 1212 and the Zing outlet. He walks up to Zing, introduces himself to the cashier, and asks for the outlet manager. The cashier points out a woman in a cheongsam with a high slit, showing plenty of slim, milky-white thighs, sharing a public-relations laugh with some male guests at a table. He waits until she finishes, strolls toward her, introduces himself, and asks if there is anywhere he can speak to her in private. She points to the entrance and they walk toward it. Once outside she asks, "How may I help you, Inspector?"

"Did you know Mr. Robert Tham?"

"Yes. I read in the papers he was killed during a robbery a few days ago? Is it true?"

"Yes. Did he come here often?"

She nods.

"Who did he come here with?"

"Many people I didn't know. I mean, who they were or what they did."

"I am told that he was always with a woman. Do you know her?"

"Jennifer."

"Jennifer who?"

"I can't remember. She did mention it, but I don't remember. It could be Mok or Mah. I didn't talk to her much."

"Who's she to Robert Tham?"

"First, I thought she was Mrs. Tham. But later, I learned she was not. Maybe his girlfriend or something."

"Can you describe her?"

"Five-three or four, thin, shoulder-length hair, straight, too much makeup, good dresser, all branded clothes."

"Age?"

"Maybe thirty-seven, thirty-eight. Hard to tell with the makeup. Forty max."

"Has she been here lately? I mean, the last couple of days?"

"If she has, I have not noticed."

"I need you to call me if she comes here, or if you see her in the hotel or anywhere. Call me anytime, okay?" he says, handing her his call card.

"Sure."

"Thank you. Please pass the word on to your staff."

He calls Kamil's office using the house phone, and Johan says they're about to finish. He tells his assistant about Jennifer and asks if Kamil can get some footage of her. Meanwhile, he goes to get his parking ticket validated. Stepping into the parking lot, he lights another cigarette, inhales deeply, and thinks, "Maybe this time my hunch is right." His cell phone rings. "Mislan," he says.

"Inspector, Nathan. I've got the image of the outsider and mailed it to you. Did you get it?"

"Hi Nathan, I'm out of the office. I'll check it when I get back. Is the face clear?"

"Yes, it looks like an Indian guy. He is captured talking to the technicians and working on the Cayenne. He is handling the diagnostic system, that's for sure."

"Good job. Thanks, really appreciate your putting time on this."

"No sweat, glad to be of help. Let me know if you need me to do anything else. Good night."

The time is 23:05 on his car clock. The sergeant slides in and asks if he has found out anything unusual. He updates him about his conversation with the manager of Zing and about Jennifer Mok or Mah.

"I think we've got her on camera," the sergeant says, tapping his bag. "The vic was always with a woman. Yah, she's about that height, with shoulder-length hair. It has to be her."

"Jo, I need to learn more about this woman. I need you to hit the ground, start with the hotel. I'm sure there's someone who knows more about her. Find out how she comes to the hotel, whether she drives, takes a cab, or gets a ride from someone, if anyone has seen her shopping, buying something, anything. We have to pin her down. She could be our best lead. I'll talk to ma'am and see if she can give us more personnel."

"Tell you what, when we get back to the office, I'll check with the shift and get the standby detective to start with the hotel."

"Good. I want to meet Hubble and Di. Nathan said he managed to spot the outsider. I want to see if I can work that angle."

"Ricky and Ah Meng?"

"We'll work on them once we have ammunition. Better chance of breaking them."

37

FRIDAY

IT IS FIVE PAST midnight when Di and Hubble walk into the McDonald's in Bukit Bintang, and toward his table. Hubble looks worn out as he slumps his 330-pound mass on the chair, shaking the table and spilling Mislan's drink. Di laughs heartily, looking as fresh and cheery as she was in the morning. Does she ever feel down? Mislan wonders. He asks what they'd like to have and goes to get the orders: two large sets of Big Mac meals with Cokes. He is back in ten minutes. Di and Hubble are working on a notebook computer each, as he sets his tray in the middle of the table. Like the tentacle of an alien, Hubble's hand extends and grabs the Coke, bringing it to his mouth without looking away from his notebook.

"What are you doing?" Mislan asks.

"Chatting," Di says.

"Anyone in particular?"

"Some guys from our chat group. You remember how Hubble said he knows the programmer? Hubble has found out how to surface the signature," she says. She turns her notebook computer toward him and presses a few keys. The monitor goes black. Then some writing emerges that he cannot understand, in white. She keys in more commands, and the screen displays the animated word *Deepseeder* dripping blood. "You'll find the same signature in all the sleepers."

"Great, but who is he, or she?" he asks, his respect for Hubble growing with every meeting.

"Well, after you left, Hubble tried to lure him, I mean Deepseeder, into a snare. He took the bait about nine, and Hubble sent in a spybot to track him down. Hubble's good. The spybot has been bouncing around and penetrating firewalls for hours but hasn't been detected, or terminated. We think he's not aware of it, and we'll lock in on him soon," she says, smiling at Hubble who smiles back, busy working his notebook and eating at the same time.

"You mean you can ID him?"

"His IP address. With the IP address, we can learn who owns the computer. If it's not him, maybe the owner can lead us to him, or her," Hubble interjects, with his mouth full. "I've been making some inquiries with my chat buddies; one of them says he's probably met Deepseeder, but is not sure. Says Deepseeder works for a telco and is one of those computer geeks from India. About a month ago, they were at a seminar, and this one guy was talking about sleeper programs and GPSs during the break. My contact says he was boasting about developing sleeper programs for a car manufacturer for car security systems."

"Why did your friend remember Deepseeder?"

"This guy, Deepseeder, works with a telco. What was he doing writing programs for a car manufacturer? My friend felt it was a bit strange. Anyway, the guy was a show-off. That's why he remembers him."

"Did he remember which telco?"

"No, but the seminar was held in PJ Hilton, organized by Avira."

"I'll get someone to check the participants' list."

Hubble's notebook suddenly starts beeping. Hubble slams down the Coke spilling some of it, and starts frantically banging on his keyboard. "Here we go. Easy . . . easy . . . yes . . . yes, that's my girl." The beep gets louder, more rapid. Hubble presses the Enter key and the beeping stops.

"What's up?" Di leans against Hubble, looking at his screen, "What's happening?"

"What's going on?" Mislan is concerned.

"I'm in. Dude, am I good or what? Now, show Uncle Hubble your face," he says, punching more commands. "*Shhhh*, don't need to wake him, just need a peek at his face, that's all. Oh fuck!" he curses, his fingers moving like lightning on the keyboard. "*Oooh* fuck, fuck, fuck! *Aghh*, this guy's good. My spybot is toast. *Uh-oh*, he's coming after me. Shit!"

He sees panic on Hubble's face as his fingers dance on the keyboard, punching in more commands. After several minutes of profanities, cursing and banging on the keyboard, Hubble smiles, reaches for the Coke and says, "It's dead."

"What's dead?" Mislan asks his anxiety peaking.

"His hound dog," Hubble says, clearly relieved.

"Now what?"

"Now he knows someone is trying to ID him. He'll probably shut down and lie low." Hubble wipes the sweat from his forehead. "I'm telling you, this guy's good. He knew the spybot was coming, let it in within striking distance, toasted it, and jumped on its trail to track whoever was sending it. Damn, he's good," Hubble says, now able to smile.

"What about your friend? If I show him a photo, can he ID the Deepseeder?"

"Don't know, got to ask him."

Using Di's notebook computer, Mislan logs into his personal webmail, downloads the photo sent by Nathan and mails it to her. He logs off and pushes the notebook to Di.

"Can you ask your friend if that's him? Deepseeder."

Hubble leans toward Di, punches in some commands, waits a few second, punches more commands, waits again, then sits up and says, "My friend says he used to wear a mustache, but it looks like him."

"Okay, that'll do. You sure you're all right? I mean, Deepseeder cannot trace you? You got my cell number; call me if anything happens," he says, concerned for the safety of Hubble; his genius, his Merlin the Magician.

"I'm okay, his hound dog is dead. Don't worry," Hubble says, pretty sure of himself.

"Look Hubble, I appreciate what you've done. I don't want you doing anything else. From what I've seen so far, these guys are good, they are pros. I don't need another case now. I hope you guys are going to be okay?"

"Sure, we'll be here a little longer, then split," Di answers, looking at Hubble.

"Right, call me if anything happens."

38

JOHAN IS ALREADY AT his desk talking on the phone when Mislan comes into the office. He acknowledges the sergeant with a wave, sits at his desk, and switches on the computer.

"Just spoke to one of the concierge from Millennium. He says he remembers Jennifer depositing a Guess and a Burberry shopping bag with them the last time she was there. She was alone. I'm going to visit the stores in Pavilion and check them out. Maybe if I show them her photo, they'll remember."

"Good. I need to contact Avira. They held a seminar last month in the PJ Hilton. According to one of Hubble's friends, Deepseeder may have attended the seminar. They might have a participants' group photo, or maybe the facilitator will remember him."

"You want some coffee?"

"Sure. No *nasi lemak*?"

"Sorry, not today."

The front desk officer tells them there will be no morning prayer, but Mislan is required to be in the boss's office at 8:30. He asks if Johan is to join him, but the officer tells him it would be just him and ASP Ghani. His assistant gives him the don't-get-into-trouble look as the officer leaves. "Don't worry," he says with a smile. "It has to come out one day."

He sees ASP Ghani walking toward the boss's office from the corner of his eye, with his loyal sidekick. They are already seated when he knocks on the door. Superintendent Samsiah indicates for him to come in and close the door. His boss has only two guest chairs and both are taken, so he remains standing. The bozo sidekick doesn't offer him his chair, although he is junior in rank.

"You want to pull in a chair?"

"It's all right, I'll stand. This won't take long, right?"

"I called you here because I've been hearing talk around the office about the two of you, and I want it resolved," the head of major crimes starts.

Before the head of major crimes can continue, Mislan points to the assistant and asks, "Why is he here?"

"Ghani wants him here. I've no objection. Do you?"

"Yes. He's rank and file. Let's keep this between officers."

"He is my assistant," ASP Ghani objects.

"So? He is still not an officer."

"I agree with Mislan. Please leave us," says the boss.

The sidekick looks at his master, unsure of what to do. The master nods, and he leaves like a well-trained puppy.

"Right, so who's starting? Lan, sit down," Superintendent Samsiah says, and he knows better than to refuse when she is using that tone.

"About what?" He knows he doesn't sound convincing.

"You know what I mean," she snaps. "Ghani, do you have anything to say?"

ASP Ghani shakes his head.

"What went on at the emergency staircase yesterday?"

"As Mislan said, we had a private talk," ASP Ghani answers, avoiding her eyes.

"About?" She lifts her eyebrows.

They remain mute.

"Look, don't take me for a fool. I've been watching the two of you, and it's a matter of time before things get out of control. You either work it out, stop whatever is going on between you, or I'll have to let one of you go. Don't let it come to that. If you have something you're not happy with, come see me. If you want it out by yourselves, get off the property. I will not tell you this again, understood?"

They both nod.

"If I hear any of the boys taking sides, I'll personally come after your asses. That's a warning," she says, clearly upset. "You had your chance. Now get out."

Leaving her office, neither of them says anything to the other. *At least ASP Ghani kept his word*, the inspector thinks. Once at his desk, Johan comes over to ask what the meeting was about, saying he bumped into ASP Ghani's assistant storming out, blowing steam.

"What's happening upstairs, you heard anything?" he adds.

"Nope. The truth is I don't care."

"You don't care! Now, that's a first."

"Maybe I do, but not today. Let's focus on our case, the rest can wait."

He dials Di to ask her if she can get the telephone number for Avira from Hubble. Di calls back to give him the organizer's number and address. He calls the number and is passed on to someone named Sherry from the sales and marketing department. She tells him they do have details and group photos and will scan and send them to him by e-mail. He is delighted that he has saved himself a drive to Petaling Jaya.

At 9:45, Mislan updates his assistant on the latest development, and asks when he's leaving to check out the retailers. They only open at about 10:30, he is told in reply.

He then calls Forensics to speak to Nathan.

"Nathan, Mislan. I need you to look at some recordings. I think we've got the mystery woman on it. Is there any way you can do a height and size measurement?"

"I can run measurements, same as I did the last time. Then you can use it to match them."

"That's not conclusive, but I suppose it will have to do. Okay, I'll e-mail you the photo. How soon can you get back to me?"

"An hour, max. I'm getting good at this," Nathan says with a chuckle.

"That'll be fine. Thanks."

He checks his inbox, and sees the e-mail from Sherry. He opens the attachment labeled "Seminar Photos." Two group photographs pop up on the screen. He prints them, then opens the attachment labeled "Participants." A list with twenty names, designations, and companies appears. He takes out the photograph of the "outside technician" Nathan has extracted from the workshop recording, makes the match and circles a face in the group picture. He then runs through the listing, and notices there were only three Indian participants. Examining the group photograph, he identifies three Indian participants, two of them standing side by side and one standing apart. He figures the two standing together must be from the same company. He's right—the other one is from another telco. The man he wants is one of the two from the same company.

He asks the investigator on shift duty if he can use a standby detective and car for a few hours. He makes another call: "Jo, you done there?"

"Almost."

"Made the match on Deepseeder from the seminar photos. I want to pick him up. You want to come along?"

"You bet. Give me ten. I'll call you when I'm downstairs," the sergeant replies excitedly.

Mislan walks to Superintdendent Samsiah's office, asks if he can have a moment. She closes the file she is working on and gestures him in. "Yes?" she says sternly, probably still upset with the morning meeting.

"You okay, ma'am? You look disturbed; something bothering you?"

"You and Ghani, that's what's bothering me. What do you want to see me about?"

"I've identified the Deepseeder. He works with one of the multimedia super corridor–status companies in the Petronas Twin Towers," he says. "He looks like a foreigner; you know, one of those computer progamers these MSC companies usually recruit from India."

"You're expecting problems?" she asks.

"If he's a foreign national, we can expect the embassy to be informed."

"Play it by the book. Bring him in for questioning first. Besides the CCTV, do you have anything else to link him?"

"Chew lifted some prints from the diagnostic system we recovered from the workshop. We need to print him and see if they match. If it does, we have him cold."

"Do that. I'll brief the OCCI. When are you picking him up?"

"Shortly, I'm waiting for Jo to come back."

"Remember, strictly by the book. Let me know immediately if you think it is going to be a foreign affairs disaster," she says.

39

MISLAN INSTRUCTS THE DRIVER of the police car to go along Jalan Ampang and park the car along the driveway next to the Maxis Centre. They show their identity cards at the security post to collect their access passes, go through the automatic turnstile, up the escalator, take the elevator to the fortieth floor, and locate Beyond Infotech. The inspector pushes the glass door, smiles at the woman at the reception counter, and says, "Hi, I'm Inspector Mislan. Can I speak to the person in charge?" He notices that the word *inspector* makes her eyebrows atch higher.

"Please take a seat," she says, picking up the phone and punching a few numbers. "Mr. Thana, there is a police inspector here to see you. . . . I don't know. . . . Okay." She replaces the phone and tells him Mr. Thana will be out soon. A minute later, a beer-bellied man in his early forties appears and extends his hand to Johan, saying, "Inspector, I'm Thanaraju the general manager, how may I help you?"

Johan takes Thanaraju's hand, nods toward his boss, and says, "I'm Sergeant Johan, that's Inspector Mislan."

"So sorry," he says awkwardly, extending his hand again. "I'm Thanaraju."

"Mr. Thanaraju, is there somewhere we can talk?"

"Yes, follow me, please." Thanaraju swipes his identity tag, the door clicks open, and they follow him to a small discussion room while the detective waits at the reception.

"Major Crimes, what's that?" Thanaraju asks, puzzled. "Is it an immigration task force?"

"No, we're from the police. Can you tell me who this person is?" Mislan asks, pushing Deepseeder's photograph toward him.

"That's Logan. Sivalogan Phaniti, one of our programmers. Why? What has he done?"

Mislan detects an edginess in Thanaraju's voice but lets it slide as a normal reaction from a foreigner dealing with the police.

"We need to talk with him. Is he here?"

"Yes. Why do you need to talk to him? What is he involved in?"

Again, Mislan detects the nervousness in his voice.

"Is he local, I mean Malaysian?"

"No, he's from India. He has a valid work permit under the MSC-status program."

"We don't doubt that. How long has he worked here?"

"Two years. You still haven't told me what he is involved in."

"It's an ongoing investigation. I can't reveal anything yet. What's his area of expertise?"

"System programming. He is the best we have."

"Okay, can you tell him to join us here?"

Thanaraju punches in a few numbers on the phone, speaks to someone, replaces the receiver, and says, "He is coming."

"Sorry for asking, are you local?".

"No, I'm from India, too. Most of our employees are from India."

"What does your company do?"

"We specialize in telecommunication systems design."

They hear a soft knock on the door. It opens, and Sivalogan Phaniti pokes his head in. Thanaraju invites him in, and Johan immediately stations himself next to the door. Sivalogan Phaniti looks at them suspiciously.

"This is a police inspector, and he wants to talk with you," Thanaraju says.

Mislan detects a fleeting look of worry on Sivalogan's face and fear in his eyes. He leans forward holding the chair's backrest to steady himself. "Why do you want to speak to me? What did I do?"

"Mr. Phaniti, I'm taking you to our headquarters for questioning."

"Is he under arrest?" Thanaraju is aghast.

"No, but if he refuses to come voluntarily, I'll have no alternative but to arrest him. So what will it be?" He looks at Sivalogan.

"What did I do?" His voice quavers.

"I'm asking if you are coming voluntarily with us for questioning."

"I want a lawyer," he says, panic in his eyes.

"Mr. Phaniti, why do you feel you need a lawyer? Did you do something illegal?" Mislan smiles, convinced he's shaking the right tree. "I'm asking you for the last time: are you coming with us willingly for questioning?"

"I'm entitled to a lawyer. I want a lawyer," he answers in a shrill voice.

"Okay, I'll take that as a no. You're now under arrest in connection with an ongoing murder investigation." The inspector nods to the sergeant, who takes a step forward and in one fluid movement places his left hand on Sivalogan's shoulder, grabs his right hand, pulls it back, and cuffs him. Surprised, Sivalogan protests but it is too late. The stainless-steel bracelets are securely in place.

"Why are you handcuffing me?" he cries, shaking his cuffed hands violently behind him.

"Do you need to do that?" Thanaraju asks, motioning to the handcuffs.

"It's procedure. We could have avoided it if he had come voluntarily. There's no reason to worry. If he is not involved, he'll be released immediately."

"Stop twisting your hands, you'll only make the cuff tighter."

The sergeant leads the detainee out of the room with Thanaraju and Mislan following amid stares and whispers from other employees. At the inner door, Sivalogan says something to Thanaraju in an Indian language, with the latter nodding repeatedly. The inspector hears the words "promise" and "lawyer" mentioned several times in the rapid burst of words. He figures Sivalogan is making Thanaraju promise to get him a lawyer.

"Where did you say you're taking him?" Thanaraju asks.

"Kuala Lumpur Police Contingent headquarters, Major Crimes."

In the car, Sivalogan keeps insisting he wants a lawyer, claiming he is entitled to one, and threatens to sue the police. After a while Johan says, "If you've not done anything, why do you need a lawyer?"

"I want a lawyer. I've done nothing wrong. I'm here legally," Sivalogan persists.

"Just shut up, will you? You'll know in detail why you have been arrested once we reach headquarters."

Sivalogan stops talking, stares outside the window, and keeps mumbling.

When he passes Superintendent Samsiah's office, she calls out for him, "How did it go?"

"He was not willing to come in, and I had to place him under arrest."

She nods, saying, "Make a report and process him. Expecting any problems?"

"Maybe a call from his lawyer. He is insisting on a lawyer, and I think he has asked his GM to call a lawyer. I don't know what they spoke, but the words 'promise' and 'lawyer' were mentioned several times. The GM, Mr. Thanaraju, is an Indian national as well."

"The OCCI called about your suspects, Ricky and Ah Meng. What're your plans?"

"I'll do Sivalogan first, then start on them."

"You need any help?"

"I'd like the interviews to be handled by Johan, and he may need help."

"Okay, let me know when you need assistance. Lan, be careful. There are many eyes watching your moves. I don't have to remind you."

Johan escorts Sivalogan into one of the interview rooms and instructs the detectives to watch him. Walking back to the office he bumps into the remand team and asks about Ricky and Ah Meng. They tell him both were granted three days' remand by the magistrate and are in the detention cell. Back at the office, the sergeant puts a call through to Records, asking for the three suspects to be processed, starting with Sivalogan.

40

MISLAN COMPLETES HIS ARREST report, feeling elated at the potential breakthrough. "Has he been processed?" he asks his assistant.

"Still with Records. Are you not joining us?"

"I'll take the second chair. It's time you flew solo," he says, smiling. "Got all the stuff you need?"

Several shouts of "Officer taken" are heard from the detective room, followed by the sound of personnel rushing about. A detective runs into his office shouting, "Sir, your detainee took the man taking fingerprints hostage!" The inspector jumps off the chair and runs out the door. "What's happening?" he asks, and one of the rushing detectives tells him that a D6 technician has been taken hostage by a detainee in the processing room.

"Who's the detainee?"

"I heard it is an Indian man."

The elevator lobby is jammed with officers and men waiting to go down to level six where Criminal Records is housed. He signals Johan, and they take the staircase down to a corridor crowded with onlookers. Mislan shouts, "Clear the area," as they push their way through the mass of bodies. Entering the office, he instructs one of the uniformed personnel to clear the corridor and elevator lobby of onlookers and civilians.

"What's going on in there?" he asks the front desk officer.

"The tech was processing a suspect when the suspect jumped him and grabbed his gun. He's demanding a lawyer."

"Who's OC?" he demands, asking for the officer in charge.

"The OC is talking to the detainee over there," the front desk officer says, pointing to a man crouching behind an overturned desk.

"Okay, clear the office and call for a standby medic. No one comes in, I don't want casualties. Who's the tech?"

"Lance Corporal Manan. He is due for retirement in two months."

"Let's hope Manan gets to enjoy his retirement. Now move!"

Mislan moves cautiously into the general office. Johan stays close behind him. Several Major Crimes detectives, uniformed personnel, and the OC of Criminal Records crouch behind desks with weapons drawn, aimed at the processing room's door. "What's the situation?" he asks.

"He has locked the door; I don't know what's going on in there. He has been asking for a lawyer," comes the answer.

"Does he have a gun?"

"We think so."

"You don't know? Did Manan carry his gun on him?"

"I don't know," the OC answers angrily.

"Does anyone know if Manan had his gun on him?" he asks, looking at those crouching. No one seems to know. "Can someone check his desk drawer and see if his gun is there?"

One of the uniformed personnel checks Manan's desk drawer and says, "It's here," holding up a standard-issue Smith & Wesson.

"He is fucking unarmed," Mislan hisses, walking slowly to the processing room, hugging the wall as he moves toward the door. He peeks through the edge of the triangular glass peephole. He sees Manan on his stomach, his face turned sideways, bloodied, with hands cuffed behind him. He notes that the lance corporal is still breathing, his oversized belly heaving laboriously. Sivalogan sits on the floor next to him, hands wrapped around his knees with his head hidden between them, either crying or praying. He still wears the handcuffs on one hand and holds a motorcycle helmet in the other. He figures the detainee must have used the helmet to knock Lance Corporal Manan out cold. Keeping his eyes on the suspect, he reaches for the doorknob and tries to turn it slowly, it is locked. The sound jolts Sivalogan, making him lift his head and look at the door. Moving away from the door, he asks if there is a spare key to the room. Not surprisingly, no one knows.

ASP Ghani's voice booms across the office, asking who is in charge, as he and his bozo sidekick arrogantly barge in.

"I am," the inspector answers, stepping up to them.

"I am now," ASP Ghani says condescendingly. "The OCCI put me in charge."

"Stay out of this! That's my suspect in there. It's my case. You can go tell your boss I'm in charge," he says defiantly standing in ASP Ghani's path. Like a wrestling tag-team partner, Johan stands next to him.

"You can tell him yourself, he's on his way down," ASP Ghani dares. No sooner has ASP Ghani spoken, SAC Burhanuddin emerges at the door with Superintendent Henry, Superintendent Samsiah, and his two PR dolls. Like a spoiled brat, ASP Ghani rushes toward them, whimpering about not being allowed to take charge. Mislan and Johan stand firm as the red-faced OCCI and his entourage march toward them.

"Ghani says you refuse to hand over command to him? Is it a willful defiance of my order? Who do you think you are?"

"This is my case, that's my suspect. He is unarmed, and you know damn well if Ghani goes in, my suspect is as good as dead. I need him alive. He's the only lead I have to the killers. After I'm finished with him, you can do whatever you want. And, for that matter, you can do whatever you want with me," he says, knowing he is tempting the charge of insubordination. He is not going to lose a key witness, or a life. He will deal with whatever they decide to do with him when the time comes.

"You fool! Get him out of here," SAC Burhanuddin shouts. No one moves, and he shouts again, "Get him out of here!"

"No. Everyone calm down. Mislan is right. This is his case. That," Superintendent Samsiah says, pointing to the processing room, "is the best lead he has. The suspect is unarmed, and he is an Indian national. We don't want to invite the Foreign Ministry into this, do we? Let him take the detainee down. We'll prosecute him once that is done."

Everyone in the room breathes easier except ASP Ghani and his sidekick. The OCCI signals the head of major crimes to follow him to the outer office. Mislan waits, unsure of what to expect. How many times has he dragged his boss into a face-off with her boss? If something should happen to her because of his defiance, he would never forgive himself. He wants to leave and let them have their way. To hell with the case; the victims are dead, but his boss is alive and needs to go on living. He makes a move toward the outer office just as the Superintendent of Police comes back in, saying, "Mislan, you're in charge. The rest of you stand down. Only those the inspector picks stay, the rest please clear the room. Ghani, you and your team stand by in the outer office. You'll take over on my command. Until then, it is Mislan's show."

The expressions of disbelief on the faces of the D7 entourage and the frustration on ASP Ghani's face are unmistakable. Superintendent Henry and the two PR dolls slither away without saying a word.

"Mislan, you have one hour to end this. One hour, that's all. After that I'll pass it on to Ghani," she says.

"Thanks, ma'am."

Shaking her head, she says, "Don't thank me, this is not over yet."

"How did you do it?"

"That was easy. I offered your head on a platter, and threw in Johan as bonus after all this is over." She laughs. When she finally stops laughing, she says, "Go do what you're good at doing and leave the human skills to me."

He selects two detectives and lets the rest go. He discusses with them the plan to take Sivalogan down without firearms. They agree and move into position. He walks to the door, sticks his face against the glass peephole, and calls out to Sivalogan, who is still in his sitting position, watching the door.

"Sivalogan, we need to talk."

Sivalogan reaches for the helmet, rises, and asks, "Why?"

"Look, I'm here to help you. If you're not willing to cooperate, I'll leave and hand the situation to the UTK."

"What's UTK?" Sivalogan is confused.

"It's our SWAT. You know what SWAT is, right? Special Weapons and Tactical Team," he says slowly, to ensure the words *Weapon* and *Tactical* are heard clearly.

Sivalogan starts shouting and crying: "Why do you want to call the SWAT for? I'm going to die," and rattles on rapidly in his native tongue.

"Sivalogan, listen. I can get you out of here. Come nearer so we can talk. You need to trust me."

The detainee steps over Lance Corporal Manan and moves closer to the door. "I want a lawyer," he says. "I want a lawyer, now."

"You got any lawyer in particular that you want me to call?" he asks softly, making sure that Sivalogan can only hear part of it.

"What? I can't hear you."

He waves his hand, signaling for Sivalogan to come closer and repeats softly, "Any lawyer in particular?" This time, only the word "lawyer" is clearly heard.

The detainee steps closer to the door and leans against it sideways with his face at the peephole. "What? My lawyer? I don't know. You call Mr. Thana. He knows."

"Okay, let me call him." Without looking around, he signals his assistant. The sergeant takes a step back from the wall and with one smooth motion delivers a forceful kick, sending the flimsy plywood door flying inward, slamming into Sivalogan and throwing him over Manan. Sivalogan screams in pain as he falls flat on his back. Johan rushes in, kicks the helmet from his grip, flips him onto his stomach, and cuffs him. Sivalogan screams, "My shoulder, you broke my shoulder. You lied to me, I want my lawyer now. You tricked me," followed by something in a language they cannot understand.

Mislan dashes to Manan, and shouts for the paramedics to come in. A bottle of smelling salts is pushed under his nose, making him groan, while others prepare the stretcher-bed. They struggle to get the overweight lance corporal onto it and wheel him out. One of the paramedics steps over to Sivalogan, pulls the shirt off his shoulder, looks at it, and says, "It's just a bruise. He'll live." Holding the detainee's arm, Johan pushes him into a chair and shouts, "Can I have another tech and detective in here?" A female technician appears with a detective. "Are you the tech?"

"Yes," she answers, showing her security tag.

"Get him processed, and you!" he says to the detective, "are you his escort?"

The detective nods.

Walking out to the general office Mislan spots the detective originally assigned to escort Sivalogan. "Where the hell were you?" he asks angrily, not really interested in the answer. "Go report to front office. District will deal with you later."

"That was clever," Superintendent Samsiah says. "Listen, I want you to wrap this case up. It's attracting too much attention. You said he's your best lead, work on him. I'm assigning Reeziana and Reeze to you immediatly. Use them, let them do the footwork. You and Jo focus on breaking the suspects."

"Thanks, I could use extra legs. Are you giving this incident to the district?"

"Yes, I don't need this on our plate. So far, we have been fortunate that the press is not playing your case up, but if they get wind of this . . ." She leaves her sentence hanging. "I'll talk to the district to see if they can keep this under the media radar. Who was the detective in charge, Haris? I've always wondered how he was made detective. With his attitude, something like this was bound to happen. He's lucky no one was injured or killed."

"If you ask me, half of them should not have made detective, but who am I to say anything?"

As they walk past the outer office, she says to ASP Ghani, "Your men can stand down. There'll be no body count today."

Nathan calls to tell him the measurements are almost identical to the earlier ones, and that he has e-mailed the details. He again reminds the inspector that the measurements are not scientific and cannot be used in a courtroom. Mislan thanks Nathan, logs into his computer, opens his mail, and forwards it to Dr. Safia.

41

JOHAN TELLS HIM THAT Sivalogan is done and is in interview room one. Mislan requests Records to match the prisoner's prints with those lifted by Forensics from the diagnostic system seized from Pro Care Service Center. It is confirmed, and they add that the other prints match those of Ricky and Ah Meng. With what had just happened at Records, the stand-off with the OCCI and his boss putting her neck on the line, Mislan decides to take the lead for the interview himself. His boss's implicit instruction to close the case as quickly as possible weighs heavy on his mind. His assistant will understand. He picks up a notepad and the digital recorder and walks into interview room one. He slides a document toward Sivalogan and switches on the recorder, reciting into it the case number, date, time, and those present.

"Mr. Sivalogan Phaniti, I'm going to caution you, please listen properly," Mislan starts the interview.

Sivalogan Phaniti nods.

Speaking into the digital recorder, he reads the caution: "It is my duty to warn you that you're not obliged to say anything or answer any question. However, whatever you say, whether in answer to a question or not, may be used against you in a court of law." He pauses, allowing Sivalogan to digest the caution, then continues, "Do you understand the caution?"

Sivalogan nods.

"Please answer yes or no."

"Yes, yes," Sivalogan says.

"Please sign here," he says, pushing the document nearer and producing a pen. "How do you want me to address you, Siva or Logan?"

"Logan."

"Okay, Logan it is. I'm investigating the multiple murder of Mr. Tham Cheng Loke, also known as Robert Tham, and his family. Do you want to make a statement?"

Logan glances at Johan sitting at the edge of the table and then turns to Mislan, sounding genuinely terrified, and asks, "What murder? I know nothing of any murder. What are you talking about? I want a lawyer."

"Let's drop the lawyer thing. We don't provide you with a lawyer like what you see in US movies. If you have a lawyer, you can call him after we are done here," Mislan explains.

"My shoulder is broken, I need medical attention," Logan says, contorting his face as if in severe pain.

"The medics have examined your shoulder. It's only a bruise. So, shelf the bullshit," Mislan says. "Are you a systems programmer?"

"Yes."

"What sort of system programming do you specialize in?"

"Communication systems."

"And?"

"Only communication systems."

"Do you do freelance programming?"

"No, my company does not allow us."

"Do you belong to a chat group called Hackerchat?"

"I sometimes chat there with other programmers. There's nothing illegal about that."

"What is your chat name?"

"Siva."

"What is your chat name?" Mislan repeats firmly.

Logan keeps mum.

"Is it Siva, or Deepseeder?" he asks. At the mention of Deepseeder, he detects fear in Logan's eyes.

"What Deepseeder? I don't know what you're talking about," Logan says.

"This Deepseeder," he says, pushing a program printout across the table. "You recognize this program?"

Bending over, a little low to conceal his face, Logan pretends to read the program. The inspector snatches it away. Johan, who is sitting quietly at the edge of the table, abruptly stands, knocking his chair over with a loud bang, startling both Logan and Mislan. Logan leans as far away from the sergeant as he can, with one hand cuffed to the chair, and screams, "Yes, yes."

Johan steps closer to the table, places both his hands on it calmly, and says. "Yes, what?"

"I know the program," Logan mumbles.

"How do you know it?" Johan hisses.

"I wrote it."

"Anyone could've written it. Why do you claim you wrote it?" Mislan takes back control of the interview. He pushes the program listing toward Logan again.

Logan moves cautiously back into his original sitting position and reaches out with his free hand to bring the printout closer. "Here, this line. That's my signature," he says, keeping one eye on Johan.

"What does it say, 'Sivalogan'?"

Logan hesitates before saying, "Deepseeder. It's my code name."

"We know," Mislan says, reaching for the digital recorder and switching it off. He stands, and moves next to Logan, leaning against the table, folds his arms across his chest saying, "Listen, and listen carefully. We know who you are and what you did."

Logan looks at him, unblinking, mouth open.

Seizing the moment, Mislan presses, "And the thing you did back there," jerking his head indicating at Criminal Record, "was stupid, really stupid. It's going to get you into another heap of trouble. Abetting a triple murder, assaulting and holding a police officer hostage: you'll be an old man before you're free."

Logan's eyes open wide. He starts shaking his head and crying and rambling incoherently in his native tongue. The two policemen pick up the words *"ayo,"* "mother," "brothers," "sisters," and "boss" being repeated several times.

"Stop acting, you're not auditioning for a Bollywood movie," Mislan snaps. Logan stops. "You're in big shit, bigger than you can imagine. We've all the evidence needed to link you to the murder of Robert Tham. Your prints are on the diagnostic system from the workshop, your image is on the workshop's CCTV recording, and the sleeper programs have your hidden signature. We also know about your inquiries on ECU programs. How do you think we found you?"

Logan looks as if he is choking or swallowing imaginary saliva. "I told you, I don't know what you're talking about. What murder, who is this Robert Tham?"

"Are you willing to cooperate?"

"Yes, yes, I'll tell you everything you want to know, but I don't know anything about a murder," the detainee pleads.

The inspector walks back to his chair, switches on the recorder, and asks, "You say you know this computer program. Can you explain?"

42

When his cell phone rings, Mislan switches off the recorder and answers, "Yes, Yana." Yana is short for Inspector Reeziana, who was assigned to him for the legwork.

"He's gone. The receptionist said he left immediately after you left. She does not know where he is and he is not answering his phone," Inspector Reeziana says.

"Can you find his house address?"

"Yes, got it from one of the staff. I'm waiting for his particulars. Maybe you'd want to get immigration to alert all exit points."

"Okay, try to get a photo of him, too. I'm sure there will be some on his computer. If not, check with the office staff. Get it printed, preferably in color. Once you get the information, can you proceed straight to his address? Meanwhile, I'll get someone to call all airlines and check if there's a flight booked in his name."

"I've already got Operation Center to send an MPV to his address, with orders to arrest the suspect," Inspector Reeziana says.

"Good. Let me know once you have his particulars so we can alert Immigration. I'll get someone to start calling the airlines."

Mislan finishes his interview with Logan and calls in a couple of on-duty detectives, instructing them to hand Logan to the district investigator handling assault and kidnapping cases. He tells Johan to get Ricky ready for an interview and goes to his boss's office. She signals him in. "You're done with him?"

"Yes, sending him to the district."

"Did he talk?"

"He has admitted writing the sleeper programs and uploading them into the Cayenne. Claims he did not know what they were used for. He was assigned the project by his boss, Thanaraju. He says he was told that it was a pilot project for a car anti-theft system. Yana says Thanaraju is gone; left immediately after we picked up Logan. She has asked Operation Center to dispatch an MPV to his home address. She's now waiting for his particulars. I need someone to call all airlines to check if Thanaraju has made any booking, and I need your help to alert Immigration at the exit points."

His boss picks up the phone and asks her personal assistant to come in. She gives her a piece of paper, saying, "Call all the airlines and see if that name is booked on any flight." Then she asks him, "What about buses and trains?"

"I thought about that, but we can't check them all, except at the exit points in Johor, Kedah, and Kelantan. If he takes the land routes, Immigration should spot him, I hope. I'll pass his particulars on, once Yana gets them."

"Do you think he's skipping the country?"

"I don't know, but I'm not taking any chances. If he took to the road immediately after we left, he would have just made it into Singapore by now. Thailand via Bukit Kayu Hitam or Kelantan would take longer. My guess is, if he's traveling by road, he'll head for Thailand. It's easier to disappear into Thailand than Singapore and find his way back to India."

"Okay, get me his particulars. I'll alert Immigration. Try to get a photo of him."

"Another thing: Johan visited the shops where we believe our mystery woman, or the woman seen with the vic in the hotel video, visited. The salesgirls remember her, but the company isn't willing to give out details. I'm a bit tied down, got the two suspects to interview. Can you let me have the investigator on shift to follow up? Today is Friday. The offices won't be open tomorrow."

"Sure, give him the details and tell him it comes from me. Anything else?" she asks.

"Nope, thanks."

As he comes out from his boss's office, his assistant approaches him. "Just got a call from Operation Center. Thana's car is there, but no one is answering the door. The MPV officers were told by a neighbor she saw the suspect come home about two in the afternoon. She saw a car leaving the suspect's house an hour later."

"Probably skipping town." He calls Inspector Reeziana. "Yana, have you got the photo and particulars? We need it urgently. Suspect is skipping town . . . Good . . . Okay." He asks Johan, "Did the neighbor see the suspect leaving in the car?"

"No, she heard the car leaving and tires screeching. She peeked out but it was gone."

"Is the MPV still there?"

"Yes, Operation Center's waiting for instruction. Why?"

"I don't like it. I have a bad feeling that something is not right. Tell them to stay put."

He hurries back into Superintendent Samsiah's office, tells her of the latest development, and the change in plans. He briefs the investigator on shift and tells him to proceed to the suspect's house.

"Do you think something has happened?"

"I don't know, just got a bad feeling."

The investigator calls out to his assistant, "We're in the Yee Sang Murder team. Grab your stuff, we're checking out a suspect."

"Call me when you get there. Exercise caution," he shouts after them.

"Always."

As they go toward interview room two, where Ricky is waiting, Johan asks his boss, "What is your feeling, or intuition, saying?"

"He left the office immediately after we visited him; that was what, about 11:30? But only got home around two, two and a half hours later. That's sufficient time to go somewhere and meet someone."

"So?"

"You said the neighbor saw a car leaving an hour after the suspect reached home. I'm thinking one of two things: someone is either making arrangements for him to disappear or someone was sent to silence him. I'm hoping for the first, but either way, we're screwed."

"Shit, you think they will? I mean, do him in?"

"He is a link to them and, probably, the only link. If they know we're on to him, yes, I do."

"This case is looking more unsolvable by the minute. Everything seems to lead to nothing," Johan says with a sigh.

Mislan knows his assistant is right. Now is the time for a little luck. Something. Anything. A tip-off, a call from a law-abiding citizen, a plea bargain with an incarcerated snitch, trade-off, anything. "Just one, that's all I need," he says aloud in frustration.

Mislan dismisses the detective and sits across the table facing Ricky. Johan sits at the edge of the table and observes how calm and relaxed Ricky is. He figures Ricky must be either a seasoned player or clueless. Switching on the recorder, Mislan starts with the formalities of introductions and cautioning.

"Are you known as Ricky, and do you work at Pro Care Service Centre?"

"Yes."

"How long have you been working there, and what's your expertise?"

"About five years. I'm in charge of Porsche, but I also help with other models."

"Do you know Robert Tham?"

"Yes, I've met him several times. I take care of his cars. He's my boss's friend."

"Do you know Mrs. Tham?"

"No. I know she drives a BMW. I have never met her."

He pushes the service job sheet toward Ricky, pointing to the remarks column. "Is that your signature?"

"Yes."

"What's this remark?"

"It's for work done by an outsider. Winnie told me the ECUs needed reprogramming, and that Porsche was sending their technician to do it."

"Did you know what the reprogramming was for?"

"Winnie said the car always stalled. The engine seized."

"Was it true? Did the car stall or engine seize?"

"Not when I was testing it."

Pushing Sivalogan's photograph to Ricky, he asks, "Is that the technician from Porsche?"

"Yes."

"After he did the reprogramming, did you test the car?"

"Yes, it ran okay."

"Did you notice any additional programs?"

"I don't know how to program, so I don't know how to look for them. I only know how to read the diagnostic."

"What about Ah Meng?"

"I don't think he knows. He's like me. We can read the diagnostic, but we don't know how to program or read them."

"How long has Ah Meng worked at Pro Care?"

"About one year, I think. He worked in Singapore before he joined us."

"How well do you know Ah Meng?"

"Only as a coworker. I don't go out with him."

"Did Ah Meng work on Robert Tham's Cayenne alone?"

"He is also a Porsche mechanic. Sometimes when I had other cars to do, or if I needed to go out urgently for parts, I'd ask Ah Meng to help me. But I always signed off the work sheet if the car was assigned to me."

"Can you remember the last time Ah Meng worked on Mr. Tham's Porsche alone?"

"The last servicing. I had to leave, to recover a Porsche that had broken down in Shah Alam. So I asked Ah Meng to do the servicing. It was just a routine. Why?"

"How long were you away?"

"About four hours."

"Was the servicing completed when you came back?"

"Yes. I did the test drive. Everything was okay."

"Did Ah Meng come along for the test drive?"

"No, he was working on another Porsche."

43

TAN KOK MENG A.K.A. Ah Meng looks tense and jumpy, his eyes darting wildly between Mislan and Johan, when he is escorted into the interview room. Even before he sits, Ah Meng starts badgering them about his arrest. He keeps saying his boss knows many high-ranking police officers. The detective tells the suspect to be quiet and to remain still while he removes the cuff from Ah Meng's right hand and fixes it to the chair. Once that's done, and Ah Meng quietens, the inspector goes through the formalities of introductions, stating the case number, date, time, and finally cautioning Ah Meng. He then tells his assistant to lead the interview.

"Do you know what this is?" the sergeant asks, pushing a photograph of the canister taken out from the Cayenne.

"A can?" Ah Meng answers evasively.

"Good, now try to guess where we got the can from?"

"I don't know. The workshop?" Ah Meng replies.

"Good. Where do you think we found it?"

"In the spare part store."

"Okay, wise guy, let's try again. Do you know what this is?" Johan says, dropping his good cop demeanor.

"Told you. It's a can."

"Have you seen a can similar to this?"

"No."

"Have you handled a can like this?"

"No."

"That's funny, because we lifted your fingerprints from it. How then are your prints on it?"

Ah Meng is visibly taken aback by the question, takes a closer look at the matching prints with his name on it. His eyes start blinking rapidly. The sergeant jumps at the opportunity and asks, "Have you seen, or handled, this can before?"

"I don't know," Ah Meng answers, avoiding the sergeant's eye.

"Don't give me that crap, okay? We lifted your prints from the can."

"I don't know what you're talking about. What print?"

"Your fingerprints must have been transferred to it when you handled the can, while fixing it into the dashboard of the Cayenne. Ricky said he left you to work on the Cayenne while he attended a breakdown. You had ample time to fix the can. When Ricky test-drove the Cayenne, you didn't accompany him although you serviced it. Why? Were you afraid?"

"I don't know what you're talking about. I don't want to answer any more questions," Ah Meng says, leaning back.

"Listen, now is your chance to tell us the truth. We're talking about murder. How old are you? Thirty? Are you ready to die? How much did they pay you?"

Ah Meng stares at the wall behind his interrogator, not saying anything.

Mislan's cell phone rings, and he steps out to take it. "Yes . . . What?! . . . Shit . . . Okay, can you Whatsapp me the vic's photo? . . . Sure . . . thanks." His cell phone rings again, indicating an incoming message. He opens it to see a picture of a lifeless Thanaraju, sprawled in a pool of blood. The victim's face has been brutally battered. There is also a gash cut right across the throat. He had deduced correctly. Thanaraju must have panicked after Sivalogan was picked up, told the killers about it, and was silenced to break the link. He goes back to the interview room, looks at Johan, and shakes his head, handing him the cell phone.

"Damn it! Do you think you're safe because your boss has powerful friends in the police? Here," Johan says, pushing the cell phone in front of Ah Meng. "He was one of those who helped them. You remember the programmer from Porsche? Well, that was his boss. We just found him dead in his house. I bet you'll be next."

He sees fear in Ah Meng's eyes, and his hand shakes as he pushes the phone away.

"Are you ready to meet your Creator? Your best chance of staying alive is for us to get to them first. They've silenced anyone who can lead us to them. It's not a matter of 'if' anymore, it is 'when.' Once you are out there," Johan jerks his head toward the window, "you're dead."

Ah Meng is clearly shaken. He blinks rapidly.

"Do you think they'll help you? Do you think they'll allow you to live? They, surely, love their own lives more than yours. You are nothing, disposable, only a tool."

Ah Meng remains silent.

"Is your mother alive?"

Ah Meng nods.

"Father?"

He shakes his head.

"Brothers, sisters?"

Ah Meng nods.

"Well, you can start saying your goodbyes to them. After we release you, I'll give you twenty-four hours, forty-eight max, before you're dead."

Ah Meng starts shaking his head. "You cannot protect me. He is dead, isn't he?" He nods toward the cell phone.

"He went to them. He didn't come to us. We can try. At least, you have a chance, and if we get them first, your chances of living will increase. Anything would be better than being dead the moment you hit the streets."

Mislan shuffles into his boss's office, "Ma'am, sorry to barge in, but I need to update you urgently. Thanaraju is dead, murdered in his house. That shook Ah Meng, and he has spilled it. Remember the calls you got from the OCCI and Superintendant Henry?"

Superintendent Samsiah nods.

"Well, that was on behalf of Lai, the owner of the garage. Ah Meng has confessed. It was Lai who instructed him to fix the hydrogen cyanide canister in the Cayenne dashboard. I want to pick him up, and I need you to fend them off."

The room goes silent suddenly. She gets up and walks to the window. She stands looking out at the disused Pudu Prison as he sits impatiently, but unwilling to interrupt. She finally asks tiredly, "How sure are you, Lan?"

"I'll say very sure. Ah Meng is a low-level nobody. I don't think he has access to the killers. The way I figure it, the killers are people with clout, connections, and money, way above Ah Meng's league. It's the same with Sivalogan."

"Who's dealing with Thanaraju?"

"The investigator on shift. He's there now."

"You know, I used to stand here for hours looking out at the prison, imagining the prisoners walking about, and the horrible crimes they committed. I was never inside the facility when it was operational. Were you?"

"A few times, when I was in charge of transporting the two Australians who were hanged for drug trafficking. Not pretty in there."

"I don't think it's wise to pick him up now. Maybe you should run a background on him. See if he has some secrets, and who he hangs out with. Ah Meng's words might not be enough for you to hold him for long. I think you have only one shot. What do you think?" She walks back to her chair.

"Yes, that might be best. The killers must know that Lai's place was raided, and he would be dead by now if they wanted. Since Lai is still alive, it may mean he is not linked to them, or he is untouchable," Mislan agrees.

"That's what I think. Meanwhile, I suggest you put a tail on him 24/7."

"I'll get Jo to arrange it. I'll do the digging, and Yana can work on the mystery woman."

"Okay, go with that. I'll handle the calls when the time comes."

44

It is 4:10 in the afternoon when Mislan enters the Criminal Records office. Completing the request form at the counter, he hands it to the clerk, saying it is urgent, to which he hears the clerk mumbling as she walks to her desk, "Aren't they all?" She keys in the details and points to a record review room where she wants him to wait. She deposits a thick file in front of him and leaves. He grabs the file like it is going to grow legs, jump off the table, and run away. He runs his finger through the table of contents, flips to the page he is interested in, and starts making notes. Next, he looks for previous convictions. He returns the file, signs off, and goes back to his office.

He speed-dials his assitant, "Jo, where is the suspect now?"

"At the Kuala Lumpur Golf & Country Club. Why? Do you want me to pick him up?"

"No, not yet. Look, I just read his file. Odorful. I need to verify some information, and I need a tail on him. Is he golfing or hanging about?"

"I'm not sure, we started his tail here. You want me to go in and check?"

"Yes, but not you. He knows you. Get a detective to do it. How many do you have on your team?"

"Six. I'll send one in to see what he is doing. Then what?"

"If he's golfing, I want to know his partners. If he's hanging out, with whom? Don't ask the staff, check with the management. Get their details and pass it on to ma'am."

"What's going on? Is something going down?"

"I don't know, just taking precautions. I don't want him to do a Houdini on us. Anyone watching his house?"

"Yes. It's quiet so far. Told them to call me when there is activity."

"Okay, let's not screw this up."

He stops over at Superintendent Samsiah's office and updates her on the latest. He tells her Johan will be calling her with details of those with the suspect at KLGCC, and if she could check with Criminal Records.

His cell phone rings. "Yes, Yana."

"You're not going to like this."

"Doesn't matter, just give it to me."

"The mystery woman was Mah Swee Yin, age thirty-seven, address in Ipoh."

"Was?"

"Yes, that's what you're not going to like. She's dead."

"Dead? When? How?"

"The card company told me. They said there was something about it in the Chinese papers: suicide. I checked with a friend at National Registration and she confirmed the death record."

"Shit!"

"What's the matter?" Superintedent Samsiah asks.

"The mystery woman, she is dead: suicide." Speaking back into the cell, he says "Yana, when did this happen?"

"The report was made on Monday morning, don't know when she did it. Remember the shopping she did, probably bought the dress in preparation," Inspector Reeziana replies.

"Go to the station and get hold of the Sudden Death Report. I need to review it ASAP."

"Sure. Anything else?"

"Nope, thanks."

He leans back in the chair, buries his face in his hands and takes several deep breaths. The office swirls in his head with the distant hum of conversation. It feels as if he is in a tomb, his tomb. He runs his hands over his head and locks his fingers behind his neck. Letting out a long sigh, he asks, "What the hell is this all about?" more to himself than anyone else.

"It's about not giving up. That's what the hell this is about, Lan. When was the last you slept?" Superintendent Samsiah asks.

"Eh? Oh, I did get some this morning. I'm all right. Can't sleep anyway, I keep seeing the kid's face."

"Watch it, Lan. You know what that can do to you. Why don't you go into the meeting room and get some shut-eye? I'll get someone to wake you when something breaks. Leave your cell phone here."

"I'm really okay, ma'am, thanks. There's some intelligence I need to verify."

Dropping his hands and leaning forward, he asks, "You ever had something like this before? Where you have everything, yet you've got nothing?"

"Nothing close, I'm not that lucky." She shakes her head and smiles.

"I don't think I want to be lucky if this is what it means. Thanks, ma'am," he replies. "You're ready for the assault?"

"Always am."

"Before I forget, or if I don't get the chance to say it later, I enjoyed working with you. In my book you stand tall," he says, standing. He winks at her and leaves.

"It's not that easy to get rid of me. Get out of here and go get your killers," she says with a laugh.

Back at his desk, Mislan decides to talk to a mate to verify the information from the suspect's file. The suspect has two prior convictions, both for assault with dangerous weapons when he was in his early twenties. He spent a few years in prison but has managed to stay clean since. That does not necessarily mean he has stopped or repented. Maybe he has become cleverer, learned not to get caught. He is listed as a probably active loan shark prone to breaking arms to recover debts, but has never been arrested for it. Several high-ranking triad members were listed as his contacts, and they went a long way back. He was listed as a triad member. A file was started on him, and, interestingly, the case officer was Inspector Song. The case file is still active, although the last entry was about a decade ago.

"Inspector Marzuki, please."

"Please hold; if the line gets dropped, his extension is 2445," the operator says.

After several rings, a voice answers, "Marzuki."

"Roy, Mislan. How are you?" During training, everyone had nicknames; Marzuki's was Roy.

"Fine, fine, long time no hear. What gives?"

"How's life treating you? Heard you did a tour in Kosovo. Why are you still working? You should have enough to retire comfortably," he jokes.

"It was just a brief tour. Blew all my allowances before I was shipped back," Roy replies, laughing. "I know you're not calling me about my tour. That was four years ago."

"I need some off-the-record info on one of my suspects. I would follow procedure, but don't have the time. The suspect's spooked and could skip anytime."

"Off-the-record, okay," Roy says, stressing the status. "Shoot."

"Lai Choo Kang," he says, giving all the personal details he has copied from the file. "Roy, I know you guys keep detailed records of confidential informants. I needed to know how the suspect is related to Mah Swee Yin."

"That's classified, Lan. Told you: I blew all my Kosovo allowances, and I still need my job," Roy sounds serious.

"I wouldn't be asking if it wasn't important. I'm sure you heard of the triple murder of the RT family. I'm the lead on that. I believe the suspect can assist me, but I need to be sure before I question him. I know he's connected, and the heat is going to be on once I move in on him. I only have one chance, and I can't afford to blow it."

"All right, but you have to promise me you'll keep me out of it. Call me on my cell in thirty, it's the same old number."

Lighting a cigarette, he deliberates whether to call Song. They are good friends. Song is a decent bloke, a good officer. He hopes that, by now, he realizes that Four Finger Loo's death had nothing to do with him. Song, of all people, should understand that what the brass do is not within the control of people like them; like the way they kicked him out of D7. With the clock ticking and time running out on his chance of cracking the case, he is desperate. He stubs out his cigarette and decides he would rather lose Song as a friend than let a killer go free. He punches in the numbers and, after a few rings, Inspector Song answers. "Hey Song, Mislan," he says, trying to sound as casual as he can.

"It's you again. What now?" Song says.

"Yes, it's me. I just needed some info on one of your case files, Lai Choo Kang. You were the last person handling the file. It's still active, but no updates have been made for about a decade. Any reason for that?"

"Simple, it's not updated because he is not active. Why are you digging up my case files?"

"Don't go down that road, Song. I'm not digging up your case files. My investigations led me there, and if it's your case, I have to ask what needs to be asked. What can you tell me about him that's not in the file?"

There is a moment of silence. He can hear the sound of traffic in the background and figures Song must have stepped out from wherever he was.

"Listen," Song's voice is low and harsh, "I don't know what's going on, but I know you hit his workshop. I have received several calls about it. Look, this guy's connected, and maybe even insulated."

"Who called you? What do you mean insulated?"

"People you don't want to piss off, people who can make your life miserable. I touched him once; that was a mistake. I'm still paying for it."

"Who are these people? Our people?"

Another moment of silence passes.

"Let's just say people with sharp claws, long memories, and not very forgiving. Whatever you are thinking of doing, it's not worth it, Lan."

"What is not worth it?"

"Whatever you're going to do. I'm sorry I can't help you," Song says. His voice sounds limp and defeated.

"You can't, or you won't?" he snaps.

"Think what you want. Have to go. Bye." And the line goes dead.

Mislan feels sorry for his friend. He knows Song is in a tight spot, and he put him there.

45

INSPECTOR REEZIANA GOES STRAIGHT to Mislan and drops the Sudden Death Report on his desk. Mislan flips through it, looking for the police report. The hotel housekeeping staff found the mystery woman dead in bed when she came to clean the room. She reported it to security, and they called the police. The mystery woman checked in on Sunday afternoon under the name of Jennifer Mah, paying cash for one night's stay. No room service was ordered, nor was any call made from the room. When the police arrived, they found her in bed with a blanket up to her chest, face turned to one side as if she was sleeping peacefully. She wore an earphone connected to an MP3 player loaded with English and Chinese love songs. Her left hand was spread across the bed in a patch of coagulated blood. The police recovered a suicide note in Chinese on the bedside table, together with her cosmetics and other personal items. No luggage or toiletries were found. In the bathroom, the police found a makeshift shrine with burnt-out incense sticks, ashes of prayer money, a bowl of fruits, four photographs, one of her, a man, woman, and a child. The woman's image was crossed out with black ink. They found blood in the sink, a bloody razor blade, an empty bottle of Melatrol 5-HTP, and a half bottle of mineral water. Mislan looks at the enclosed pictures found in the bathroom. They are those of the late Robert Tham, Lionel, and Mrs. Tham. The SDR photographs of the bathroom show how the pictures were arranged with Lionel sandwiched between the deceased and the late Robert Tham, while the late Mrs. Tham's picture was placed facedown.

He looks at the autopsy report. The cause of death is listed as severe loss of blood. The report indicates two deep lacerations on the left wrist of the deceased, severing both the radial and ulnar arteries. A remark made on Melatrol 5-HTP listed it as a precursor called serotonin, responsible for controlling moods. It is known to induce a positive mood, taking away stressful thoughts before sleeping.

He finds the translation to the suicide note. It reads,

My dearest darling,

I know how much you love me and I you. It's sad that we cannot be together and share this life no matter how much we want to. For the last 12 years I prayed and prayed that we could, but my prayers were not answered. I can no longer bear living without you, nor can I bear sharing you. We belong to one another and denying us our happiness is cruel.

I've made all the arrangements for us to be together, to share a life where the evil woman cannot deny us anymore. The journey to our new beginning has been paved and blessed. I've prepared a dinner blessed with longevity, prosperity, and happiness for you and darling Lionel. She will sit in witness of how happy you and Lionel are, beginning the journey to an everlasting happiness.

To my beloved family, please be happy for me, I am going to be spending an eternity with the man I love. Honorable Kai Yea, Godfather, thank you for your understanding and support.

My darling, I shall be joining you soon after I make other arrangements to fulfill our destiny.

The letter was signed, *"Your only true love."*

Flipping the file to the last page, he fails to locate a forensic report; nothing about the suicide note, the Melatrol 5-HTP bottle, razor, MP3 player, nothing. No dusting for prints, no handwriting comparison. Only one statement was recorded, and it was from the housekeeping staff who found the body. No other staff were interviewed, nor was there any mention of CCTV images or phone calls, or how she arrived at the hotel. It was a sloppy investigation. The investigator probably found the suicide note and developed tunnel vision.

He pushes the SDR away, leans back using his hands as a headrest. "Shit," he says, a little too loudly.

"You okay, Lan?"

Mislan reaches for the SDR, finds the suicide note, and pushes it to her. "Read this."

Inspector Reeziana reads it, pushing it back to him, and says, "That's a confession, a dying declaration!"

"Yes, it is," he answers.

"You have solved the case, so why the long face?" Inspector Reeziana is puzzled.

"It's a long story," he says, dismissing the conversation. He walks to the pantry, makes a mug of coffee, lights a cigarette, and goes into the stairwell. He needs to be alone, he needs to think. He leans against the wall that he once pinned the head of Special Projects against. Jennifer Mah's dying declaration might have just ended it all for him, and for Lionel.

How many have died and how many more will die, and for what? Love? How could there be love in killing? It just does not make sense. You cherish love, not take it away. What about Lionel? How do you justify killing him? Who kills in the name of love?

46

THE DOOR OPENS A crack. Inspector Reeziana pokes her head through it and gives him a phone call sign. He flicks the cigarette butt down the stairwell and follows her into the office. "Who's it?"

"Roy," she answers, walking toward her desk.

"Thanks." He picks up the phone. "Mislan."

"Lan, Roy. Call my cell phone with yours," and the line goes dead. He makes the call and is answered immediately.

"It's me. What have you got?"

"Off the record!" Roy stresses.

"You've my word."

"Your man, he is a Confidential Informer but has been inactive for some years. A file note says D7 recruited him and asked for his background. That was about fifteen years ago. I think he still is a D7 CI. We have no record of the other name you gave me. It means that the individual is not immediate family or someone of interest to your man."

"Who's his handler?"

"Listed here is—our one and only—Henry Lau," Roy says, chuckling.

One last question: "Where is he from?" He is mindful that Roy has not mentioned Lai or the mystery woman by name.

"I knew you'd ask that. He is from Ipoh."

"Anything else?"

"That's about all I can tell you. Sorry."

"Thanks, Roy. It's helpful. We should catch up one day."

"Sure, call me."

As he is about to switch off his phone, he notices an incoming message icon. He opens the message. It's a photograph of several men sitting around a table, but it is too small to make out their faces. He Bluetooths it to his computer and enlarges the image. He recognizes the suspect, who is with three others. One of the men looks familiar, but he cannot place him, while the other two are complete unknowns to him. He speed-dials Johan, "Know any of them?"

"I inquired from the outlet manager. The Malay guy is Dato' Sufi, a club member. Of the two Chinese, the chubby one is also a member, known as James, a lawyer. He does not know the other person, probably a guest."

"The other Chinese guy looks familiar, but I just can't place him. Keep a close watch on our guy, we can't let him fly."

"Sure, I'll supervise the team."

"Jo, for your info, the mystery woman is dead, suicide."

"What?"

"A hotel staff found her on Monday morning. I'll update you once I have briefed ma'am and hear what she has to say. Stay with the suspect."

"*Wow*. Are you sure it was suicide? This is getting creepier by the minute. Are you coming here?"

"Will let you know."

He prints the photograph, gathers the SDR documents, and walks to Superintendent Samsiah's office. It is late in the evening, and most civilian staff have left for the weekend. His boss is still in her office going through files when he knocks, enters, and takes a seat.

"What's new?" she asks, closing the file she is working on.

"The dead mystery woman, well . . . she left a dying declaration," he says, placing the suicide note in front of her.

She adjusts her glasses and starts reading. Lifting her head, she looks straight at him and asks, "And?"

He shrugs.

She smiles, "You know what this means, don't you? And you came to see me because?"

"Because it's my duty to inform you, to keep you up-to-date," he says perfunctorily.

She bursts out laughing, making him to laugh, too. "I see the case has made you discover your sense of humor. That's good. Now, let's have it."

"The suicide note," he says, gesturing toward the SDR with his head, "it's going to close the case, right?"

"Looks like it. The note links her to the killings. It gives us motive. What's on your mind? Do you doubt the suicide or the note?"

"The SDR investigation was slipshod, no forensic investigations or anything. A typical case of investigative tunnel vision."

"The autopsy?"

"Severe loss of blood. Two cuts to the left wrist. No external bruises recorded."

"And, that says?"

"Okay, that rules out someone holding her down, but the lack of forensic data does not rule out the presence of assistance, or the note being written by someone else," he says.

"So you're saying, she had help, and the helper wrote the note?"

"I'm saying it does not exclude the possibility."

"What're you getting at?"

"Even if she confessed to the killings, she must have had help, accomplices. Look at her. There's no way she could have carried the vics, dressed them up, and propped them unless she had help. She took her life because she wanted to be with the vic, her lover. For whatever reasons, she figured, or someone influenced her, that that was the only way they could be together. That, I can buy. Now try this; if she planned and executed it alone, why leave a suicide note to the one you have killed when you know he is already dead? Suicide notes are for the living. I believe the suicide note is to protect someone."

"That makes sense, your reasoning on the suicide aside. So you're saying the accomplice is your suspect, Lai."

"Lai is linked to the hydrogen cyanide canister. I don't know how, or if, he's linked to the mystery woman. They are both from Ipoh. Off the record, he is a D7 CI, and guess who is his handler?"

"Where did you get all this from?" she asks, raising her eyebrows.

"It's off the record. Can't reveal my source, but it's reliable."

"Okay, I don't want to know your source. Henry?"

"Right the first time." He pushes the printout over the table toward her. "This just came in. It's at KLGCC. The Malay guy is Dato' Sufi, don't know who he is. The chubby Chinese is James, a lawyer. The other one looks familiar, but I cannot place him."

"That's SAC Chua, Chua Kah Teng, a Bukit Aman deputy, Narcotics Director. Dato' Sufi is an ex-police officer, now a lawyer, Suffian & Partners. Maybe they're working on something. Maybe they're working on him surrendering, cooperating in the investigation."

"I think he knows we're closing in. I know he is an accomplice; he and the mystery woman are linked somehow. If he is innocent, why all the big gunslingers?"

"What you think doesn't count for anything. You know what's going to happen: he'll come in with a powerful crony, give us a prepared statement, and that'll be the end of the case."

"No way, I'm not letting that happen."

"Yes, way. They'll not be coming to you, they'll be going up there," she says pointing up, indicating the OCCI. "You or I will not be part of it, and will only be duly informed. You know how these things work."

"I want in. I want to be there when he reads his statement."

She laughs. "There's your sense of humour again. My advice is, use whatever time you have before they arrive to link him to the mystery woman. The suicide note implies love as the motive. Find the link between her and your suspect that proves abetment; otherwise he is going to play dumb. He'll say he received the canister from the vic or the vic's wife, who instructed him to fix it in the vehicle. He passed it on to Ah Meng, and his worker fixed it. Where is the crime? Thanaraju could have been the accomplice. He's dead now. How's that for a theory? Believable?"

"I don't buy that theory."

"You don't buy it, I don't buy it, and the public won't buy it, but none of that matters. It's a theory and they," jerking her head up, "buy it. There'll be something about it in the papers, some concerned and bleeding hearts will make noise, and after a while no one will care anymore. That's how it is, and that's how it will be. The music has stopped, we can continue dancing if we want to, but there will be no one in the gallery. So stop beating yourself up with what you cannot control. You gave it all you had, did the best you could. Now it's time to let whatever happens happen. Your time is up this Monday. Take the weekend off, spend time with your family. I'm sure they miss you."

47

IT IS FIVE MINUTES to six in the evening, and he is still at his desk, thinking of what the head of Major Crimes said, toying with an unlit cigarette, when Johan calls, saying excitedly that Superintendent Henry just joined the group. He tells Johan to withdraw his team and keep his distance to make sure Henry does not see them. He drops the cigarette on the desk, leans back, and closes his eyes. It is just as his boss had predicted. The wheels are in motion, and soon Lai will be out of his reach. The case will be closed, stamped "solved." Lionel's death will not be avenged. He hopes the mystery woman is right, and they will be reunited happily as a family in whatever afterlife there is. Now the *yee sang* makes sense: prosperity, longevity, abundance, and vigor. A last dinner set for her lover and Lionel, while for Mrs. Tham, it is a journey she needs to go on alone.

The ringing of his phone startles him. He grabs it and answers, "Mislan."

"They're leaving."

"Forget the rest, stick with the suspect."

"Okay."

He looks at the clock on the wall; it is ten minutes past seven. "Shit, I must have dozed off." He goes to the restroom, takes a leak, and washes his face. On the way back he notices that his boss is still at her desk. Would he have joined the police if he were a woman? he wonders. Criminals have so many aces in their deck: corrupt officials, politicians, human rights and civil rights activists, lawyers, statutes, weapons. . . .

What do victims have? Someone like Superintendent of Police Samsiah Hassan.

His cell phone rings. "Yes, Jo."

"The suspect left with two of them in one car. They have just gone into Wisma Budiman. I don't think we can follow them in."

"How about the rest?"

"Superintendent Henry and the other Chinese guy left together."

"Okay, give them about ten minutes. Then, go in and check the tenant listing on the board. See if there is a Suffian & Partners, Solicitor and Advocates, listed. If there is, I'm sure they're headed there. If not, go down to the parking lot, check out the car, ask the security or parking attendant whose car it is, and which company he is from. Jo, I don't think anything much will happen tonight. You make the call to stand down your team if you want."

"What's happening? What did ma'am say?"

"I think they're going to build a brick wall around the suspect before he gives himself up. They'll probably be there a while."

"You okay?"

"I'm fine. Thought of going home, catching up with Daniel, and getting some sleep. I suggest you go home, too."

"I'll be around a little longer. If nothing moves, I'll stand down the team."

He gathers the SDR, switches off the computer, grabs his backpack, and leaves. His boss is still at her desk, working. He sees her lifting her head as he walks past, flashing an understanding smile, and she goes back to whatever she is working on.

Stepping out of the elevator at the ground floor, he bumps into Superintendent Henry coming in. He stops and stares at him. He needs every ounce of restraint to stop his hands from grabbing him by the shirt collar and dragging him out of the elevator cab and smashing him. His body trembles with rage. He loathes the very existence of people like Henry and all that they represent. The elevator door closes, protecting the object of his rage. He walks toward his car, breathing in the cold night air deeply to calm his nerves.

48

He calls home, and Daniel answers, "Daddy! Where're you?"

"On my way home, kiddo. Why?"

"Are you nearby? I have finished my Vitagen. Can you buy some more?"

"Sure, you want anything else? Ask Sis if she needs anything?"

He hears Daniel shouting to the maid, "Sis, Daddy asks if you want anything, he will buy," and the maid shouting back, "Eggs."

"Sis says she wants eggs."

"Okay. You had your dinner?"

"Yes, bye."

He stops at Giant supermarket and buys two six-packs of Vitagen, a dozen eggs, a loaf of bread, and two packs of cigarettes. Although he hasn't eaten since lunch, he has no appetite; he will probably make an omelet later. His mind is preoccupied with losing the case through the dying declaration. Going by what his boss said, his suspect is plotting a strategy to insulate himself, and Superintendent Henry's presence at KLGCC confirms it. In times like these, he misses Lynn, his ex-wife. Misses having a person he can talk with. A detached person who does not care about the internal politics, the ingredients of law, and the chain of evidence. Someone who sees things through a layperson's eyes, someone having no interest in the result of police investigations.

Daniel is in the living room when he opens the door, and he's instantly bombarded with questions. He puts away the groceries in the kitchen cabinet and goes to his bedroom with Daniel on his heels, repeating the questions. "Did you go outstation?" "Are you going to work again?" "Did you buy my drink?" "Can we play?" "Can I watch my channel?" and goes straight for the remote control and switches the TV on.

"Kiddo, Daddy needs to take a bath," he says, dropping the backpack and placing his sidearm in the drawer. "You want to sleep here with me tonight?"

Daniel nods.

"Go get your blankie."

The refreshing cold shower and the comfort of Daniel's presence take his mind off the case. They wrestle a little in bed. He lets Daniel pin him down several times and do his wrestling winner thing after each pin-down. When Daniel is satisfied he has beaten his father hollow, they lie in bed watching *Tom and Jerry*. His cell phone beeps; it's a message from Johan. "*Sufian & Partners is listed on the building information board,*" and he says he is standing down the team for the day. He sends his assistant a message, telling Johan to take a rest, turns to Daniel, and hugs him.

"Who was that?" Daniel asks, not taking his eyes away from the TV.

"Uncle Johan."

"Are you going out?" Daniel sounds disappointed.

"No, kiddo. Uncle Johan's just telling Daddy something about work. I'm hungry. You want to eat with me?"

"Fried Maggi?" Instant noodles, his son's favorite meal now.

"No! Enough of Maggi. Let's have some bread and eggs."

"Nay, I'm not hungry." He goes to his room.

He makes his way to the kitchen, takes two eggs from the fridge, slices some onions, mixes it with the eggs, and makes himself an omelet. Then, with a mug of black coffee, he sits at the table to have his dinner. Daniel comes out, sits next to him, and watches him eat.

"You want some?" he asks, pushing his plate closer to him.

Daniel shakes his head. "What was it that you always cooked for mummy?"

"Scrambled eggs?"

"Yes. Why don't you do that?"

"I don't like it. Why, do you want some?"

"Nay," Daniel says, gets up, and disappears into his room again. A moment later he hears Daniel laughing with the maid, probably watching another rerun of a P. Ramlee movie.

After two slices of bread, he doesn't want to eat anymore. He picks up his coffee mug and walks to his bedroom. He switches on the news channel, but his mind drifts. Sitting at his work desk, he retrieves the SDR and starts reading it again, chronologically. Nothing in it, just as he expected. Nothing linking the suspect to the mystery woman. His cell phone rings; it's Dr. Safia.

"Hi," he answers, trying to sound cheerful. "What's up?"

"What's with you? Haven't heard from you in a while, are you avoiding me?" Dr. Safia teases.

"Sorry, was a little busy. So how have you been?"

"Usual. What's the latest; found your mystery woman yet?"

"Yes and no. Found her, but she's dead. Suicide."

"Sorry to hear that. What happened?"

"Last Monday. A hotel staff found her loaded with Melatrol 5-HTP and a slit wrist."

"Melatrol, *wow*. She knows how to pick them. That stuff is a stress reliever. Most suicides I've encountered use aspirin. Was the autopsy done here?"

"No, at GH. Hey, are you working tomorrow? Want to come with me for a drive to Ipoh?"

"Ipoh? What's over there?"

"It's been a long time since I had Ipoh *kweh teow*," he says, laughing. "Pick you up, say, about nine. We can be in Ipoh by eleven. Spend a few hours there and be back in the evening. What say you?"

"Sounds like fun. Sure."

"Great. I'll see you then. Night."

"Lan," she says, followed by an awkward silence.

"Yes."

"You take care. Night."

49

LEAVING THE HOUSE, HE takes the Kesas Highway, exiting at Cheras. He heads back toward the city and makes a left to Taman Midah toward the condominium. Traffic is light. He speed-dials her number.

"Good morning. I'm downstairs, a little early," he says.

"Excited to see me, eh?" Dr. Safia teases. "I'm ready, will be down in a minute."

Three minutes later, he sees her walking toward the car, dressed casually in jeans and a crew-neck T-shirt. Simple, but looks stunning. Her hair in a tight ponytail, she wears sunglasses and the ever-present smile. She spots him and gives a little wave. "Hi," she says as she slides into the car.

"Hi, you look nice," he says, meaning it.

"Thank you, and you look like hell. Sorry, I mean you look beat," she says, chuckling. "You want me to drive?"

"Thanks for the compliment." He smiles. "I'm fine, thank you. Have you had breakfast?"

"Yup. You?"

"Coffee, before I left. Saving my appetite for the *kweh teow* later," he answers, putting the car into gear. Soon they are passing Istana Negara toward Jalan Damansara and Duta.

They drive in silence until they hit the North-South Expressway. Dr. Safia leans sideways against the car door and faces him, "I know we're not driving all the way to Ipoh just for *kweh teow*. We could've easily had it at one of the stalls in KL." She smiles. "So, are you going to tell me why we're really going to Ipoh, or are you going to be the tough cop and keep me in the dark?"

"Not any *kweh teow*, it's Ipoh *kweh teow*," he replies, laughing.

She gives him the "yah, right" look.

"All right. On the back seat," he says, "is the SDR. Look at it."

She unhooks her safety belt, kneels on the seat, bends over, and reaches for the file. In the process, she presses on his shoulder for support, squeezing it lightly. He watches her through the rearview mirror and smiles. That's what he likes about her; every move she makes is so natural. She returns to her seat, buckles up, and starts going through the SDR.

He drives quietly as she reads the report, flipping through the pages for about twenty minutes. She finally closes the file and looks at him.

"What?"

"Explain why we are going to Ipoh?" she asks, without taking her eyes off him, her smile disappearing.

"To know more about the deceased," he answers, avoiding her eyes.

"Because?"

He is silent as he thinks of an answer that may be acceptable to her.

"Because?" she snaps.

"Because I don't think she did it alone. She had help, and she is protecting the helpers."

"Who are these helpers?"

"I don't know."

"Don't give me that crap. We wouldn't be making this trip if you didn't have someone in mind."

"I mean, I don't know if he's the helper. He is linked through the hydrogen cyanide canister, the one planted in the Cayenne, but it could have been an innocent act."

"I don't get you."

"The owner of the workshop where the Cayenne was serviced is a Mr. Lai. The mechanic who installed the canister has made a statement that his boss instructed him."

"So pick up the boss."

"I wish it was that simple. His lawyer will punch a thousand holes in the story if it's based on the mechanic's statement alone. I need something to tie him to the mystery woman and uncover a motive. I have a feeling the two are linked, but I don't know how." He knows it's unfair of him to burden her with his office politics. He is sure she has her share of them. Their work did cross paths, but for either of them to be involved in the other's work problems, or office politics, will only complicate matters.

"Want to know what I think?" she asks.

He glances at her. "Nope, but somehow I think you are going to tell me anyway."

"I think you're not willing to accept that you have been beaten. Beaten by this woman. She closed the case for you. She beat you to it, so you're looking for something to keep the case open because you want to close it. You're obsessed with the case. My advice is, don't let it consume you."

He pulls out the cigarette pack and she snatches it from his hand and lights two sticks, handing one to him. They smoke in silence, pretending to listen to the radio, barely audible over the noise of the wind. When they approach the Tapah rest area, she asks him to stop, saying she needs to use the restroom. He can see she's upset, and wonders if he should have invited her for the trip.

He pulls into the rest area and parks the car. Dr. Safia steps out and heads toward the restroom without saying a word.

He kills the engine, steps out, locks the car, and walks slowly behind her. He finds a shady spot and waits for her to come out. When she finally emerges, he strolls toward her and smiles, "You okay?"

She nods.

"Like to have a drink before we continue?"

She nods.

Taking her hand, he leads her toward the food outlets. He orders one coffee and a *teh tarik* while she finds an empty table. Joining her, he asks if she wants anything to eat.

She shakes her head.

"We're now down to sign language, eh?" he remarks.

She stares at him, saying nothing.

"Oh, come on, Fie, this is supposed to be a fun trip, for *kweh teow*," he teases her. "Let's not get all worked up over a minor detour, okay?"

"You! Lan, I may not have known you a long time but, believe me, I know you. You're not the type who can sleep with dangling ends. I can appreciate your drive but . . ." she leaves the sentence hanging.

"I'm sorry, Fie, really. If you want to turn back, we'll turn back."

She looks at him, shakes her head, and cups her face with her hands. He thinks he sees tears welling in her eyes. Without lowering her hands, she says, "You just don't get it, do you?"

"Get what?"

"I just don't want to see this case consume you, your life. It'll destroy you if you let it. You cannot solve every case. Some of them are just not meant to be solved. Do you know how many dead people I examine daily? If I let them get to me, into my head, into my life, I'll think of nothing but them. I do my best, treat them as dignified a manner as I can, then let go. It's not easy, I know. They come to me in my sleep and, sometimes, even when I'm wide awake. But I just won't let them close in on me because I know what they can do. Now, I'm seeing what they're doing to you, and it hurts me just as bad." She slowly stands and walks back toward the car without touching her *teh tarik*.

50

THEY CONTINUE THE JOURNEY in awkward silence, him chain-smoking, stealing glances at her as she stares out of the window. He gets off the expressway at the Ipoh South interchange and drives toward Perak Police Contingent Headquarters. When he stops for a red light, he notices the time, 10:40. They have made good time. They could probably check out the mystery woman's address before going for their *kweh teow*, that is, if Dr. Safia is still in the mood for it. His cell phone rings. Looking at the screen, he sees it's from his boss.

"Morning, ma'am."

"Morning. Lan, where are you?"

"Ipoh, why?"

"Ipoh? Perak? What're you doing in Ipoh?"

"Had an urge for some Ipoh *kweh teow*," he answers evasively. "Anything the matter, ma'am?"

"Funny. You're checking on the suicide woman, right? Well, you can drive back immediately, and I'll buy you Ipoh *kueh teow* right here in KL. The OCCI wants a meeting, and if my guess is right, it'll be about your suspect. You said you wanted in, now you're in. So make the U-turn and be in the office by two."

"You're serious? It's Saturday. Is he not golfing?" he asks sarcastically.

"Not now, Lan. If you want in, be at the office before two," and the phone goes dead.

Turning to Dr. Safia, who is watching him, he tells her they're turning back. Her eyes narrow as if asking, why?

"The OCCI is calling for a meeting at two. We still have time. Maybe we can have lunch before I send you home."

"It's Saturday. I thought your admin is closed on weekends." She is prying. "It's your case, isn't it? Is there something you're not telling me?"

He lights a cigarette, offers it to her. She refuses, pushing his hand away. He takes a long deep drag, unsure if he should tell her his fear. He had just listened to one lecture from her, and he would only be inviting another by telling her.

"Is there?" She nudges his shoulder.

"Remember, I told you about the workshop boss?"

She nods.

"Remember I told you it's not that simple? Well, he is well-connected and, I mean, really well-connected. At this point, all I have is his mechanic's statement linking him to the canister. With his connections, I don't stand a chance of picking him up for questioning, much less holding him. He'll be back on the street before we even reach the office."

"The OCCI is one of his connections. So the reason for the meeting is a stop-order," she states rather than asks.

"I don't know. I think he's making his move to insulate himself from being implicated. You see, I put a tail on him yesterday. He was seen with several influential people at KLGCC, after which they went into a lawyer's office. My boss thinks he'll waltz in with a prepared statement that'll end his link to the case. I told my boss that I want in if he comes in. I am guessing that's what the meeting is about, for him to surrender himself to the OCCI. As the lead investigator, my presence is just decorative, like a flowerpot."

He keeps to the right lane, looking for an opening to make a U-turn, when she says, "We still have about three and a half hours before the meeting. Why don't you do what you came here to do?" Her smile reappears.

He looks at her, surprised. He sees her smile, the understanding in her eyes, and knows that Fie is back. He squeezes her thigh and accelerates toward the Perak Police Contingent HQ.

51

WITH FIVE MINUTES TO the meeting, Mislan goes into his boss's office just as she's getting ready to go in herself.

"Thought you weren't coming," she says.

"Wouldn't miss it for anything," he replies, following her to the elevator.

He expects her to grill him about his trip to Ipoh, but she makes no mention of it. As they step out of the elevator at the floor of the OCCI's office, she abruptly stops, making him bump into her. "Look, I think you already know what's going to happen in there." She nods toward the OCCI's office. "We have had this conversation before, and I don't want to have it again. So hold your tongue and keep your thoughts to yourself. I don't need this to become a circus."

He wants to respond but thinks better of it. He nods.

They're warmly greeted by the OCCI himself as they enter his outer office, "Glad you could make it. Sorry to spoil your weekend. My secretary is not here, and I didn't want to bother her. If you want coffee or tea, it's over there, please help yourself," SAC Burhanuddin says, pointing to the pantry.

"No thanks, we're fine," she answers for them.

"Okay then, let's get the ball rolling. They are waiting in the meeting room." He walks ahead of them.

Mislan sees four men in the room: the suspect, Superintendent Henry, and the two men he recognizes from the photograph Johan sent. The OCCI makes the introductions: "Dato', gentlemen, this is

Superintendent Samsiah, Head of Major Crimes, and this is Inspector Mislan, the lead investigator in the Robert Tham murder case."

The two Major Crime officers nod in acknowledgment and take their seats.

"This is Dato' Sufian from Sufian & Partners, and that's Khoo Kai Beng of Khoo & Associates."

"Call me James," Khoo Kai Beng says, smiling.

"And, I think, you have already met Mr. Lai Choo Kang, the owner of Pro Care Service Centre," the OCCI continues. "I don't have to introduce Henry, do I?" he says, letting out a hollow laugh echoed by the other four.

They look and sound like four performing seals, eager to please their trainer. The room is so thick with smugness and pompous self-righteousness, it is nauseating. Their faces are plastered with fake smiles, their eyes fixed endearingly on the OCCI, who rambles on with his silly remarks. The inspector examines them, one by one, before settling on the suspect. None of them look at him, though he catches the suspect stealing odious glances at him through the corner of his eye. What would he not give to have an hour with the suspect alone?

"Shall we get on with the business?" the head of Major Crimes says, disrupting the silliness and obnoxious laughter, getting a disapproving look from the OCCI, who seems to be enjoying the ass-kissing.

"Dato' is an ex-police officer, I'm sure you know him," the OCCI says, looking at Superintendent Samsiah, then at Mislan. She nods while Mislan keeps his eyes fixed on the suspect. "Dato' and James are representing Lai. Lai has come in voluntarily and has given us a statement about his innocent role in the Robert Tham murder case—sorry, the Yee Sang Murders. That's what it's called, isn't it?" The OCCI smiles, contagiously infecting the other four. He taps on a piece of paper in front of him and pushes it toward the head of Major Crimes.

She pulls it closer, looks at the suspect, and says, "Mr. Lai, why don't you tell us what is in your statement?"

"It's all in there. Just read it," the OCCI snaps.

"I don't want to hold up the discussion. I'm sure they are all busy people, and I don't want to take more of their time than necessary by reading it, then passing it on to Inspector Mislan to read it," she answers sarcastically.

"It's okay, Burhan," Dato' Sufian interjects, giving the OCCI a reassuring smile, "Lai, why don't you tell them what's in your statement?"

Mislan notices discomfort in the suspect's manner, and he figures it is not what he is expecting, or what has been promised. Lai hesitates, looks at his two high-priced lawyers, but it is Superintendent Henry sitting next to him who whispers something, perhaps telling him not to worry. The suspect pulls out a piece of paper from his shirt pocket, unfolds it, and starts reading from it.

"That's not what I meant, Mr. Lai." Superintendent Samsiah stops the suspect. "If you are going to read from the statement, I can do it, too. Why don't you tell us your involvement, in your words?"

"My client's involvements are mentioned in his statement," Dato' Sufian counters. "But if you insist, we must put it on record that if there are any discrepancies, deviations, or conflicts between what is said by my client here and what is in the written statement, the written statement shall prevail as the true statement. The discrepancies, deviations, and conflicting verbal statements given here are a matter of choices of words and added clarification. Is that understood and agreed by all?"

"Yes, yes," the OCCI says readily.

Mislan shakes his head in disbelief at what is going on.

"I see that Inspector Mislan is shaking his head. Are you not in agreement?" Dato' Sufian asks. All eyes turn to him.

"That's crap. If he wants to give a statement, let me record his statement. If he claims to have unknowingly played a role—"

"Mislan, if you do not wish to be here, you can leave," the OCCI retorts. "Otherwise, watch your language. Why don't you listen, and, maybe, you can learn a thing or two about police work?"

His boss leans toward him and whispers, "Calm down. Let me do the talking." He nods, and she sits up saying, "No promises. Let's hear what Mr. Lai has to say before we deliberate on your request; shall we, Dato'?"

Mislan smiles, noting his boss has not offered an apology for his outburst. The two lawyers and the suspect band together for a private consultation. Then, Dato' Sufian says his client maintains that his written statement is the true statement, and is invoking section 112 of the Criminal Procedure Code, and that he would not answer any questions that could or may incriminate him.

"Nothing Lai says will leave this room!" the OCCI says angrily to Superintendent Samsiah, prompting satisfactory smiles and nods of approval from the four.

"Whatever pleases you."

Still hesitant, the suspect says, "Robert was the one who gave me the canister to be fixed into his Cayenne. I didn't know what was inside it, and I instructed Ah Meng to install it. That's it."

"When and where did Robert give you the canister?" Superintendent Samsiah asks.

"In my office. I can't remember the exact date, but it was last month."

"Did you ask Robert what was the purpose or function of the canister?"

"No, I assumed it was a new Porsche gadget, or something."

"Did you or Ah Meng check with Porsche?"

"No."

"Is that normal? You and your mechanic did not know what the canister was for, yet no one bothered to check with the vehicle's manufacturer or its representative?"

"What's there to check? The client asked us to install it, we installed it," the suspect answers angrily.

"If you and your mechanic did not know what the item was for, how did you or Ah Meng know where to fix it, or what to link it to?" Superintendent Samsiah asks sardonically. The suspect's face becomes red, his eyes shift wildly between Dato' Sufian to James. Mislan notes small beads of perspirations on the suspect's forehead as he leans toward Dato' Sufian. Another whispering session ensues, punctuated by dark glances toward the two of them. After some head-shaking and nodding, Dato' Sufian says to them. "My client chooses not to answer the last question, invoking Section 112."

"It figures," Mislan sneers.

"That was uncalled f—" Dato' Sufian snaps but is cut off by Superintendent Samsiah, who raises her hand to stop him before he can finish.

"Let's move on. You said Robert gave you the canister in your office. Was the canister in a casing, a box, or was it wrapped?"

"No."

"So it was just the canister?"

"Yes."

"That being the case, can you explain why Forensics was unable to find Robert's prints on the canister?"

The suspect, taken aback by the question, again leans toward Dato' Sufian for a whispered conference. Dato' Sufian nods several times and says, "My client chooses not to answer the question."

The inspector shakes his head. "Do you know a woman named Mah Swee Yin, also known as Jennifer Mah?" he asks before his boss can continue.

"Jennifer who?"

"Jennifer Mah, or Mah Swee Yin?"

"No, I don't think so," the suspect says.

"You are from Ipoh, aren't you?"

"Yes, I was born and grew up there. Why?"

"And you're saying you do not know who Jennifer Mah is? She committed suicide last Monday. It was in the Chinese press."

He sees the suspect beginning to perspire heavily, stalling and groping for an answer. He pulls a weathered black-and-white photograph from his shirt pocket and places it on the meeting table. Pushing it slowly toward the suspect but not taking his hand off it, his gaze never leaving the suspect's face. He notes recognition, followed by surprise as the suspect reaches out for it, but he presses it hard to the table, refusing to release it.

"You know her, or shall I say, you knew her."

"What game are you playing?" James barks.

"Ask your client. Ask him to tell you who the woman in this photo is standing beside him."

"That's enough," Dato' Sufian snaps, standing. "This meeting is over. My client has given his statement, and I have been made to understand that you have a dying declaration from the murderer. Isn't that right, Superintendent Samsiah? If my memory serves me right, that means the case is closed. My client has come forward voluntarily to give his statement to assist you and your investigator, and you interrogate him like he is a criminal."

"How do you know about the dying declaration?" Mislan brusquely asks.

Soon as he asks, the room falls silent. The OCCI and Superintendent Henry gawk at Dato' Sufian, stunned.

"How did you know about the dying declaration?" Mislan repeats, keeping his eyes on the OCCI and Superintendent Henry.

"It's public record," Dato' Sufian says, looking at Superintendent Henry.

"Like hell it is." He notices Superintendent Henry shifting in his seat. "It was Henry, wasn't it? He told you of the dying declaration yesterday at KLGCC, didn't he?"

"Burhan, what is your position on this? You said the case is closed. Is it closed?" Dato' Sufian asks the OCCI.

"No, it's not." Mislan answers before the OCCI could.

"Yes, it is," the OCCI snaps back. "I'll inform the district to link the SDR to this case and close it for filing. It is solved, that's official."

"I will close the file the minute I receive your written instructions," Superintendent Samsiah says. "Is there anything else?"

"No," the OCCI says, getting up and going toward the door, followed by a panic-stricken Superintendent Henry.

The two teams remain sitting, looking at each, not saying anything. Although Mislan desperately needs his nicotine, he simply sits, staring unblinking at them. Superintendent Samsiah stands, gathers her notepad, nods toward the other team, and starts to leave. Mislan does not make a move until he feels a hand on his shoulder. He looks up at the head of Major Crimes as she beckons him to follow. He requires all his energy to stand and follow his boss. As they reach the door, he hears Dato' Sufian say, "You think you know it all, don't you, Inspector?"

Mislan swings around, steps back toward the table and says, "No, I don't, but I know the woman did not and could not have done it alone. And he," he adds, pointing to the suspect, "is guilty as hell, and you know it."

"How many years of service do you have? Ten, twelve? What makes you an expert? I've done more years, and I have a law degree to top that. You're just a kid compared to me. You don't know who you're dealing with."

"You may have more years and a law degree, but that means nothing if you don't have a conscience. Have a good day, gentlemen." Then he leaves.

52

THEY TAKE THE ELEVATOR down, and his boss invites him to her office. She drops her notepad on the desk, walks to the cabinet, makes two mugs of coffee, and takes out the ashtray. Mislan slumps into the chair, confounded by what has just transpired. She offers him one mug and places the ashtray on the desk in front of him.

"Thanks," he says, taking out a cigarette and lighting it.

She sits, sipping the hot coffee, watching him taking long drags on the cigarette without saying anything. When he finally squashes the cigarette in the ashtray, she asks, "You all right?"

"Nope," he answers shaking his head.

He takes out another cigarette and lights it.

"How many a day?"

"I don't know. Stopped counting."

"Twenty, thirty?"

"Maybe, maybe more."

She sips her coffee, then puts the mug down. "What happened in Ipoh?"

"We found the mystery woman's, I mean Jennifer's, house. Met her family. Her mother is dead, but the father is still alive. He told us that he and the suspect grew up together. They were good friends, and, when he had his first daughter, Jennifer, Lai became her godfather. But, soon, the suspect left for KL and they lost touch with one another. After Jennifer finished school, she came to KL and linked with Lai, and the father believes he took care of his daughter. He does not know much of the suspect's businesses or activities, but he says he heard the villagers say he was a *Taiko*, a gang leader."

"You said 'we'; who did you go with?"

"Dr. Safia." He smiles.

"So you think Lai is an accomplice?"

"I have no doubt he is. She couldn't have done it herself. Let's not even talk about carrying and moving the vics. How about the remote control? Did she have enough knowledge to handle the remote control that killed the engine, jammed the locks and discharged the gas? Even organizing a programmer and the hydrogen cyanide, I'd say, would have been too much for her." Mislan pauses to calm himself. "Apart from having the right connections with the right people to obtain the gas, the remote, the killers must have resources—money. This is not a garden-variety murder, this is a masterpiece, a work of art. It was very well planned and executed. It costs a lot of money, to pay the programmer, the gas, the embalming, and others. I don't think Jennifer could have done it by herself. Too many things just don't fit. I can accept that she may have wanted it, I mean for them to be dead, but someone did it for her."

"Well, you may be right, but that's not how they see it."

"Ma'am, what is the chance of keeping this case alive?"

"You heard what the OCCI said. What do you think?"

He lights another cigarette.

"Look, Lan, I know this is not how you want the case to close. You did all you could, but sometimes things don't work out as we want them to. As you said, it's the conscience that matters, and I'm sure yours is clear."

"What is the chance of reopening the case?"

"I don't get what you mean?"

"When a case is closed, can it be reopened?"

"I suppose so, if new evidence emerges. What are you thinking?"

"Nothing."

"Don't give me that 'nothing' shit. I know you, and I know you're thinking of something."

"I was thinking: since the file is going to be closed, I might as well hang on to some discoveries I've made. I'll produce them when the time is right, and in the event the case is reopened."

"You can be charged for withholding evidence. And when is the right time?"

"No one will know. When *he's* gone," he says, jerking his head up, indicating the OCCI.

"All right. We did not have this conversation?"

"What conversation?"

53

LEAVING THE OFFICE, MISLAN calls Johan to update him. He listens patiently as his assistant pours out his frustrations, holding back his own. After Johan has calmed down, he tells his sergeant to get some rest, as it will be their turn for the twenty-four-hour on Monday. He calls home and tells Daniel to get ready. He will be back in twenty minutes to pick him up.

"Where are we going, Daddy?"

"Where do you want to go, kiddo?"

"Bowling."

"Sure. I'll call you when I'm downstairs."

"Can Sis come?"

"Sure."

They go to the Ampang Point Bowl, where he gets a lane with a guard rail, pays for two games, and sits watching his son bowl. Daniel uses two hands to throw the seven-pound ball, which bumps against the railing a few times as it makes its way down the lane. He gets four pins. He looks around, smiling widely, proud of his achievement, and runs up to his father to give him a high-five. *Life is so simple when you're Daniel's age*, he thinks. You play the game the way you want to play it. Scores do not matter.

It is Saturday evening, and the bowling alleys are crowded with children running, playing, laughing, crying, eating, and otherwise making a ruckus. It's like family day, with fathers, mothers, children, and even grandparents, spending time together. He longs for Lynn to be with them, watching their son enjoying himself. *How could she not want this?* He sighs.

Just then, his cell phone rings. It is Dr. Safia. "Hi," he answers.

"Hi. What's the noise? Where are you?"

"Ampang Point Bowl, watching Daniel bowl."

"Oh, all right. How did it go?"

"As expected."

"You okay?"

"Yup, fine."

"You don't sound okay. Look, if you want to talk or something, you know where to find me."

"Sure. Thanks. Fie."

"Lan . . . you take care, okay?"

Dr. Safia's call brings him back to the case, the reality of life. Yes, some people do get away with murder. They are the "untouchables." It's reality. But how does one accept it, stomach it as a police officer, a father, and a human being?

54

ALTHOUGH HE IS AWAKE at his usual time, 6:30 in the morning, Mislan has no desire to jump out of bed. He hugs Daniel, who is sound asleep, and takes comfort in his soft rhythmic breathing and his tiny hands that hug him back.

When his cell phone rings, he notices the call is from a landline he doesn't recognize. Having decided to have a lazy day, he decides to let it ring. Then the cell phone beeps. It is a text message from one ASP Kumar of Major Crimes in Bukit Aman, the headquarters of the Federal Police, asking him to return his call. Why is Major Crimes from Bukit Aman calling him? He dials the number, and a voice answers after one ring, "Kumar."

"ASP Kumar, Inspector Mislan."

"Mislan, sorry to disturb you on a Sunday."

"No problem."

"I understand you were the lead in the triple murder of Robert Tham and family."

"Yes, but the case has been closed."

"Yes, I was told unofficially of that. I am the lead for Thanaraju's case. As the vic is a foreigner, it was deemed of public interest, so Bukit Aman is handling it. I understand your case is related to mine, and since your case is closed, I would appreciate it if you can pass on to me whatever evidence or intelligence you have that has not been filed?"

"What makes you think I have any?" Mislan is shocked.

"A reliable source."

"Who may this source be?"

"Someone who cares."

His decision to have a lazy Sunday is shelved, and they meet for breakfast. They talk about his case, his findings, and obstacles. He hands over everything to ASP Kumar. No mention is made of ASP Kumar's source. He offers ASP Kumar his help should it be required and wishes the Federal officer luck.

Driving home, he is in good spirits. He knows who the source is. In his eagerness to get closure, he had gone head-on against adversaries who were far too formidable for a frontal assault. He lost sight of available alternatives, but his boss did not. She knew what was ahead and made sure that she identified an alternative route. She had handed over Thanaraju's case to Major Crimes in Bukit Aman, knowing it would be linked to the Yee Sang Murders, and out of the reach of the OCCI.

Mislan speed-dials his boss. She answers after several rings. "Yes, Lan."

"Thanks, ma'am."

"You deserve a better closure," she says.

"Thanks." He feels tears welling up. There is only one rule of law, and it can still prevail when there are people like Superintendent Samsiah and ASP Kumar. He can now go home, play with Daniel, and sleep restfully, knowing Lionel will not be visiting him anymore. Mislan reaches for his cell phone and speed-dials Dr. Safia.